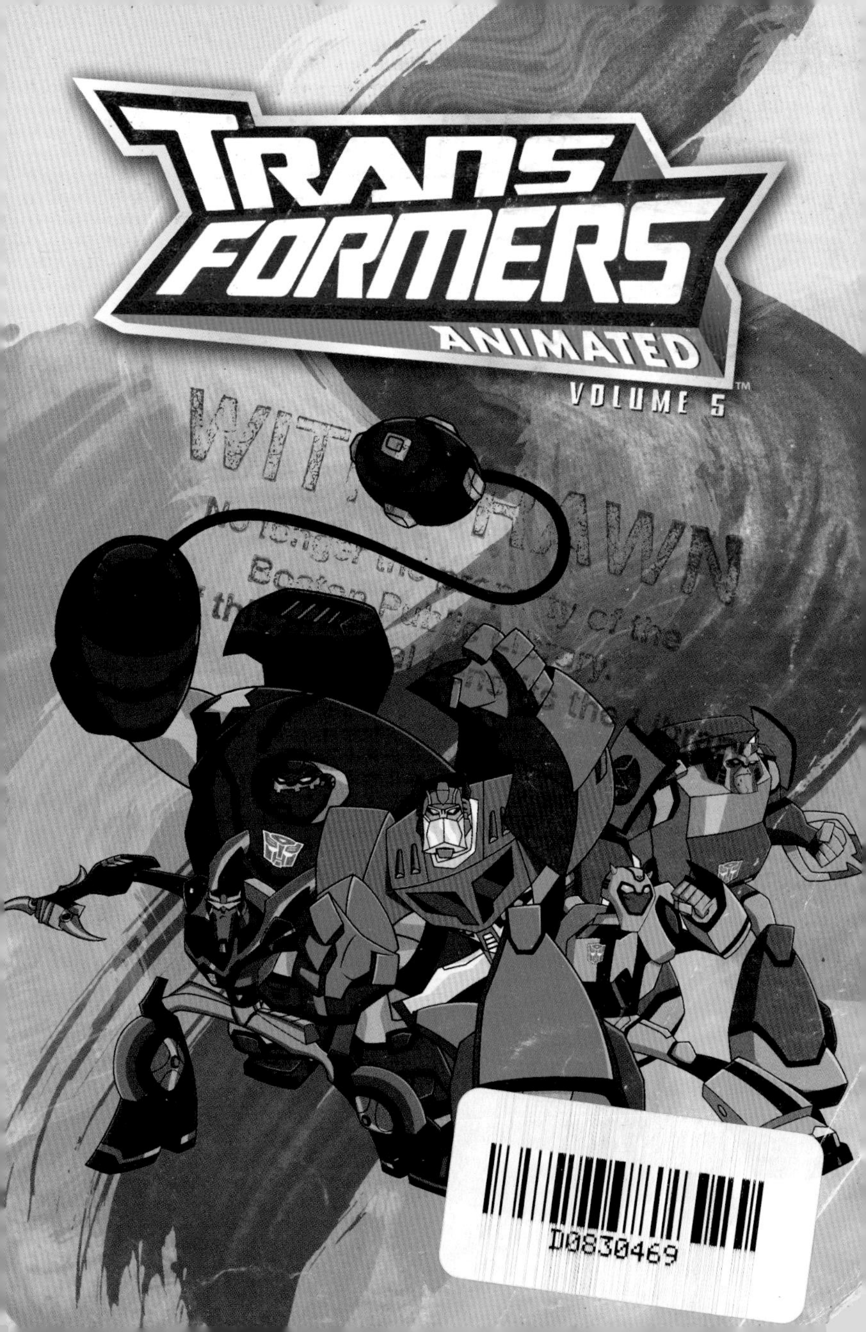
TRANS FORMERS
ANIMATED
VOLUME 5™

SURVIVAL OF THE FITTEST
WRITTEN BY:
STEVEN GRANT

LOST AND FOUND
WRITTEN BY:
RICH FOGEL

ADAPTATION BY:
ZACHARY RAU

EDITS BY:
JUSTIN EISINGER

LETTERS AND DESIGN BY:
TOM B. LONG

ISBN: 978-1-60010-243-1
11 10 9 8 1 2 3 4 5

Licensed by:

Special thanks to Hasbro's Aaron Archer, Michael Kelly, Amie Lozanski, Val Roca, Ed Lane, Michael Provost, Erin Hillman, Samantha Lomow, and Michael Verrecchia for their invaluable assistance.

IDW Publishing is:
Operations:
Moshe Berger, Chairman
Ted Adams, President
Matthew Ruzicka, CPA, Controller
Alan Payne, VP of Sales

Lorelei Bunjes, Dir. of Digital Services
Marci Hubbard, Executive Assistant
Alonzo Simon, Shipping Manager

Editorial:
Chris Ryall, Publisher/Editor-in-Chief
Scott Dunbier, Editor, Special Projects
Andy Schmidt, Senior Editor
Justin Eisinger, Editor

Kris Oprisko, Editor/Foreign Lic.
Denton J. Tipton, Editor
Tom Waltz, Editor
Mariah Huehner, Assistant Editor

Design:
Robbie Robbins, EVP/Sr. Graphic Artist
Ben Templesmith, Artist/Designer
Neil Uyetake, Art Director

Chris Mowry, Graphic Artist
Amauri Osorio, Graphic Artist

To discuss this issue of **Transformers**, or join the IDW Insiders, or to check out exclusive Web offers, check out our site:
www.IDWPUBLISHING.com

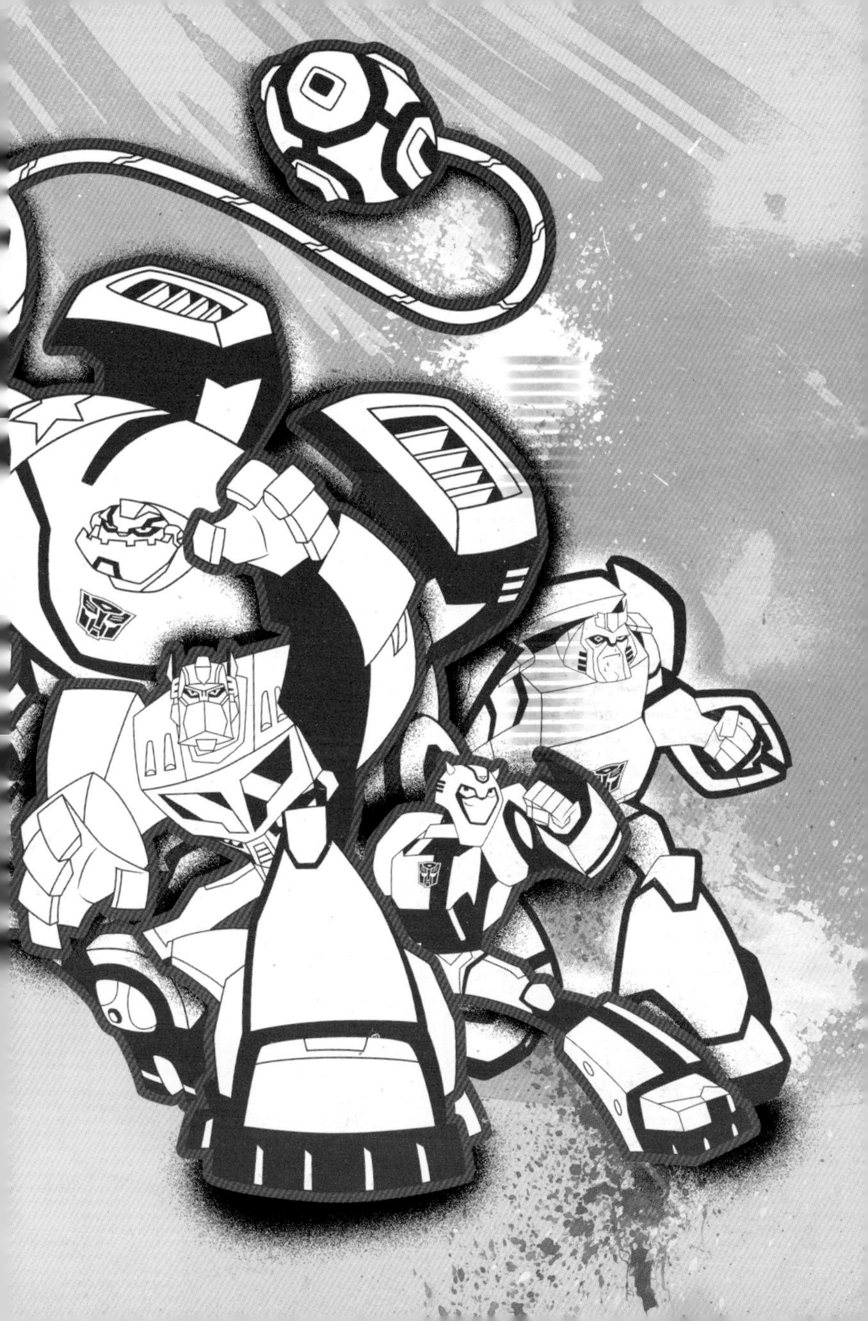

Roll Call

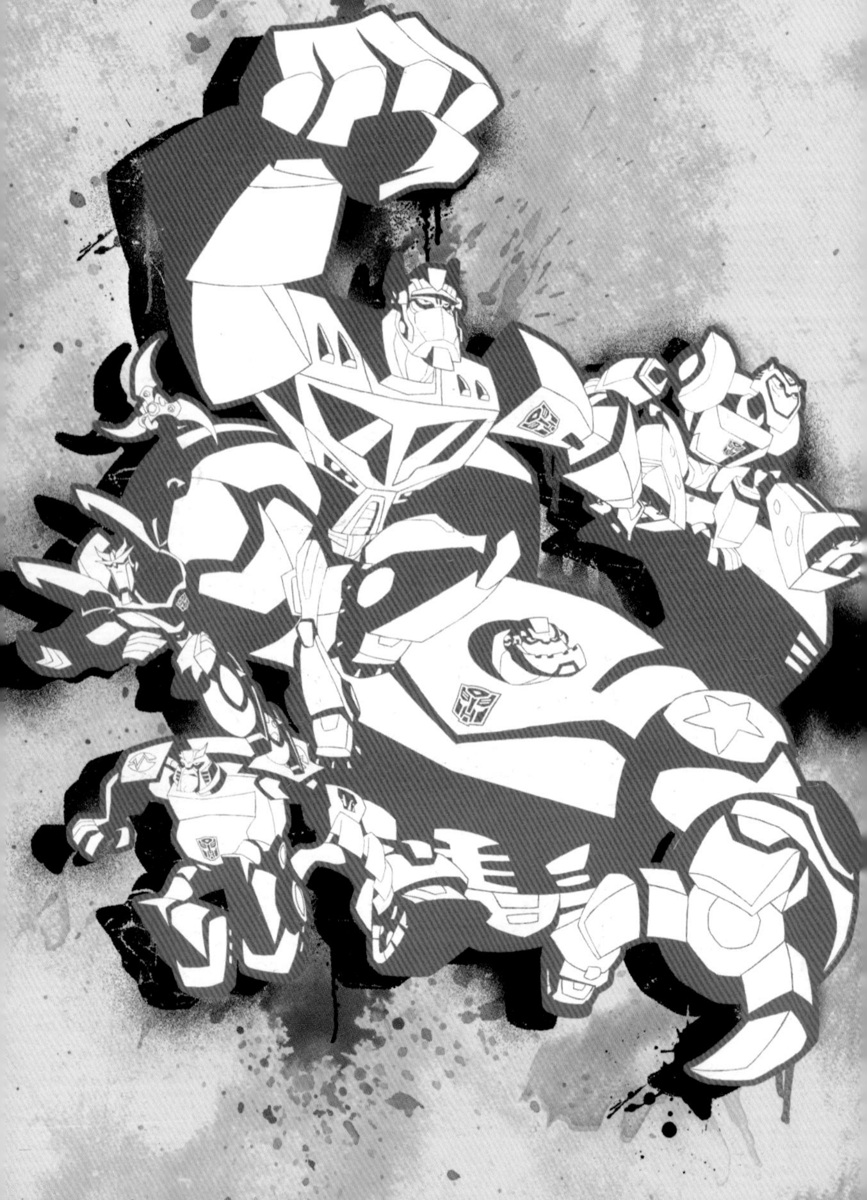

Optimus Prime

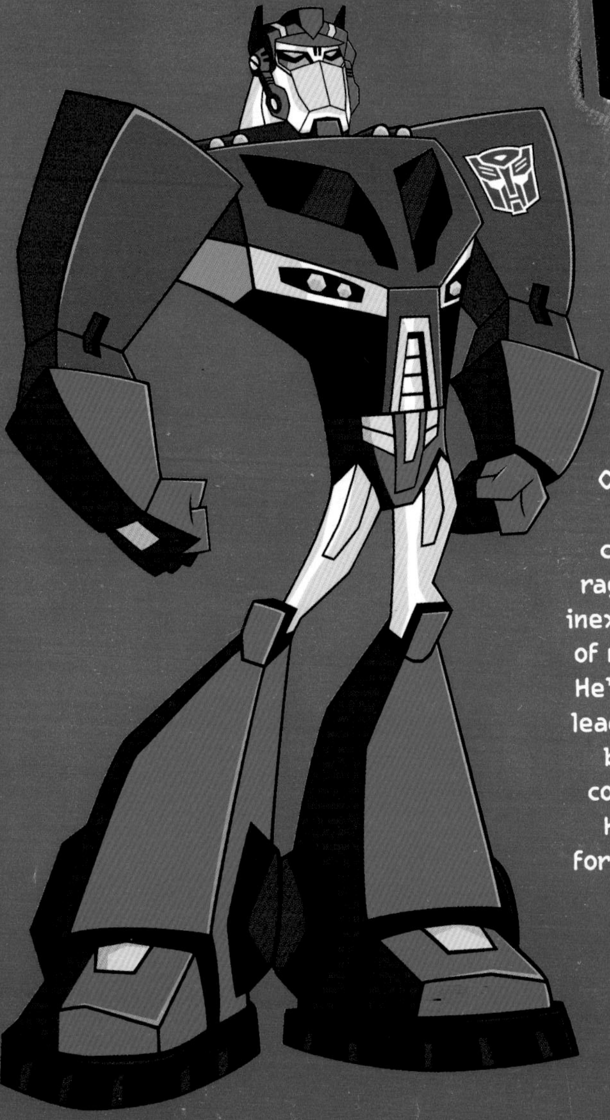

OPTIMUS PRIME
is the young
commander of a
ragtag and largely
inexperienced group
of misfit AUTOBOTS.
He's not the kind of
leader who needs to
bark orders to
command respect.
His mechanized
form is a fire truck.

Ratchet

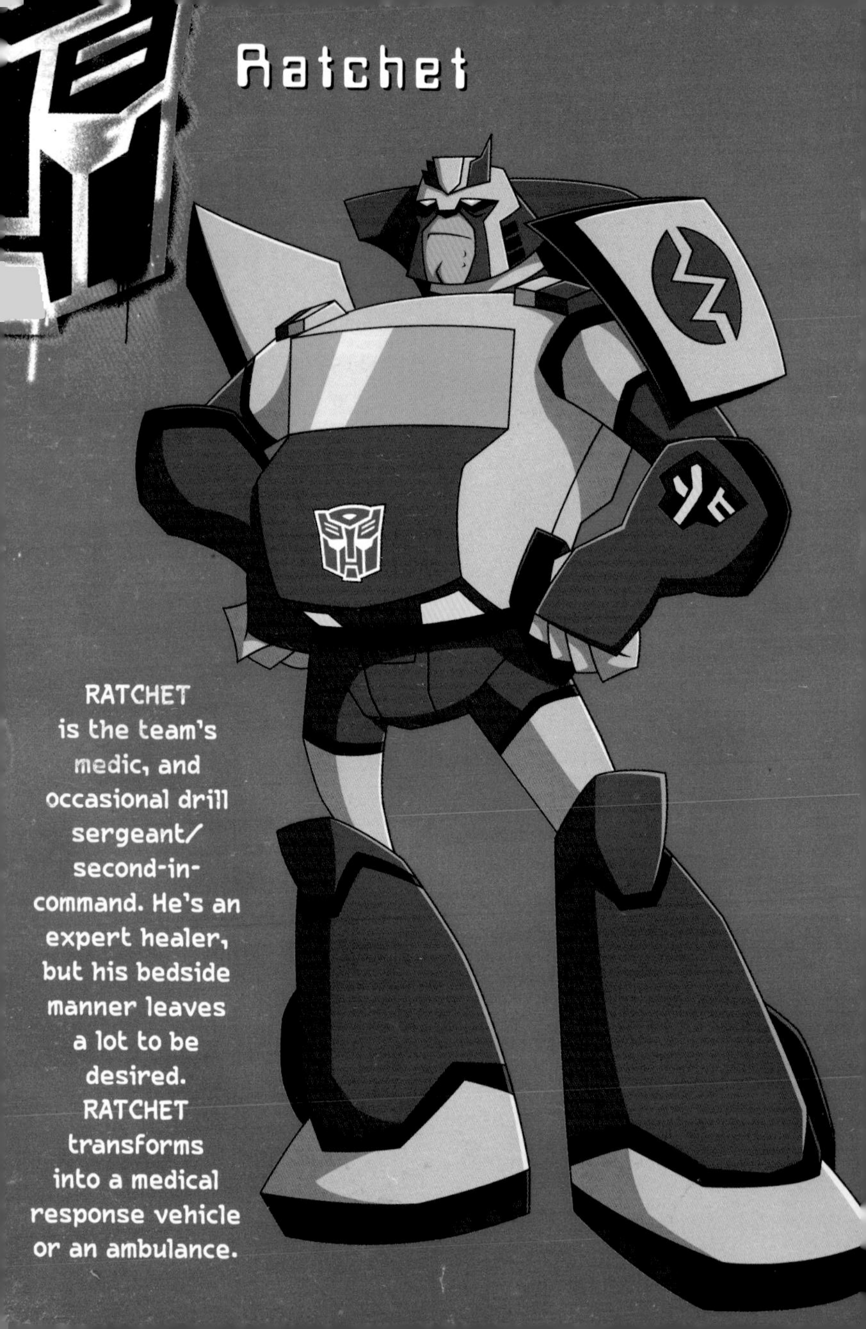

RATCHET is the team's medic, and occasional drill sergeant/ second-in-command. He's an expert healer, but his bedside manner leaves a lot to be desired. RATCHET transforms into a medical response vehicle or an ambulance.

Bulkhead

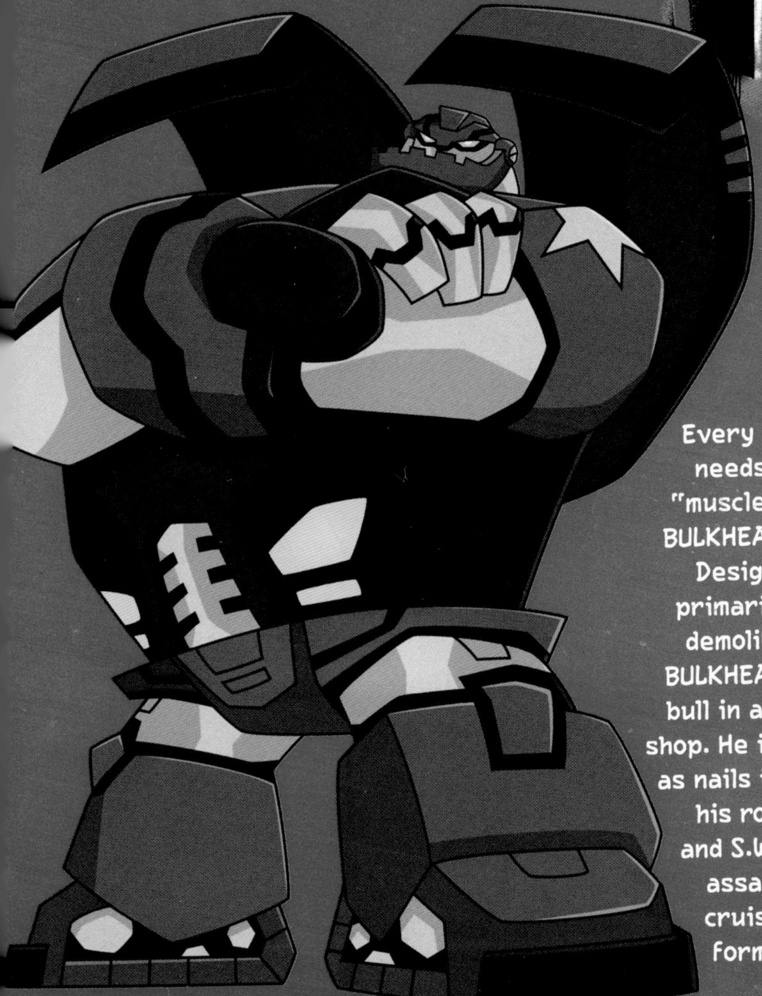

Every team needs its "muscle" and BULKHEAD is it. Designed primarily for demolition, BULKHEAD is a bull in a china shop. He is tough as nails in both his robot and S.W.A.T. assault cruiser forms.

Bumblebee

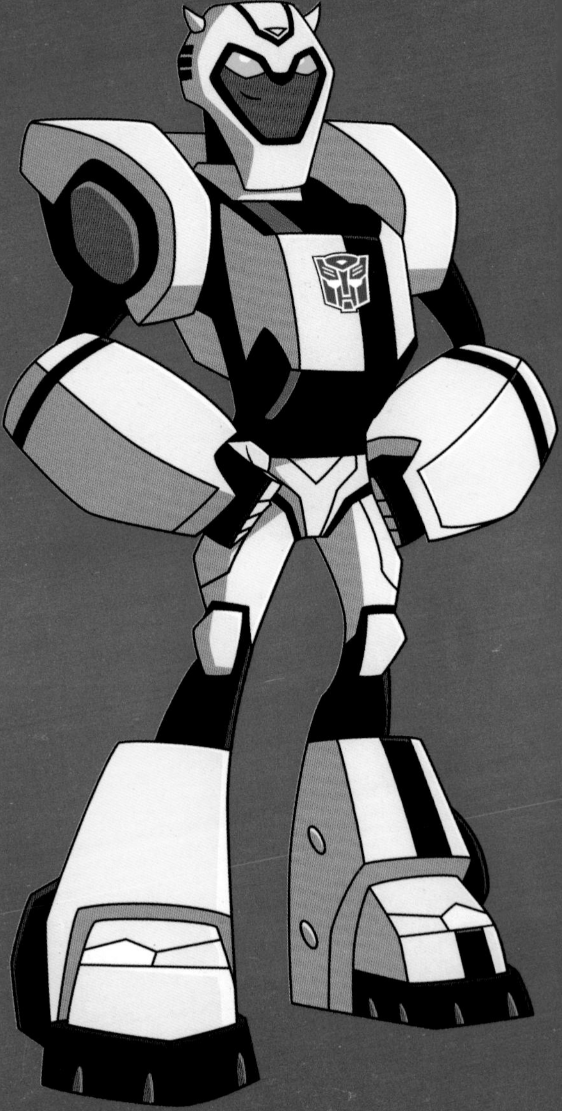

BUMBLEBEE is the "kid" of the team, easily the youngest and least mature of the AUTOBOTS. He's a bit of a showoff, always acting on impulse and rarely considering the consequences. But he looks awesome in his undercover police cruiser form.

Prowl

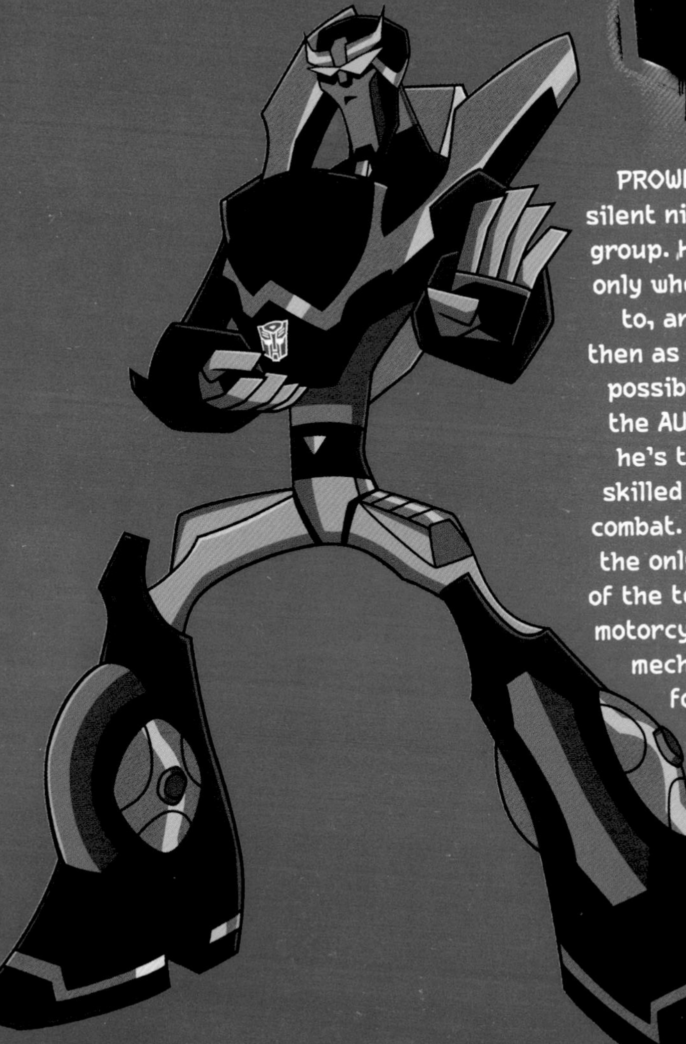

PROWL is the silent ninja of the group. He speaks only when he has to, and even then as briefly as possible. Of all the AUTOBOTS, he's the most skilled in direct combat. He is also the only member of the team with a motorcycle as his mechanized form.

Sari

SARI is the adopted daughter of Professor Sumdac. Call it an accident or call it destiny, but the AllSpark projected part of itself onto her in the form of a key. Wearing it on a chain around her neck, SARI can use the key to absorb the AllSpark energy and store it like a battery, providing an emergency power supply and healing source for the AUTOBOTS in battle. It also provides her with an almost psychic connection to the AUTOBOTS.

Professor Sumdac

One night in the late 21st Century, the young SUMDAC thought he saw a falling star cascade into his back field, but it was something much better. It was the smoldering, non-functioning remains of the head of an alien robot, MEGATRON. In the decades that passed while the AUTOBOTS slumbered in stasis at the bottom of Lake Erie, SUMDAC was able to reverse engineer the Cybertronian technology within MEGATRON and usher in the Automatronic Revolution of the 22nd Century.

Megatron

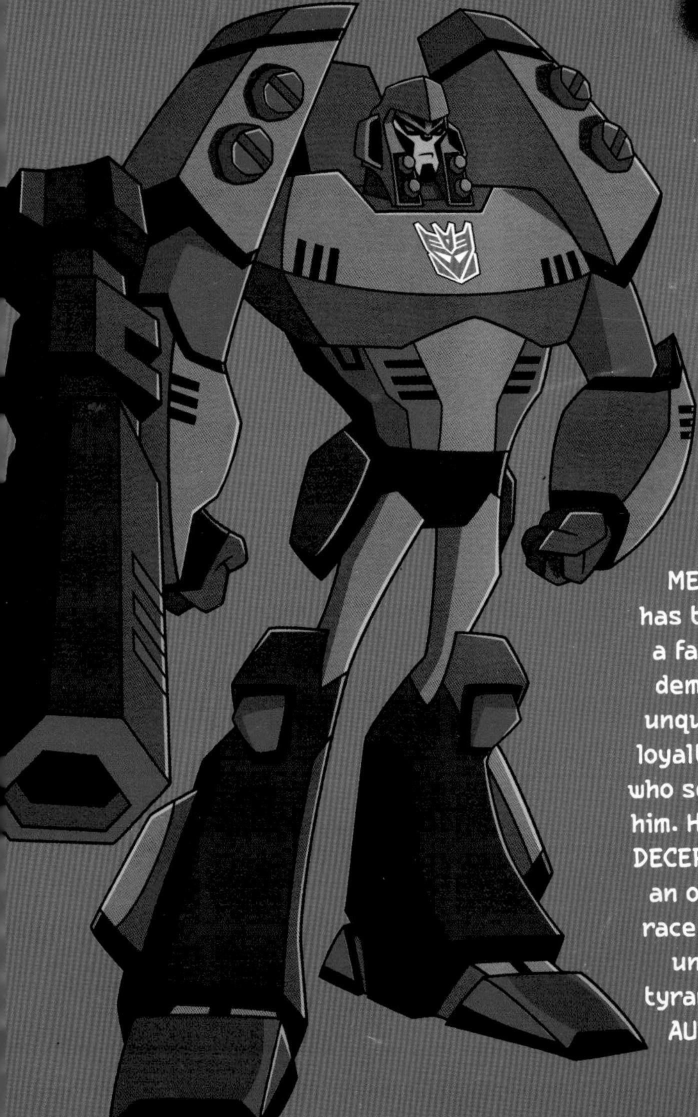

MEGATRON has the zeal of a fanatic and demands the unquestioning loyalty of those who serve under him. He sees the DECEPTICONS as an oppressed race suffering under the tyranny of the AUTOBOTS.

Blitzwing

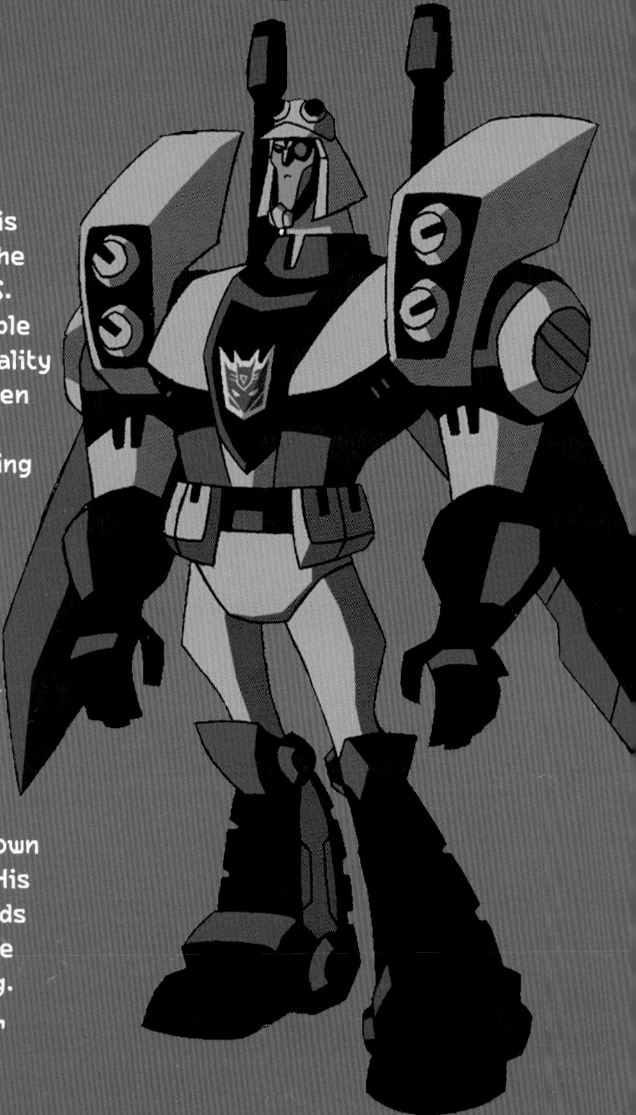

BLITZWING is the joker of the DECEPTICONS. An unpredictable multiple personality bot, he is driven mad by his constantly shifting appearance. BLITZWING is a 'triple-changer'... that is, he has three modes (one robot, two vehicles). Plus he has three faces, each with its own personality. His power depends on which face he's showing. Heat/flame, cold/ice or completely random.

Lugnut

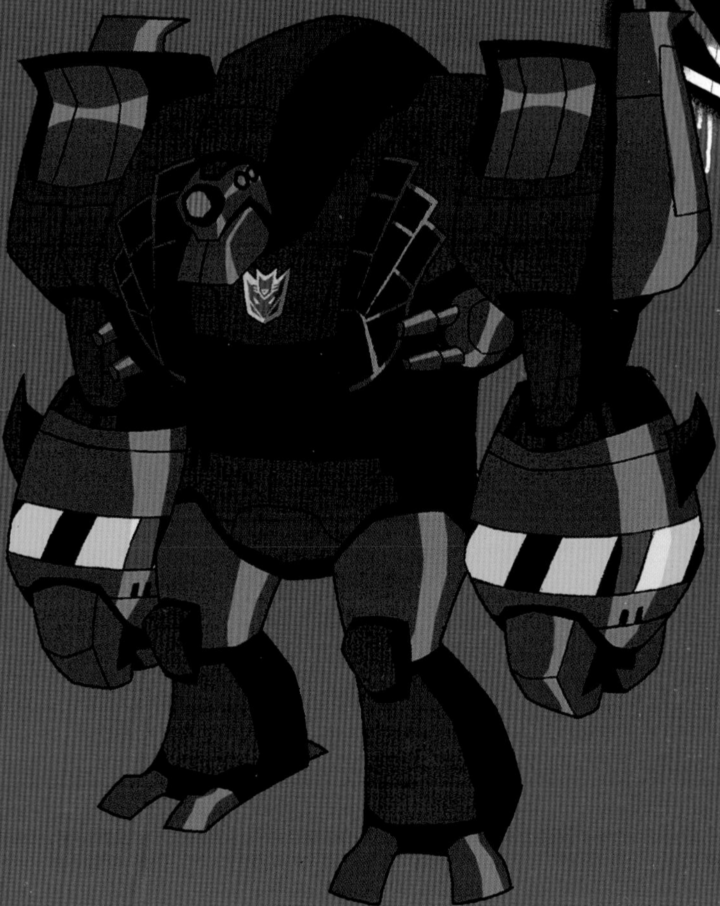

LUGNUT is more a force of nature than a DECEPTICON. MEGATRON's fiercely loyal, but none-too-bright attack dog, he would gladly follow his leader into any battle. Of the DECEPTICONS, only LUGNUT refuses to believe that MEGATRON is gone for good. Incredibly strong, LUGNUT carries a payload of mega-bombs, and can spew liquid napalm with laser-like accuracy, but he prefers to rip things apart with his bare hands.

Starscream

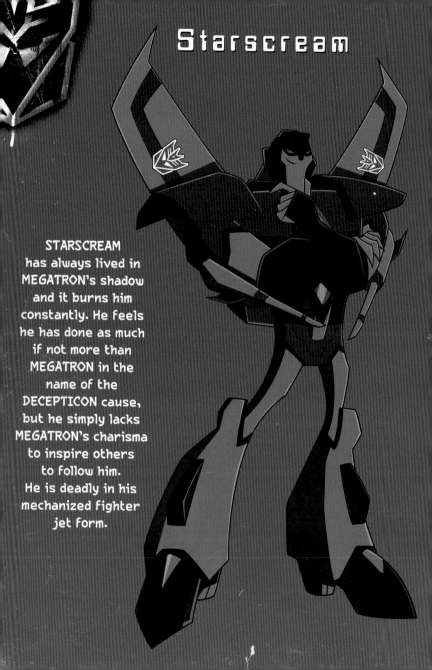

STARSCREAM has always lived in MEGATRON's shadow and it burns him constantly. He feels he has done as much if not more than MEGATRON in the name of the DECEPTICON cause, but he simply lacks MEGATRON's charisma to inspire others to follow him. He is deadly in his mechanized fighter jet form.

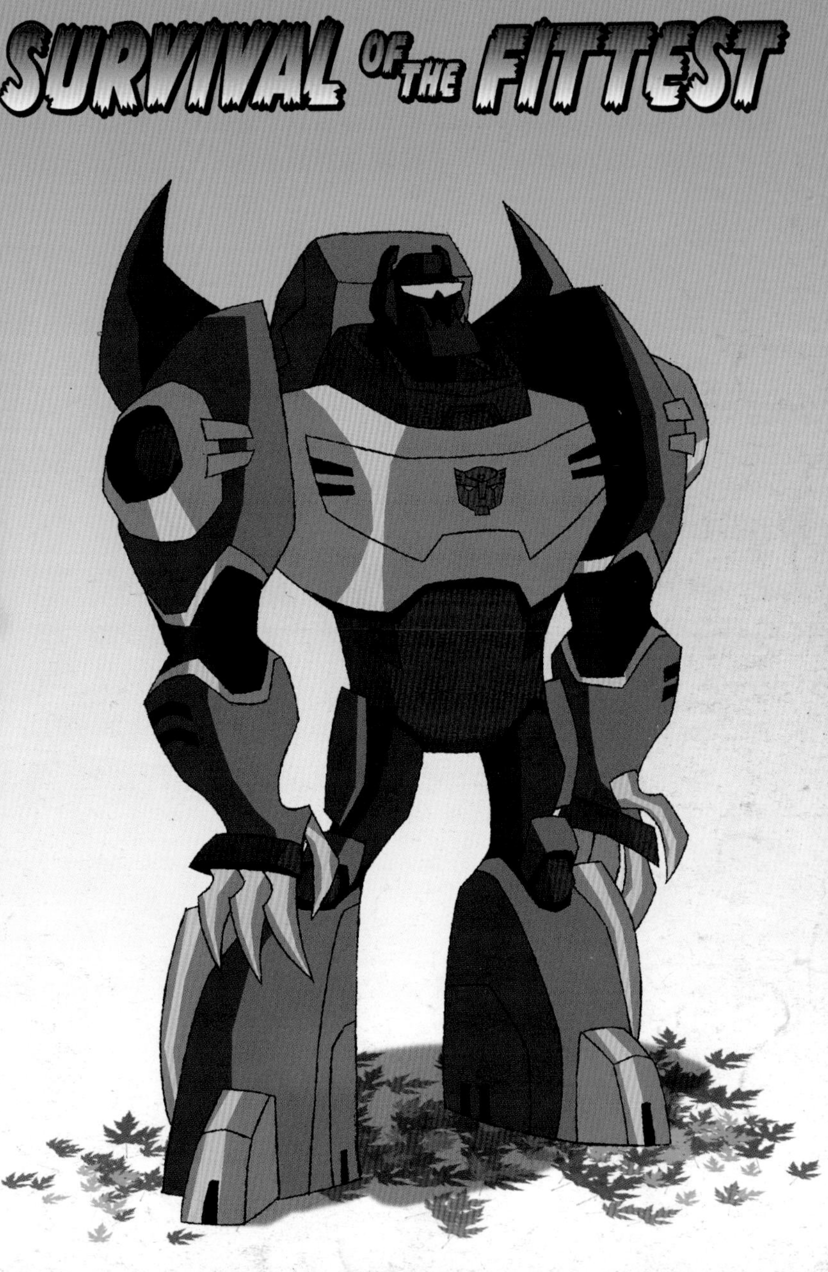
SURVIVAL OF THE FITTEST

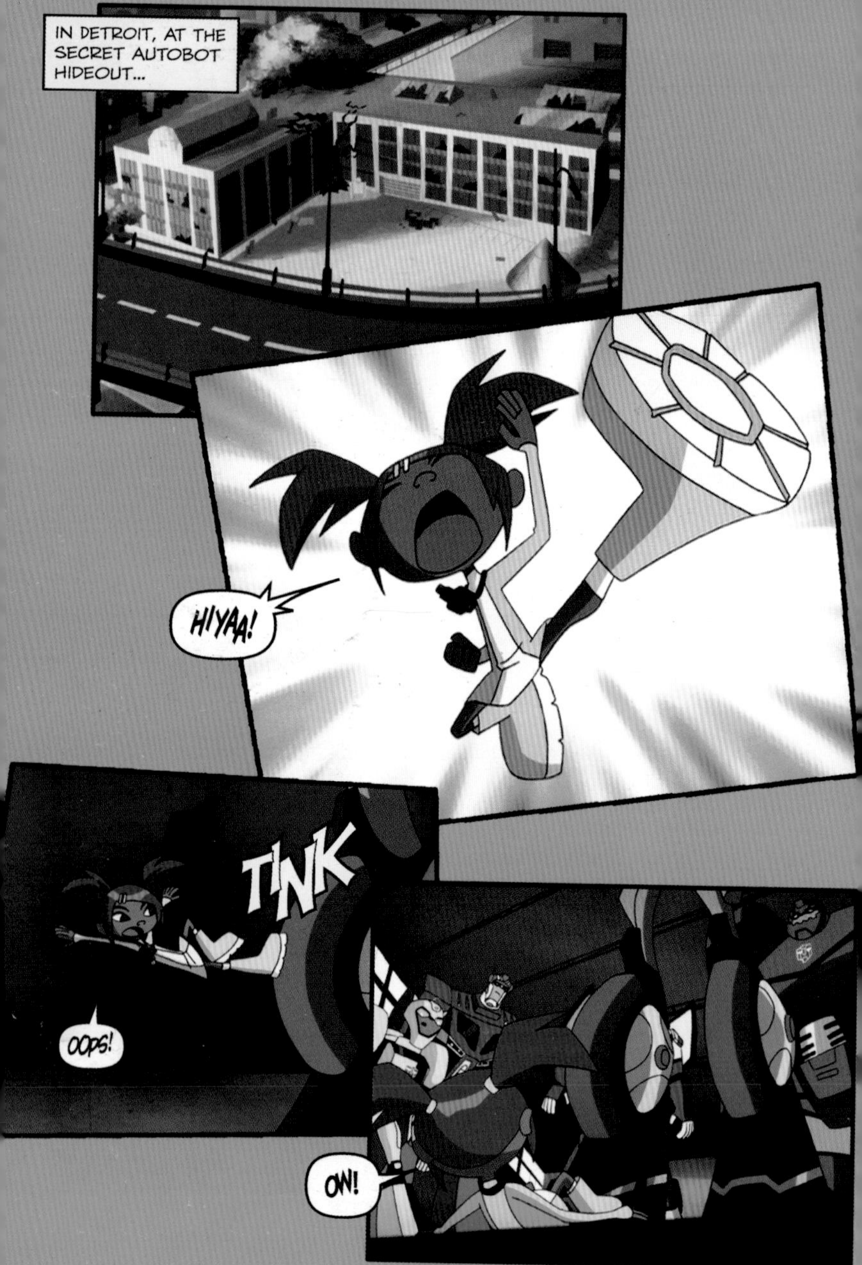
IN DETROIT, AT THE SECRET AUTOBOT HIDEOUT...
HIYAA!
TINK
OOPS!
OW!

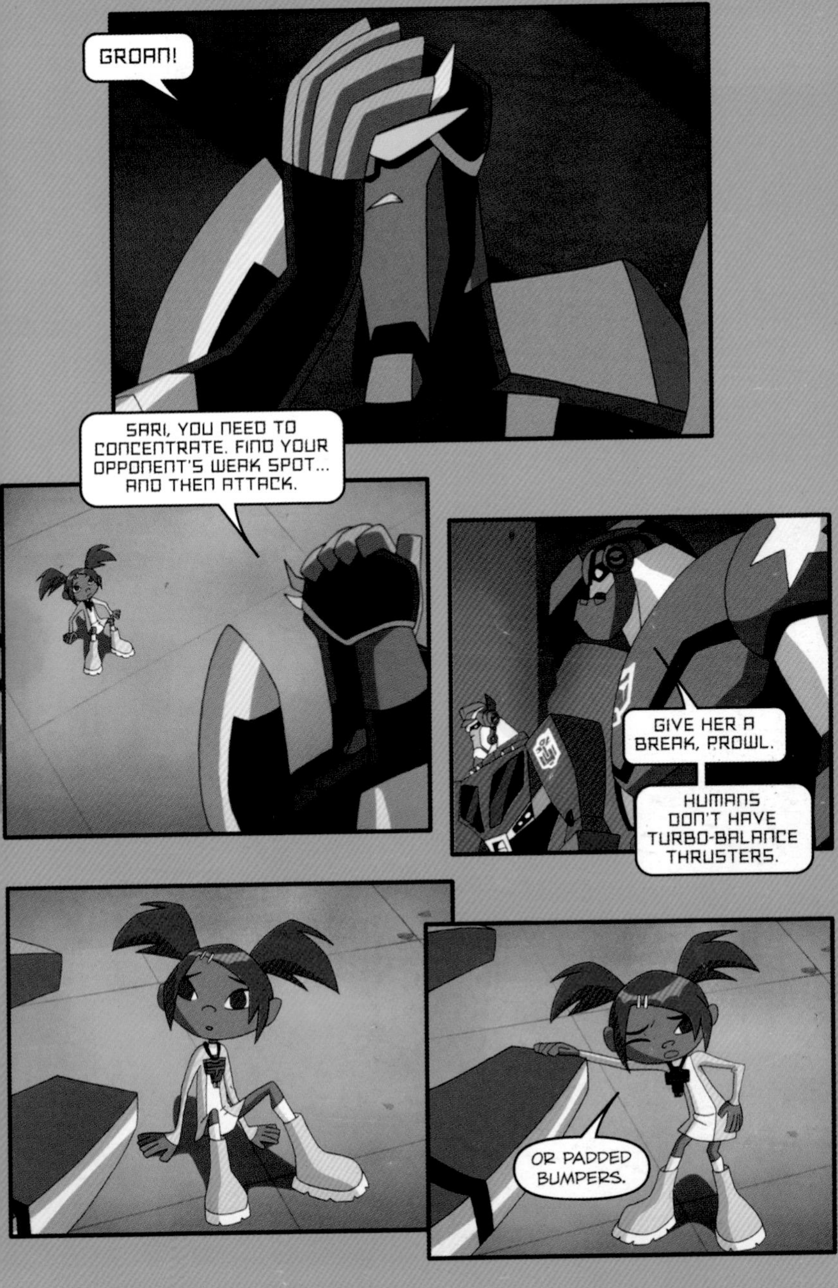
GROAN!
SARI, YOU NEED TO CONCENTRATE. FIND YOUR OPPONENT'S WEAK SPOT... AND THEN ATTACK.
GIVE HER A BREAK, PROWL.
HUMANS DON'T HAVE TURBO-BALANCE THRUSTERS.
OR PADDED BUMPERS.

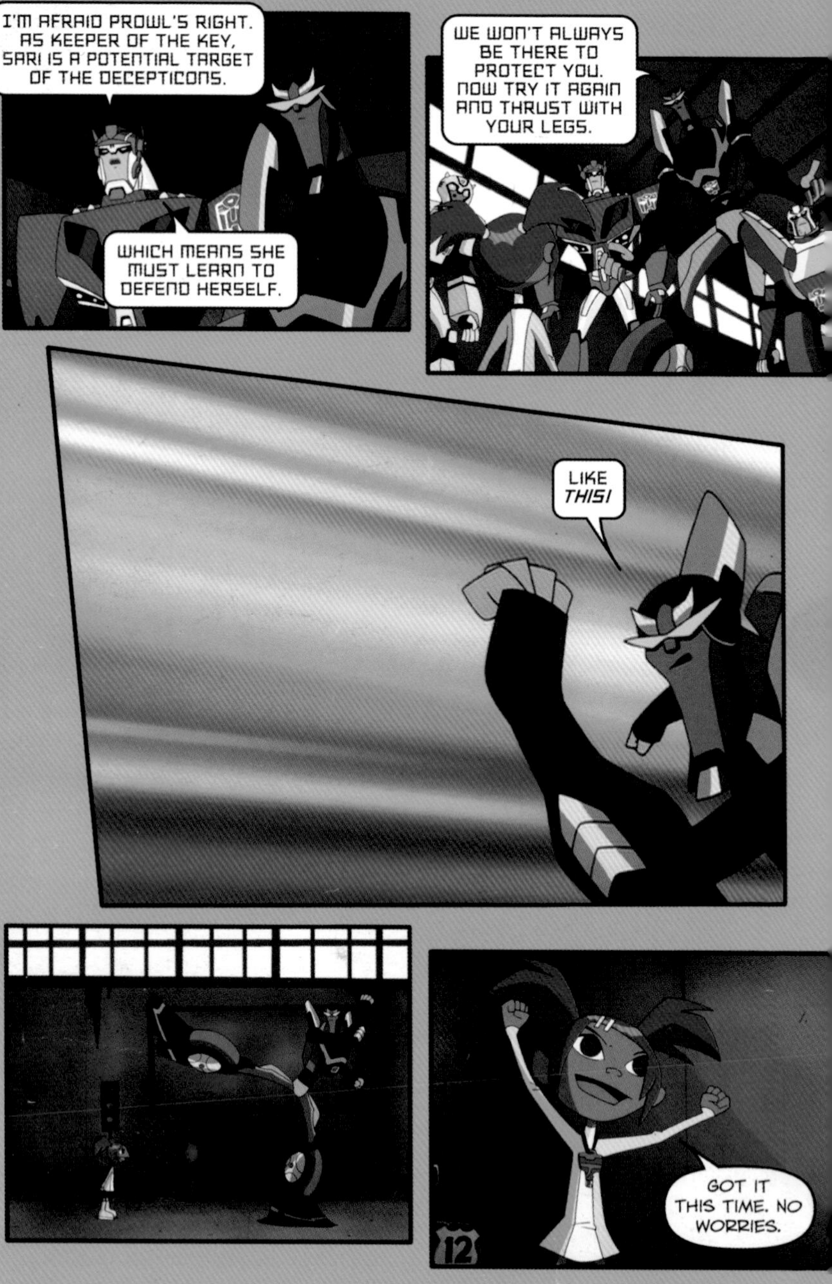
I'M AFRAID PROWL'S RIGHT. AS KEEPER OF THE KEY, SARI IS A POTENTIAL TARGET OF THE DECEPTICONS.
WHICH MEANS SHE MUST LEARN TO DEFEND HERSELF.
WE WON'T ALWAYS BE THERE TO PROTECT YOU. NOW TRY IT AGAIN AND THRUST WITH YOUR LEGS.
LIKE *THIS!*
GOT IT THIS TIME. NO WORRIES.

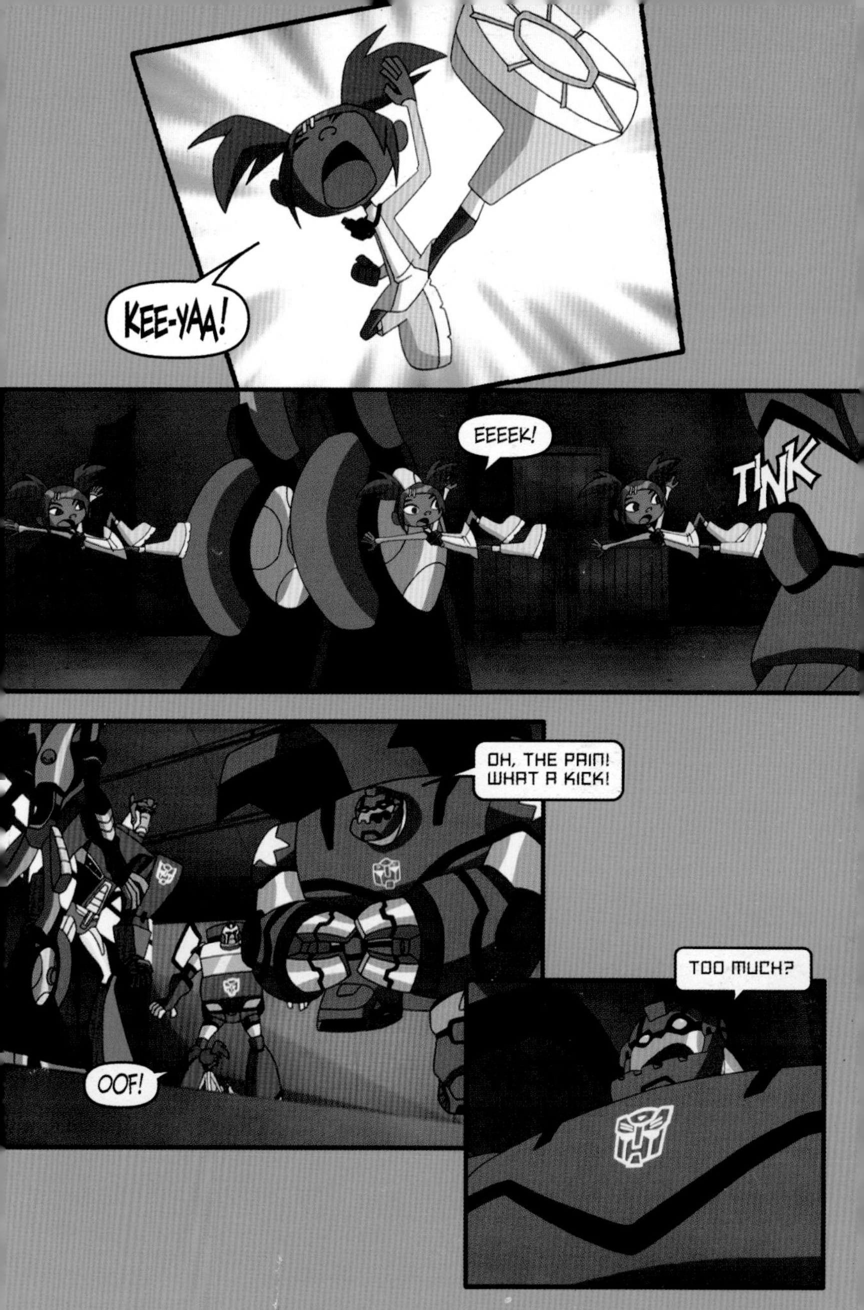
KEE-YAA!
EEEEK!
TINK
OH, THE PAIN! WHAT A KICK!
OOF!
TOO MUCH?

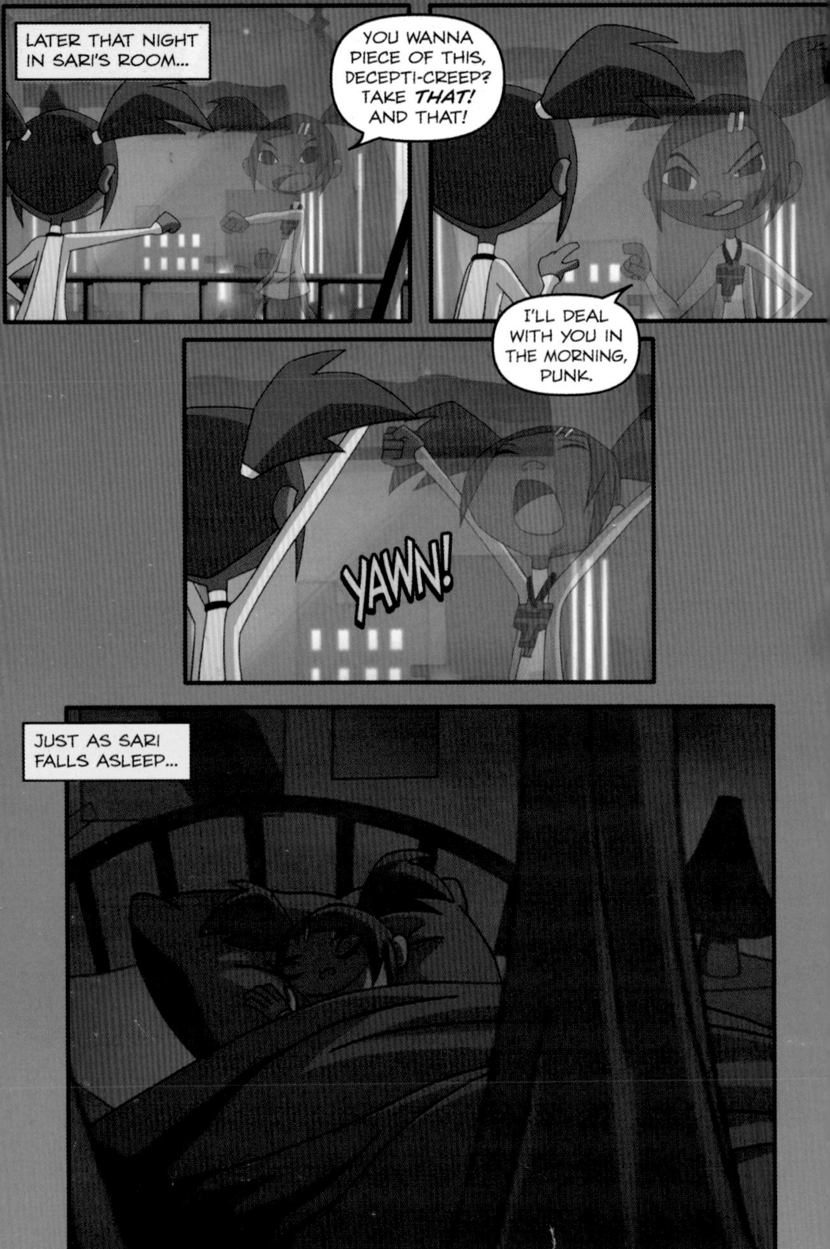
LATER THAT NIGHT IN SARI'S ROOM...
YOU WANNA PIECE OF THIS, DECEPTI-CREEP? TAKE THAT! AND THAT!
I'LL DEAL WITH YOU IN THE MORNING, PUNK.
YAWN!
JUST AS SARI FALLS ASLEEP...

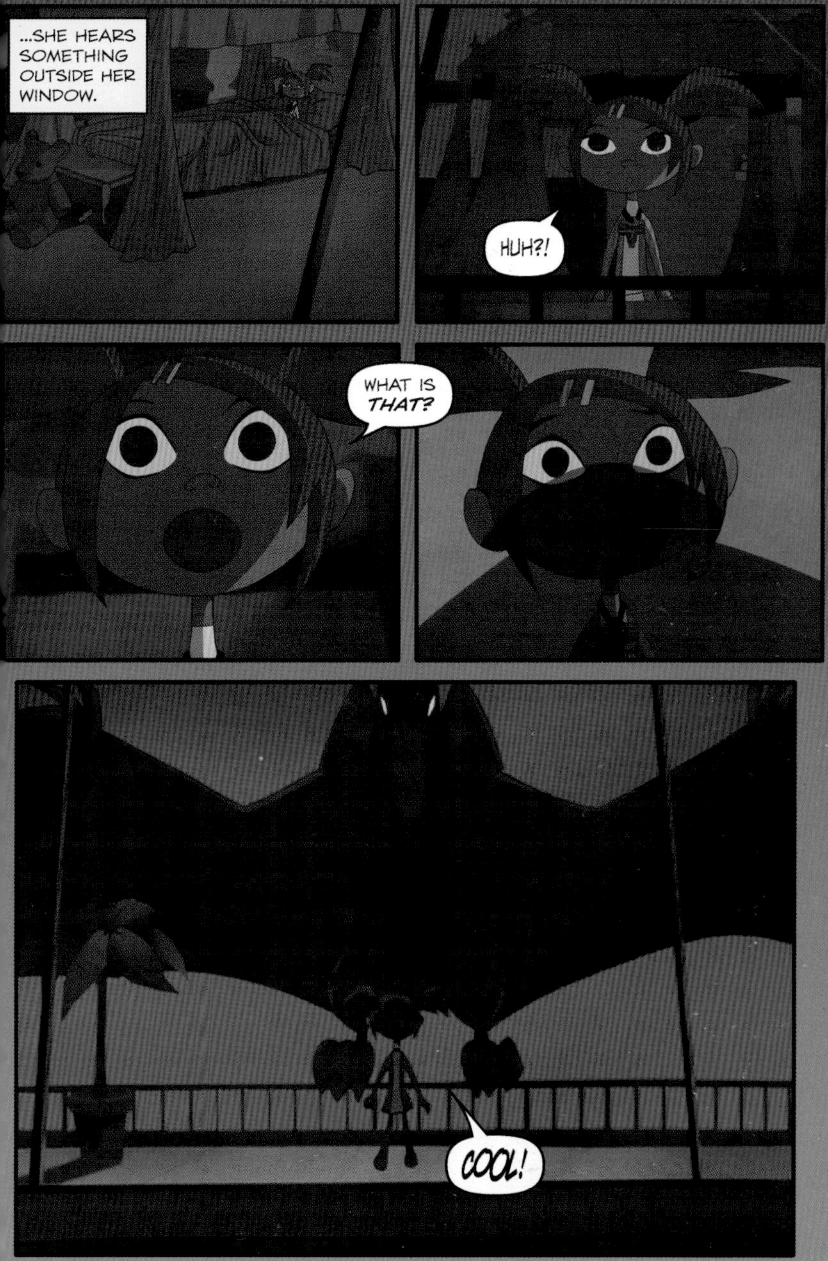
...SHE HEARS SOMETHING OUTSIDE HER WINDOW.
HUH?!
WHAT IS THAT?
COOL!

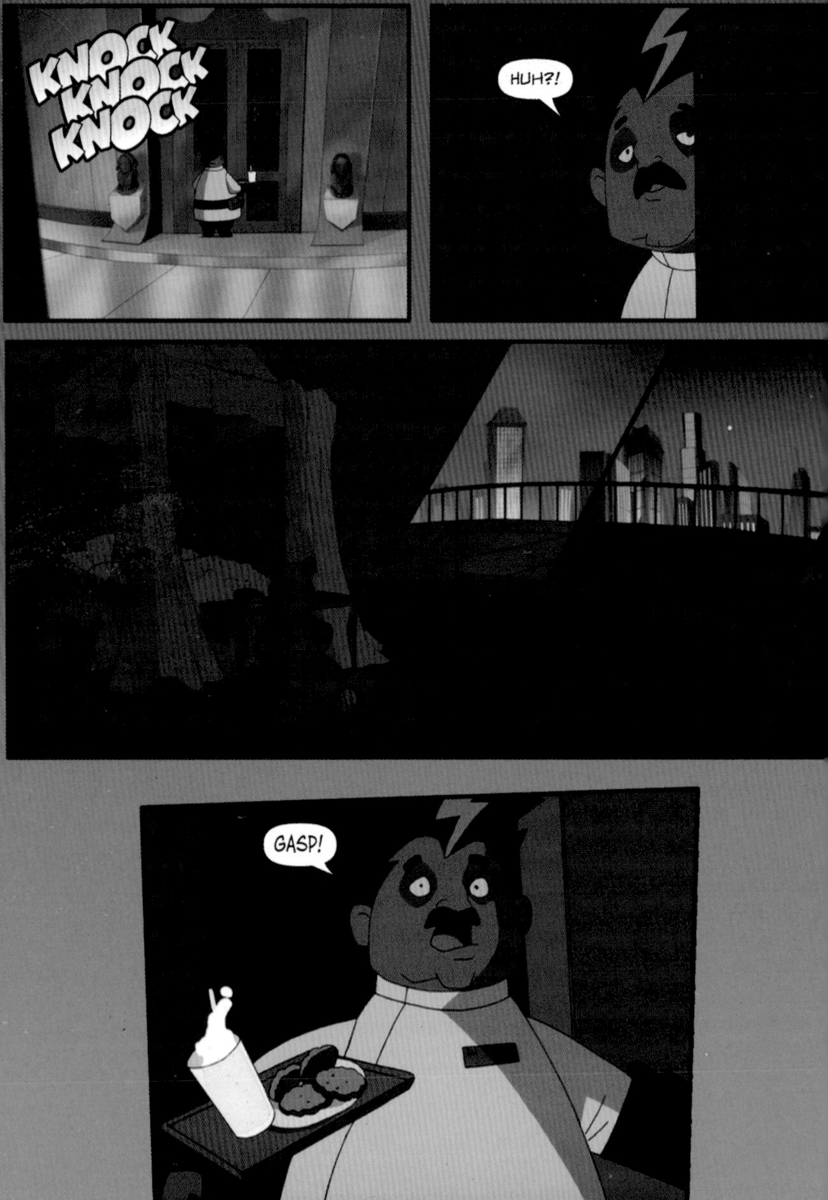
KNOCK KNOCK KNOCK
HUH?!
GASP!

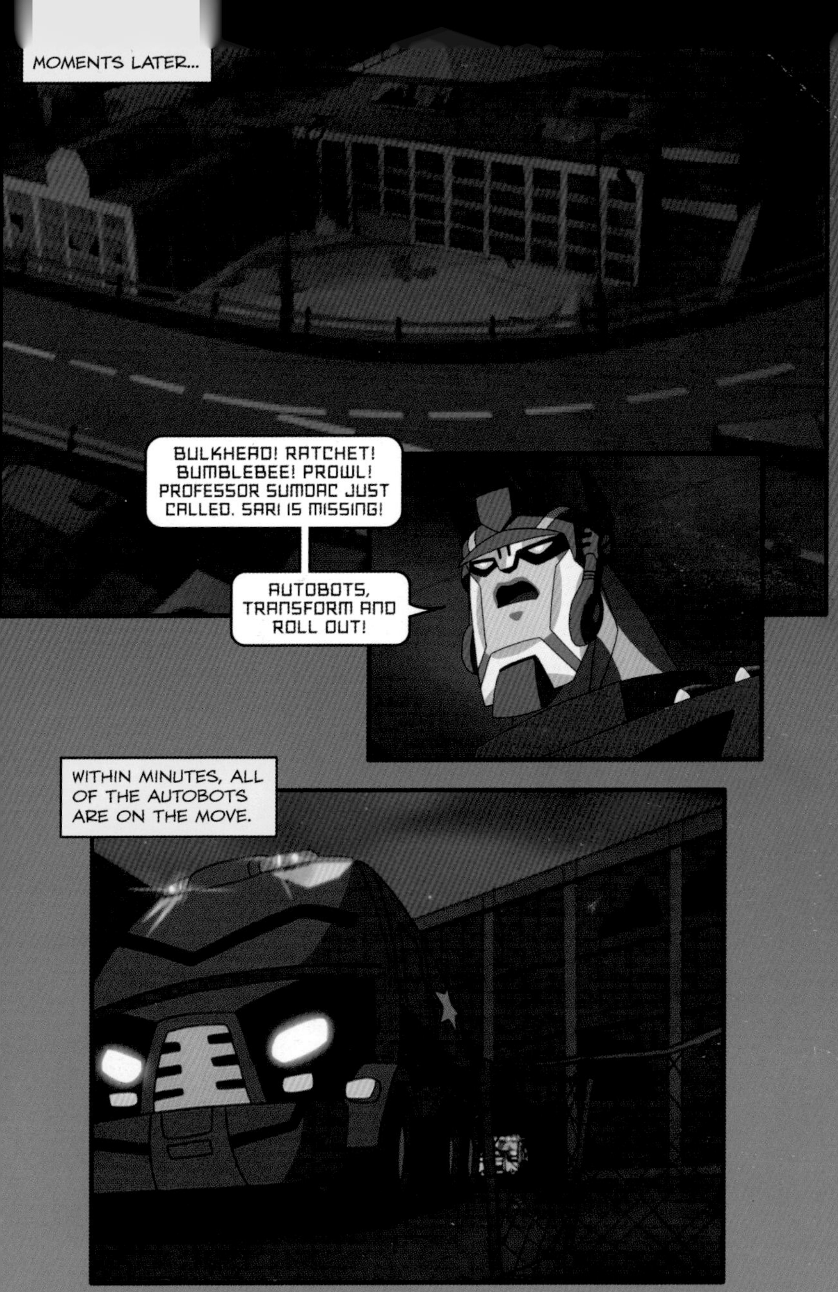
MOMENTS LATER...
BULKHEAD! RATCHET! BUMBLEBEE! PROWL! PROFESSOR SUMDAC JUST CALLED. SARI IS MISSING!
AUTOBOTS, TRANSFORM AND ROLL OUT!
WITHIN MINUTES, ALL OF THE AUTOBOTS ARE ON THE MOVE.

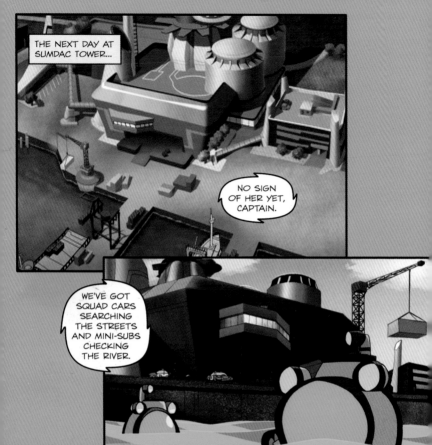

THE NEXT DAY AT SUMDAC TOWER...

NO SIGN OF HER YET, CAPTAIN.

WE'VE GOT SQUAD CARS SEARCHING THE STREETS AND MINI-SUBS CHECKING THE RIVER.

WE'RE QUESTIONING THE FATHER NOW, BUT HE SAYS HE DIDN'T SEE ANYTHING.

KEEP SEARCHING THE GIRL'S ROOM. I'LL LET YOU KNOW WHAT I FIND ON THE SECURITY VIDS.

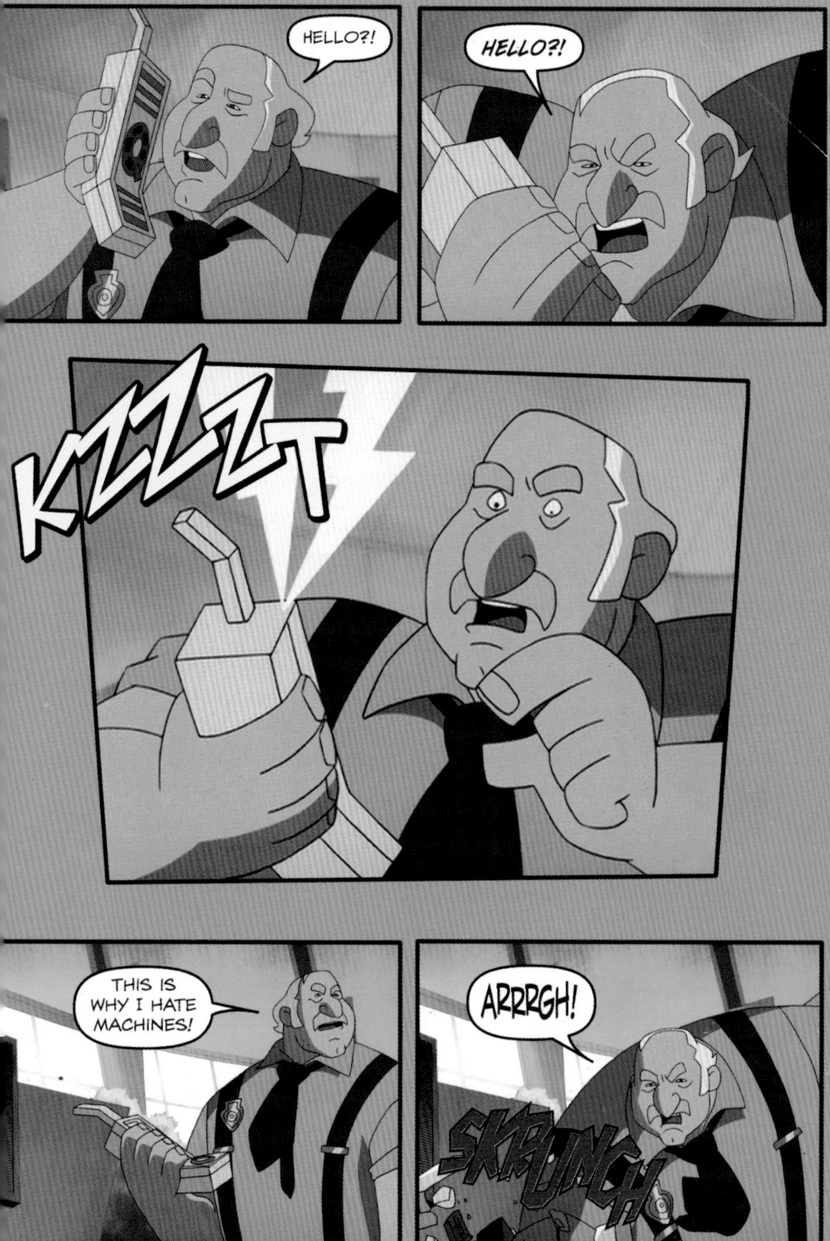
HELLO?!
HELLO?!
KZZZZT
THIS IS WHY I HATE MACHINES!
ARRRGH!
SKRUNCH

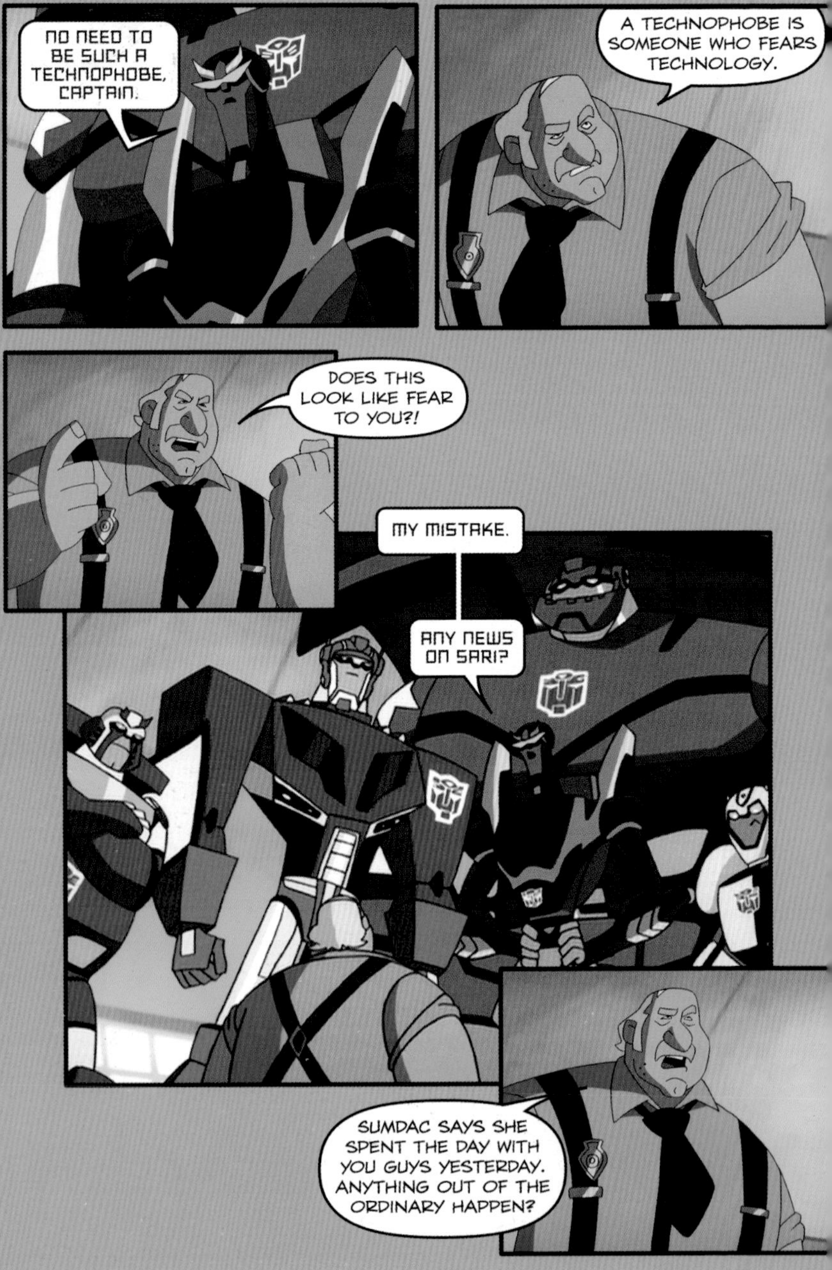
NO NEED TO BE SUCH A TECHNOPHOBE, CAPTAIN.
A TECHNOPHOBE IS SOMEONE WHO FEARS TECHNOLOGY.
DOES THIS LOOK LIKE FEAR TO YOU?!
MY MISTAKE.
ANY NEWS ON SARI?
SUMDAC SAYS SHE SPENT THE DAY WITH YOU GUYS YESTERDAY. ANYTHING OUT OF THE ORDINARY HAPPEN?

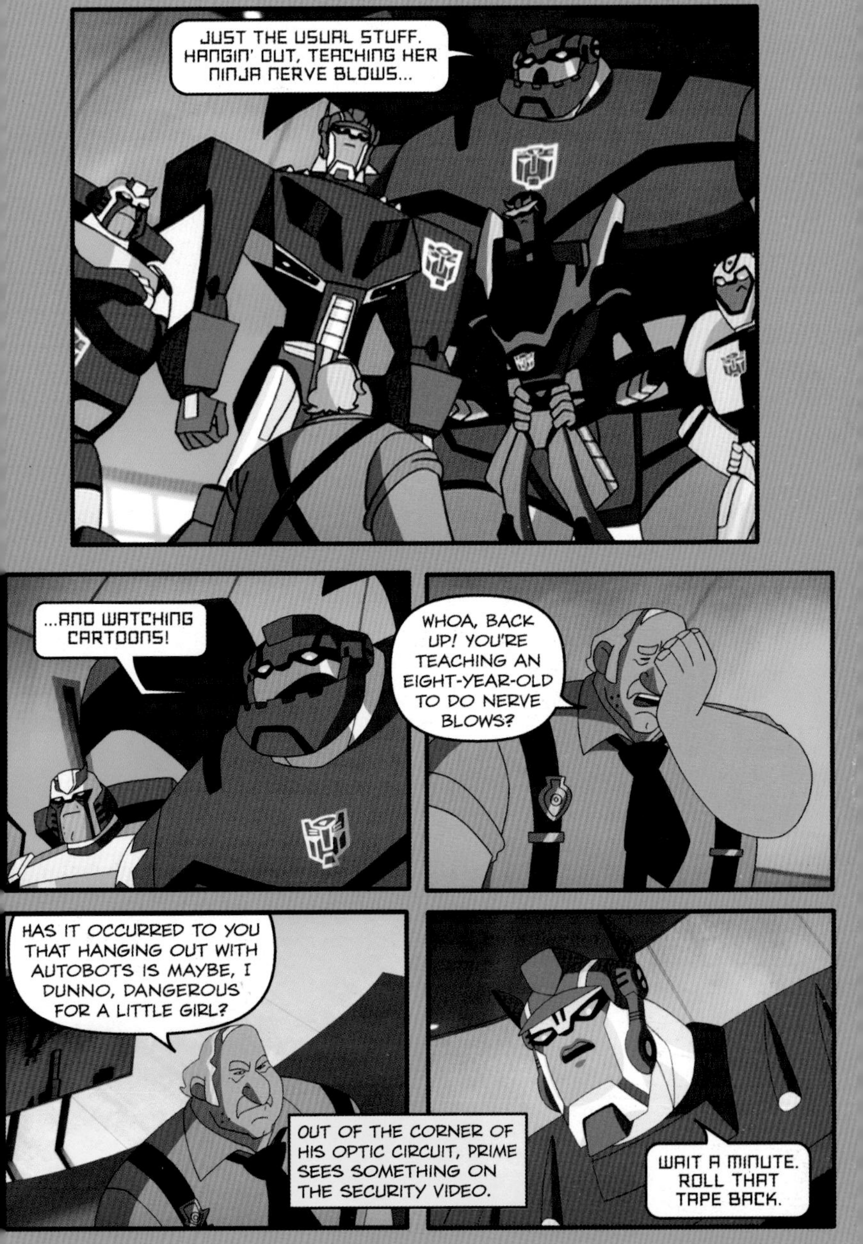
JUST THE USUAL STUFF. HANGIN' OUT, TEACHING HER NINJA NERVE BLOWS...
...AND WATCHING CARTOONS!
WHOA, BACK UP! YOU'RE TEACHING AN EIGHT-YEAR-OLD TO DO NERVE BLOWS?
HAS IT OCCURRED TO YOU THAT HANGING OUT WITH AUTOBOTS IS MAYBE, I DUNNO, DANGEROUS FOR A LITTLE GIRL?
OUT OF THE CORNER OF HIS OPTIC CIRCUIT, PRIME SEES SOMETHING ON THE SECURITY VIDEO.
WAIT A MINUTE. ROLL THAT TAPE BACK.

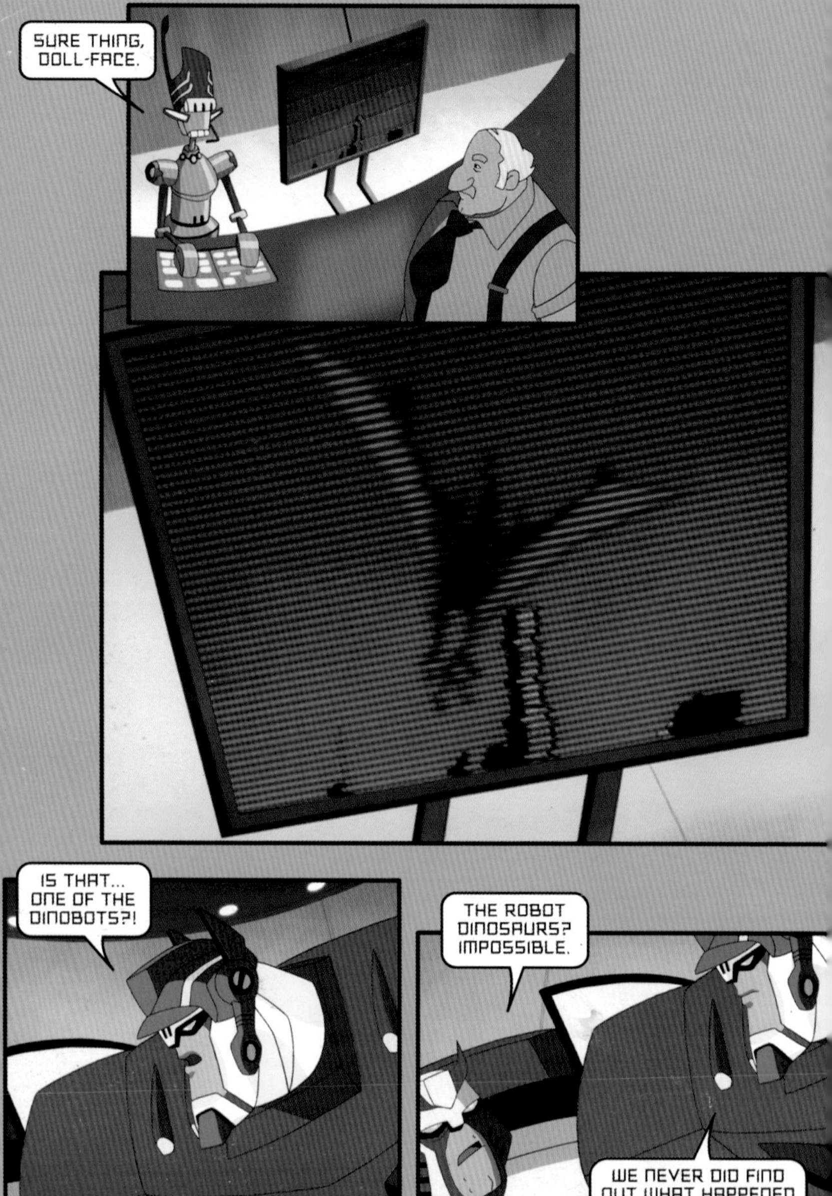
SURE THING, DOLL-FACE.
IS THAT... ONE OF THE DINOBOTS?!
THE ROBOT DINOSAURS? IMPOSSIBLE.
WE NEVER DID FIND OUT WHAT HAPPENED TO THEM AFTER THEY ESCAPED.

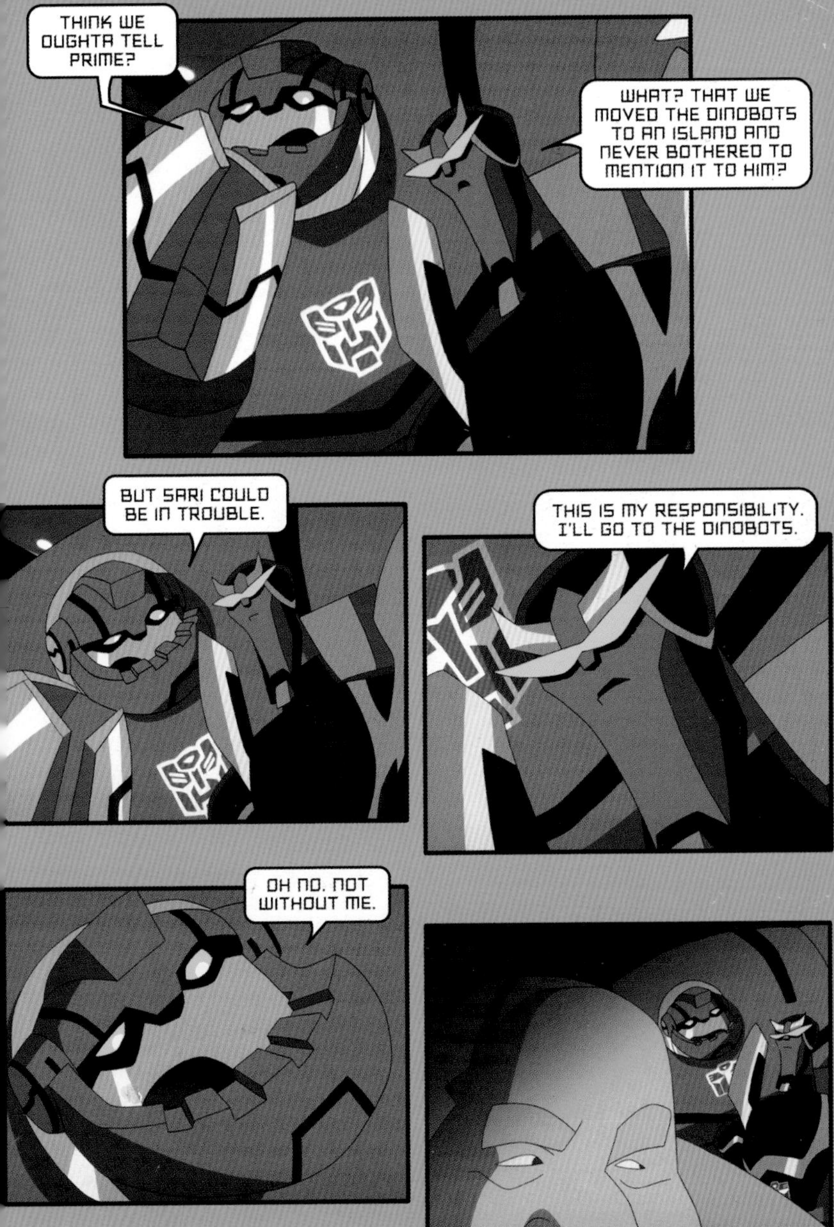

THINK WE OUGHTA TELL PRIME?
WHAT? THAT WE MOVED THE DINOBOTS TO AN ISLAND AND NEVER BOTHERED TO MENTION IT TO HIM?
BUT SARI COULD BE IN TROUBLE.
THIS IS MY RESPONSIBILITY. I'LL GO TO THE DINOBOTS.
OH NO. NOT WITHOUT ME.

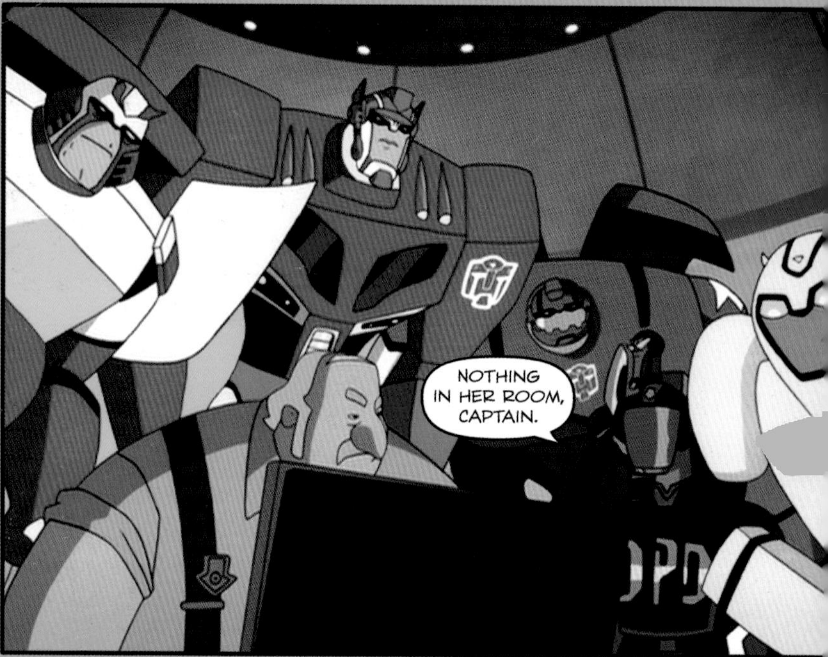
NOTHING IN HER ROOM, CAPTAIN.

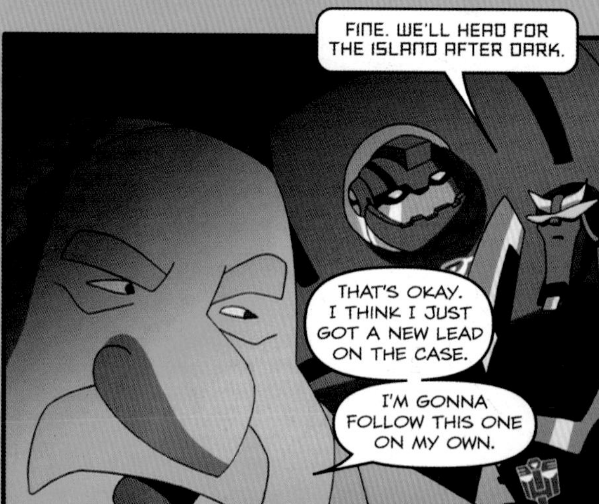
FINE. WE'LL HEAD FOR THE ISLAND AFTER DARK.
THAT'S OKAY. I THINK I JUST GOT A NEW LEAD ON THE CASE.
I'M GONNA FOLLOW THIS ONE ON MY OWN.

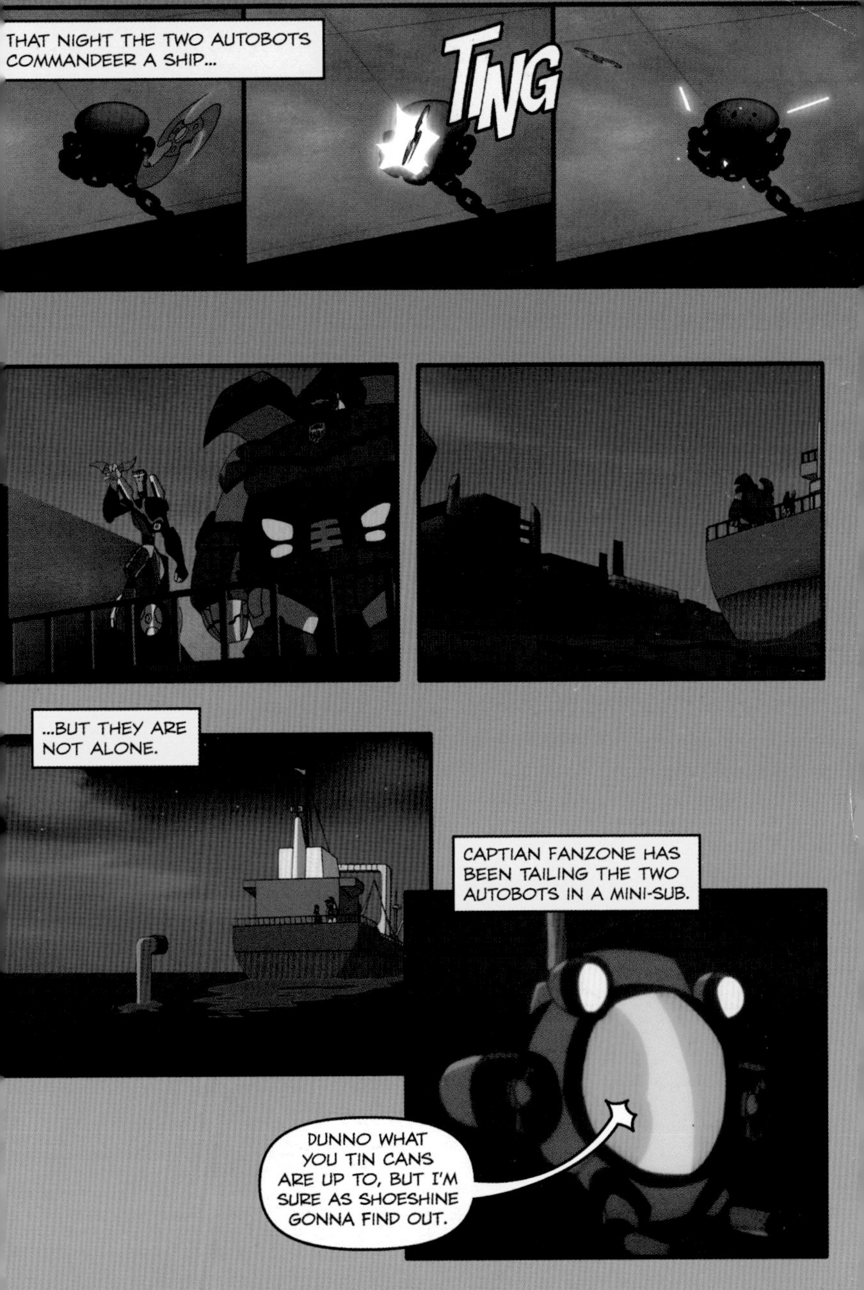
THAT NIGHT THE TWO AUTOBOTS COMMANDEER A SHIP...
TING
...BUT THEY ARE NOT ALONE.
CAPTIAN FANZONE HAS BEEN TAILING THE TWO AUTOBOTS IN A MINI-SUB.
DUNNO WHAT YOU TIN CANS ARE UP TO, BUT I'M SURE AS SHOESHINE GONNA FIND OUT.

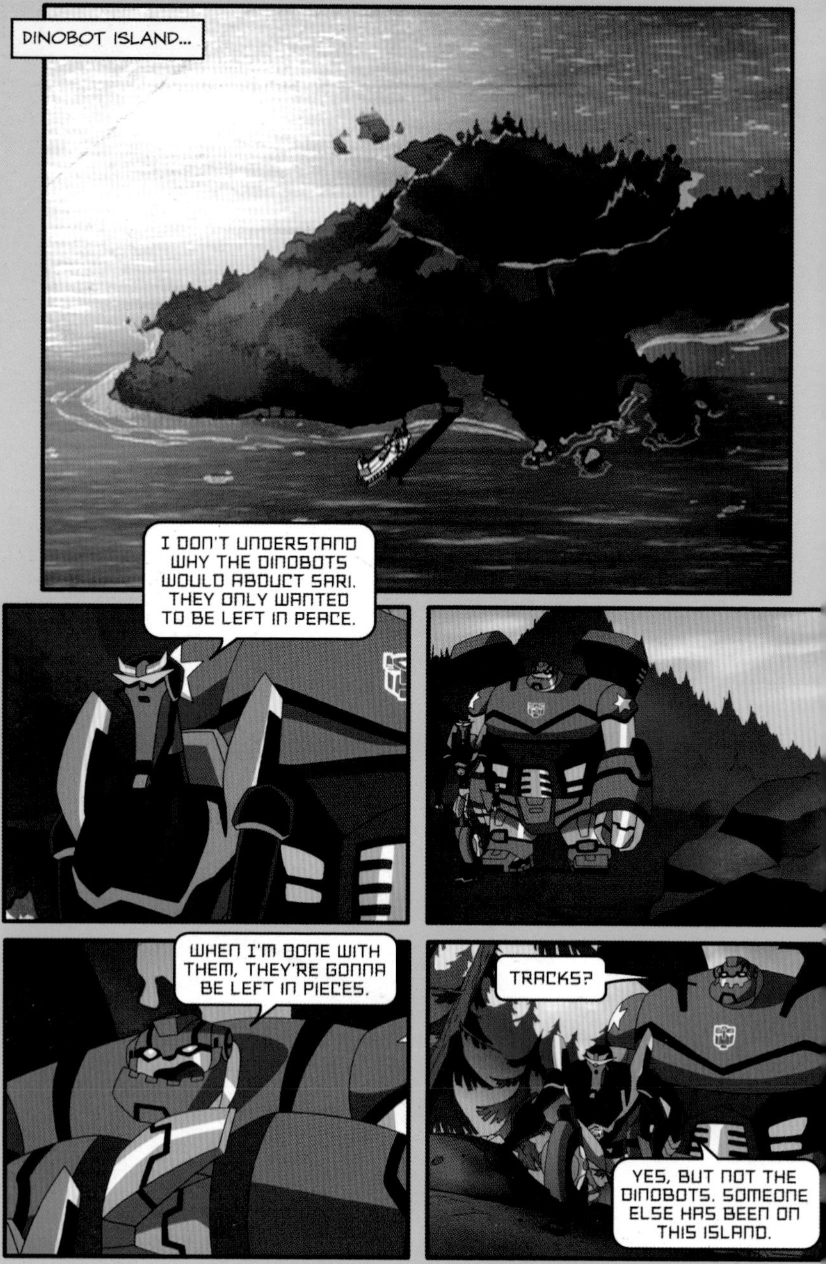
DINOBOT ISLAND...
I DON'T UNDERSTAND WHY THE DINOBOTS WOULD ABDUCT SARI. THEY ONLY WANTED TO BE LEFT IN PEACE.
WHEN I'M DONE WITH THEM, THEY'RE GONNA BE LEFT IN PIECES.
TRACKS?
YES, BUT NOT THE DINOBOTS. SOMEONE ELSE HAS BEEN ON THIS ISLAND.

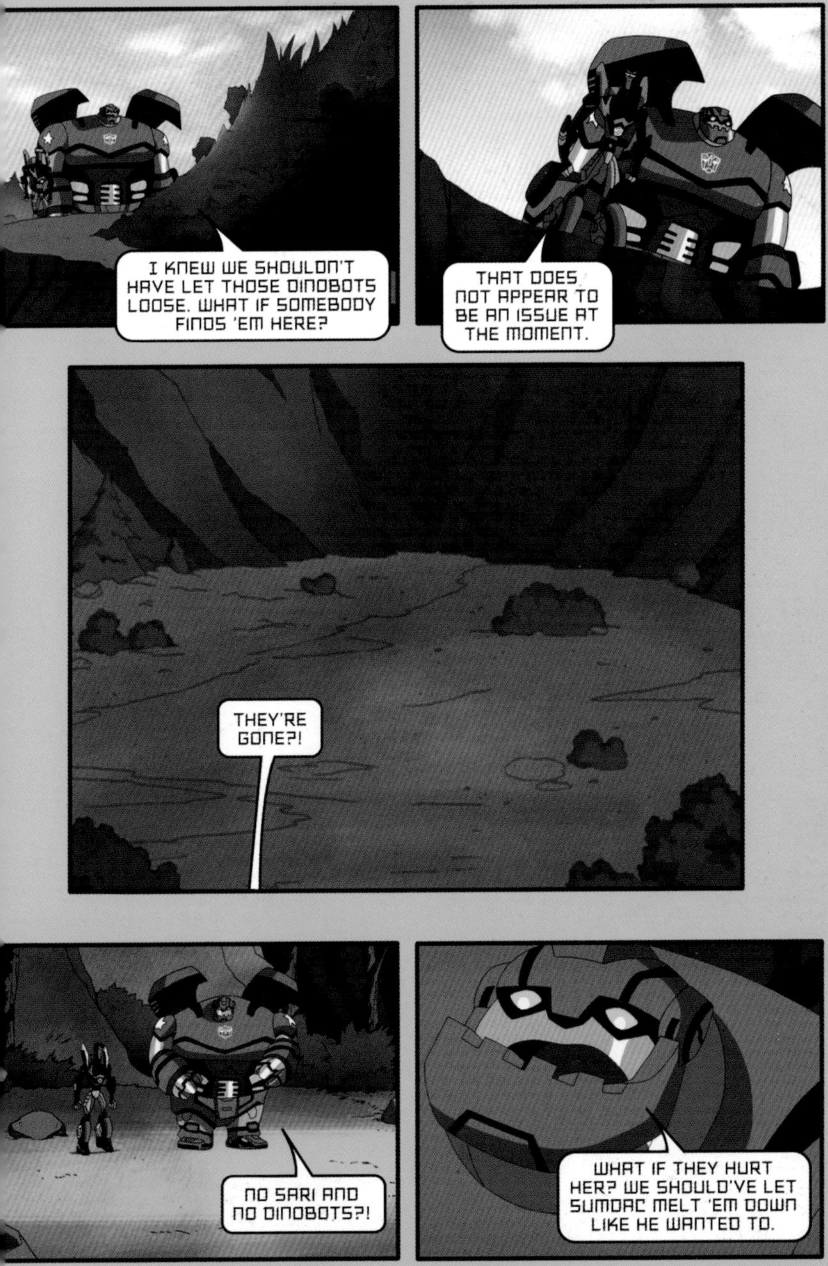
I KNEW WE SHOULDN'T HAVE LET THOSE DINOBOTS LOOSE. WHAT IF SOMEBODY FINDS 'EM HERE?
THAT DOES NOT APPEAR TO BE AN ISSUE AT THE MOMENT.
THEY'RE GONE?!
NO SARI AND NO DINOBOTS?!
WHAT IF THEY HURT HER? WE SHOULD'VE LET SUMDAC MELT 'EM DOWN LIKE HE WANTED TO.

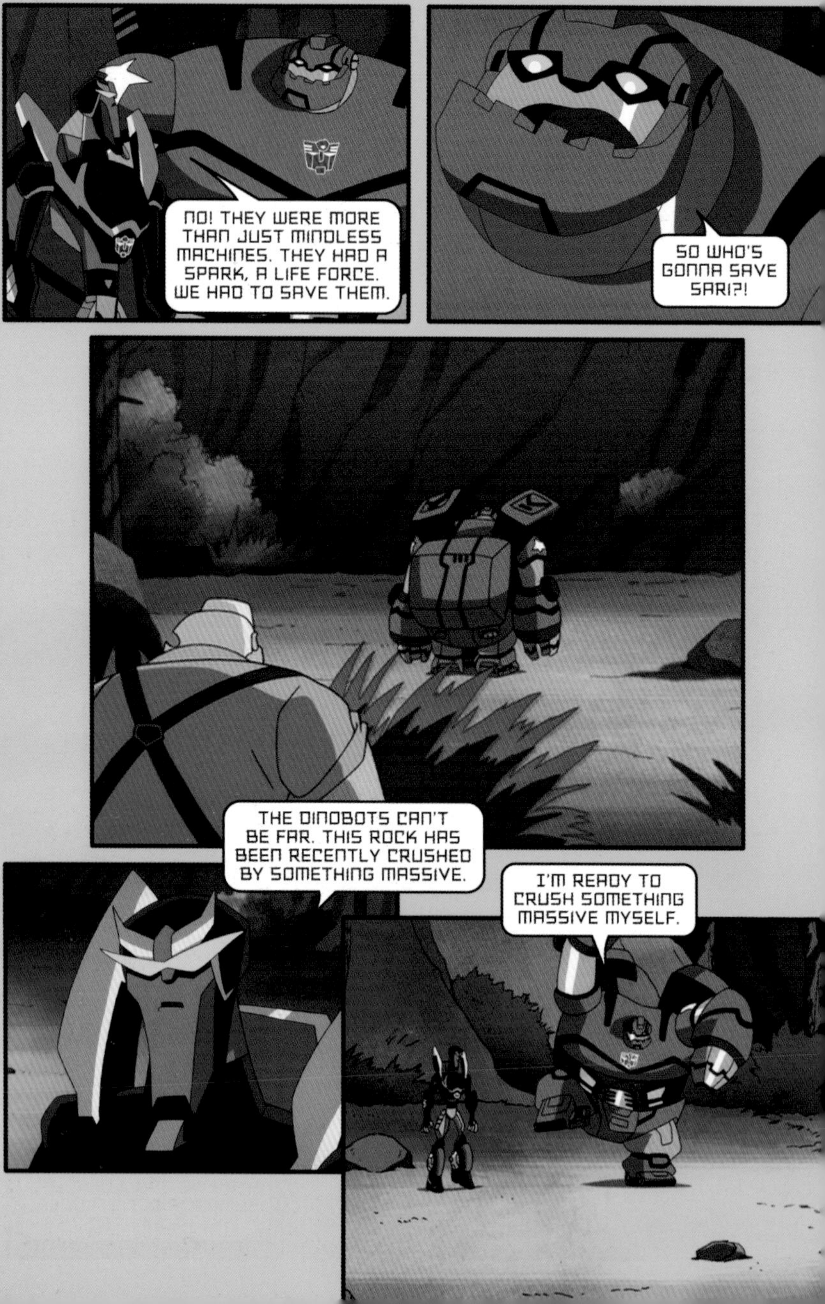
NO! THEY WERE MORE THAN JUST MINDLESS MACHINES. THEY HAD A SPARK, A LIFE FORCE. WE HAD TO SAVE THEM.
SO WHO'S GONNA SAVE SARI?!
THE DINOBOTS CAN'T BE FAR. THIS ROCK HAS BEEN RECENTLY CRUSHED BY SOMETHING MASSIVE.
I'M READY TO CRUSH SOMETHING MASSIVE MYSELF.

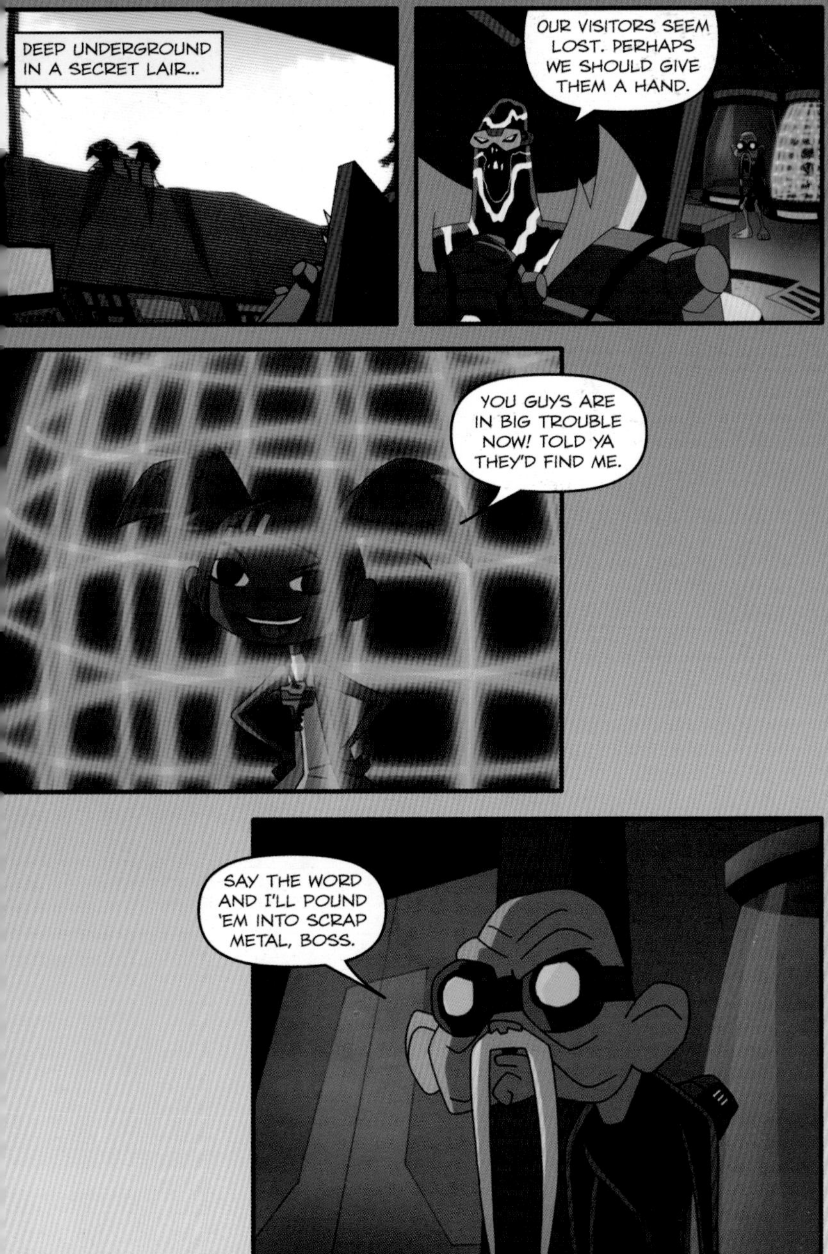
DEEP UNDERGROUND IN A SECRET LAIR...
OUR VISITORS SEEM LOST. PERHAPS WE SHOULD GIVE THEM A HAND.
YOU GUYS ARE IN BIG TROUBLE NOW! TOLD YA THEY'D FIND ME.
SAY THE WORD AND I'LL POUND 'EM INTO SCRAP METAL, BOSS.

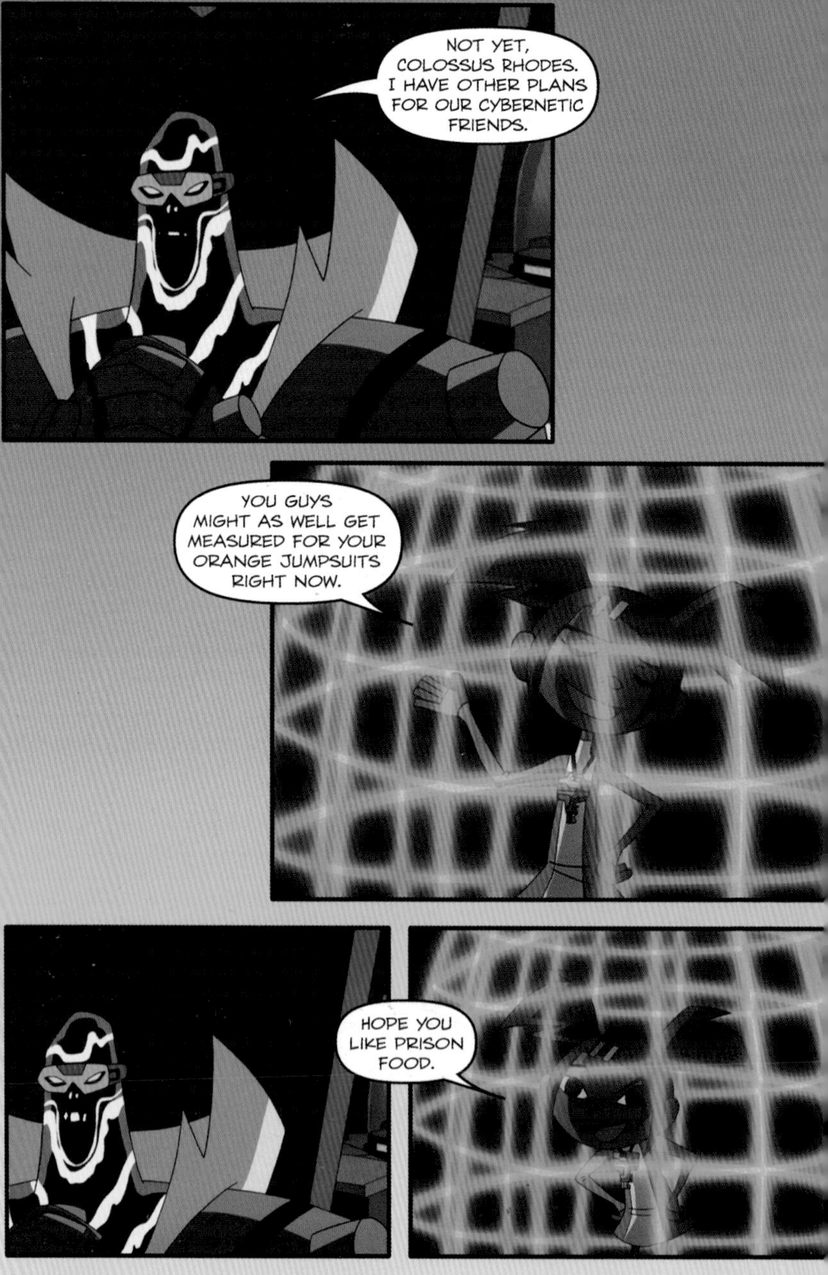
NOT YET, COLOSSUS RHODES. I HAVE OTHER PLANS FOR OUR CYBERNETIC FRIENDS.
YOU GUYS MIGHT AS WELL GET MEASURED FOR YOUR ORANGE JUMPSUITS RIGHT NOW.
HOPE YOU LIKE PRISON FOOD.

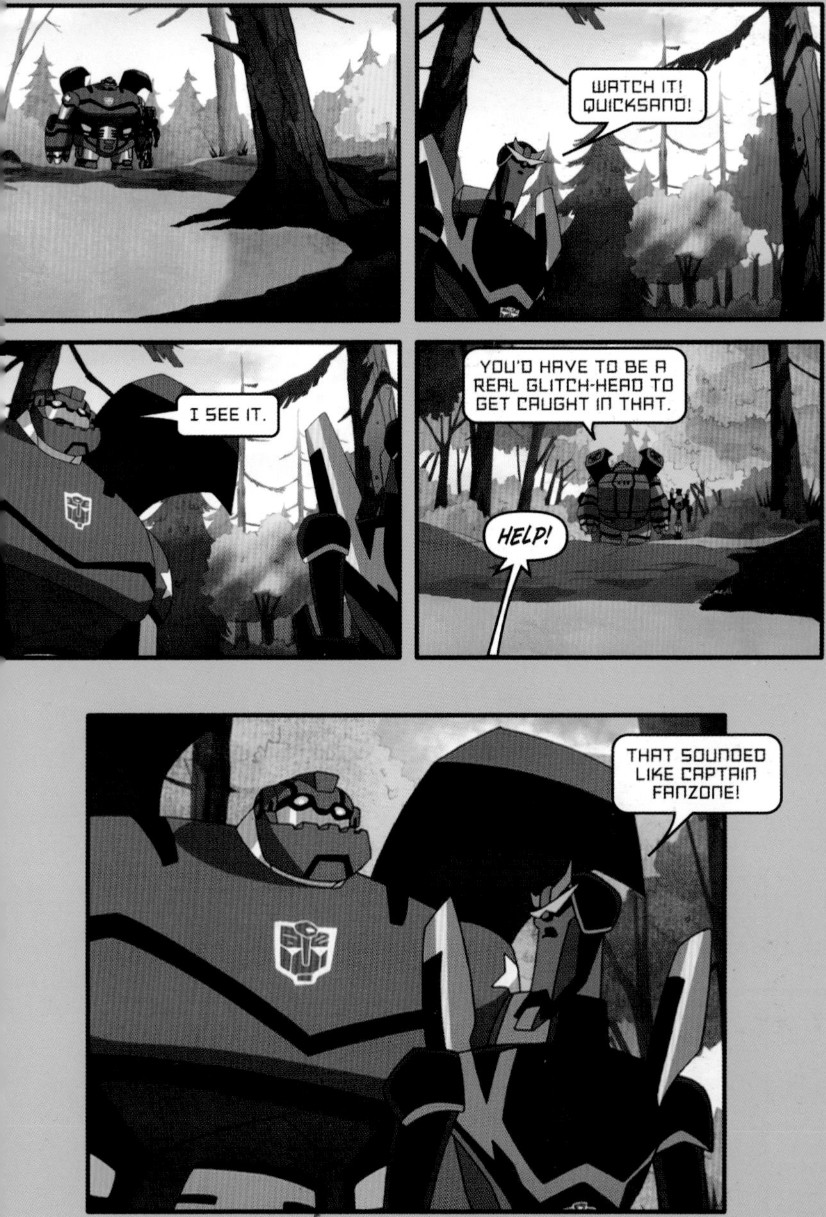
WATCH IT! QUICKSAND!
I SEE IT.
YOU'D HAVE TO BE A REAL GLITCH-HEAD TO GET CAUGHT IN THAT.
HELP!
THAT SOUNDED LIKE CAPTAIN FANZONE!

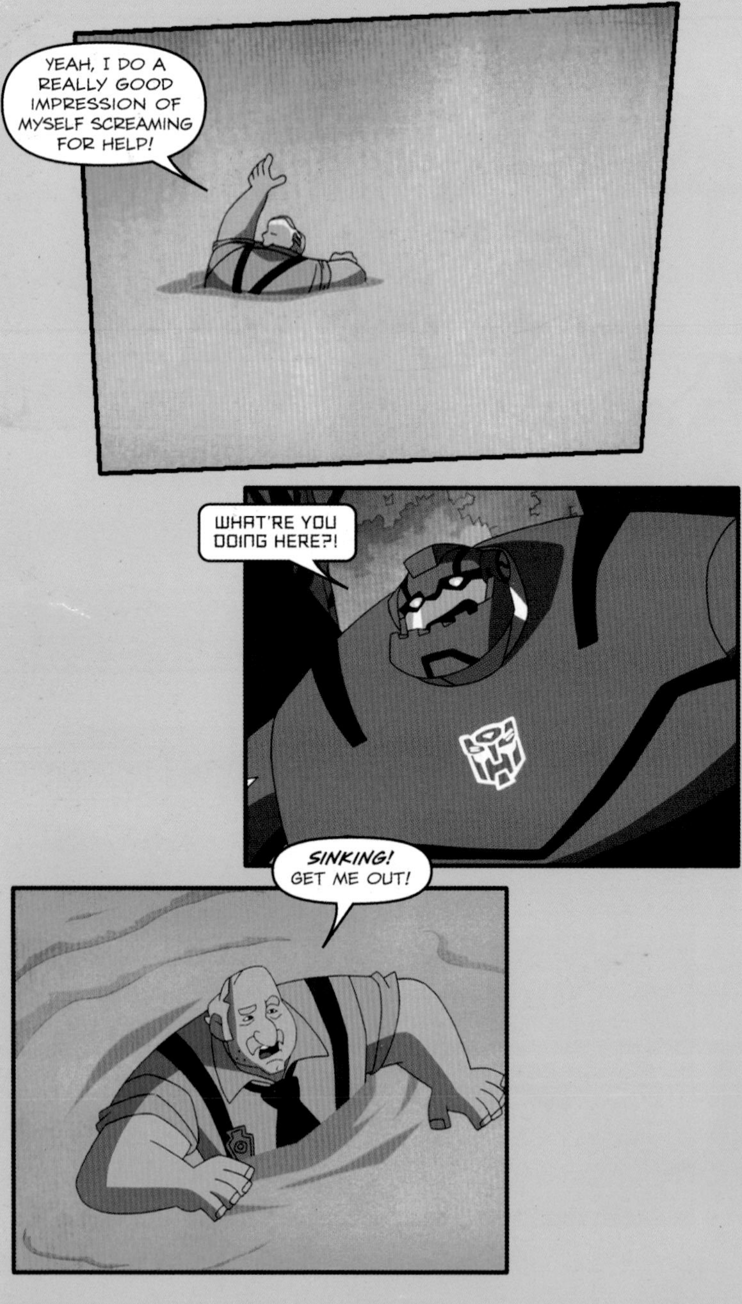
YEAH, I DO A REALLY GOOD IMPRESSION OF MYSELF SCREAMING FOR HELP!
WHAT'RE YOU DOING HERE?!
SINKING! GET ME OUT!

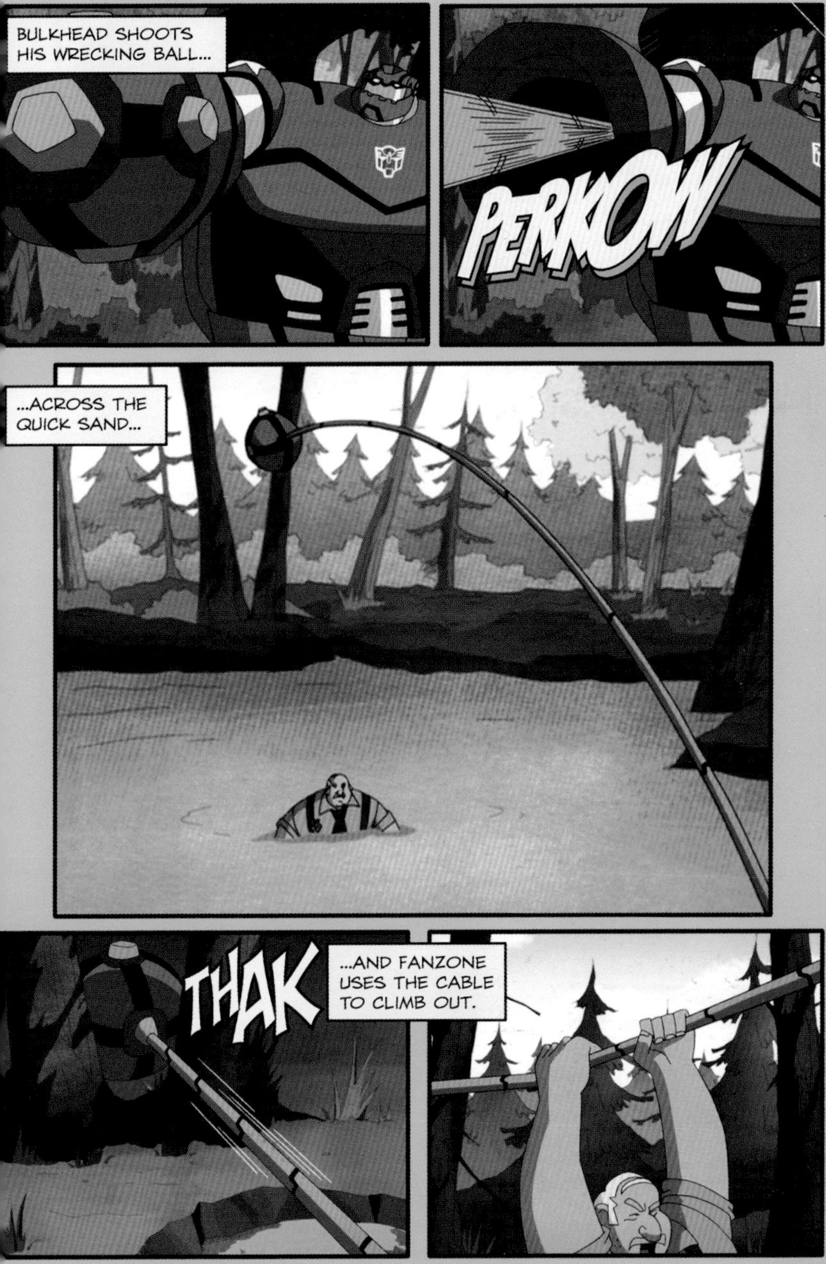
BULKHEAD SHOOTS HIS WRECKING BALL...
PERKOW
...ACROSS THE QUICK SAND...
THAK
...AND FANZONE USES THE CABLE TO CLIMB OUT.

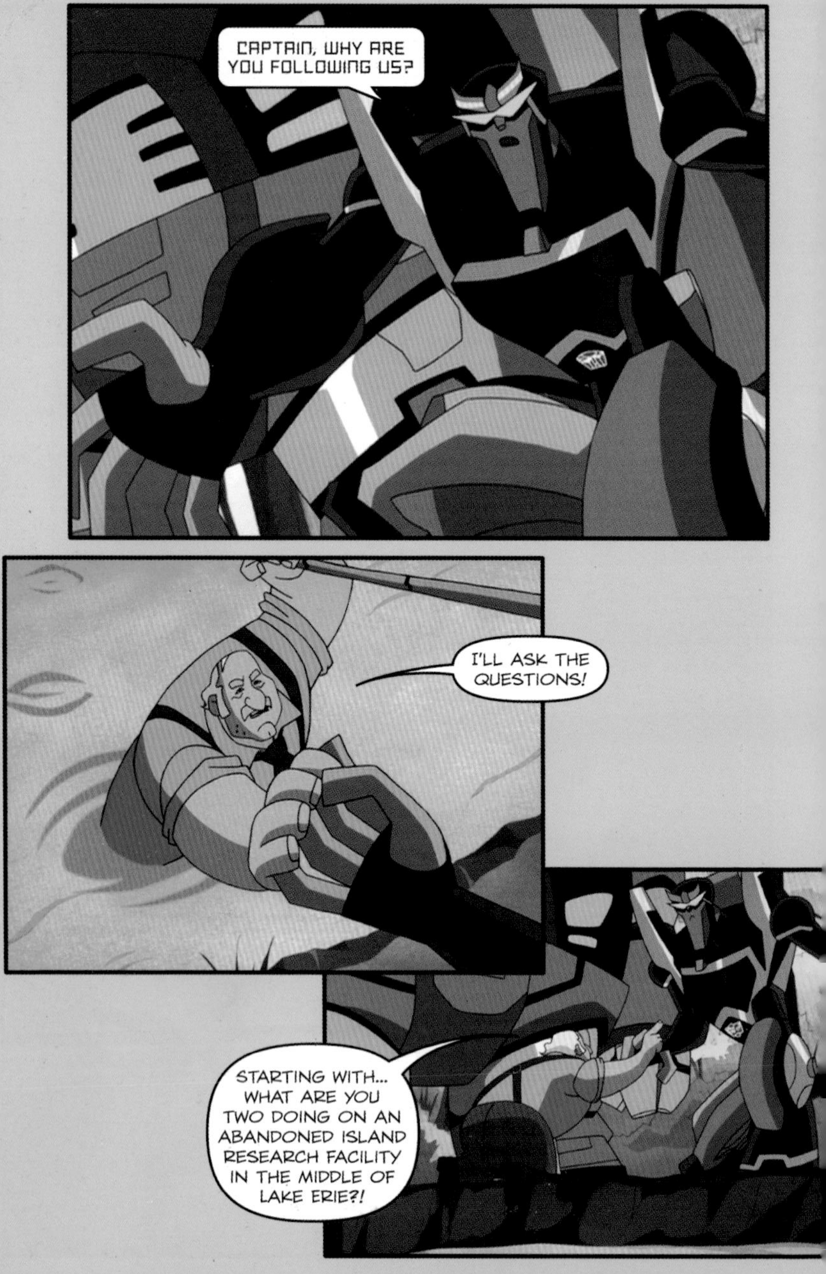
CAPTAIN, WHY ARE YOU FOLLOWING US?
I'LL ASK THE QUESTIONS!
STARTING WITH... WHAT ARE YOU TWO DOING ON AN ABANDONED ISLAND RESEARCH FACILITY IN THE MIDDLE OF LAKE ERIE?!

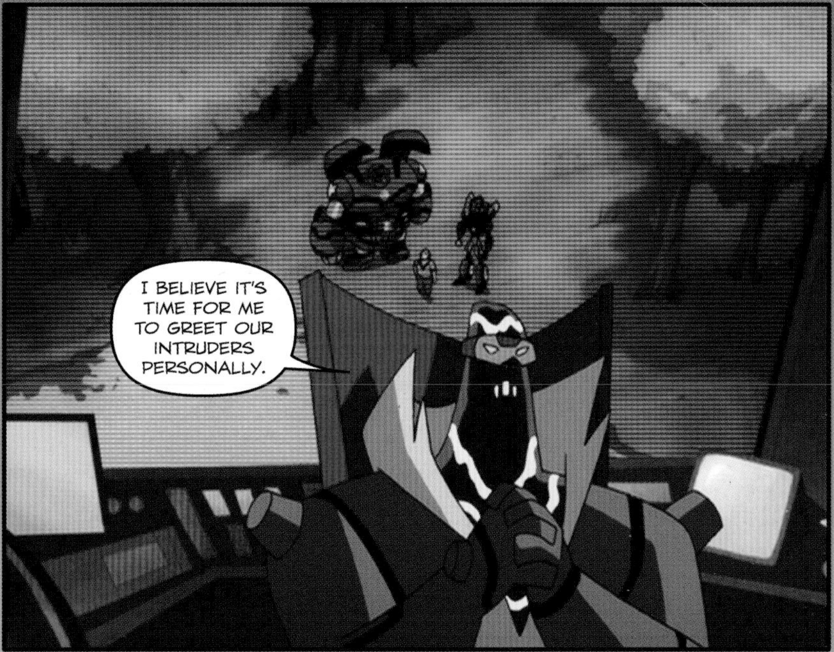
I BELIEVE IT'S TIME FOR ME TO GREET OUR INTRUDERS PERSONALLY.

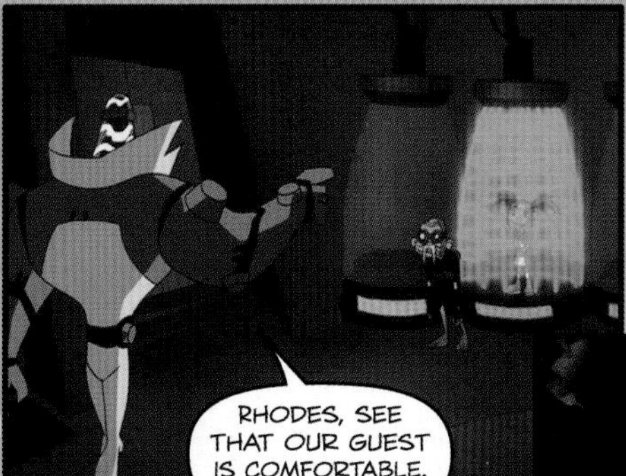
RHODES, SEE THAT OUR GUEST IS COMFORTABLE.

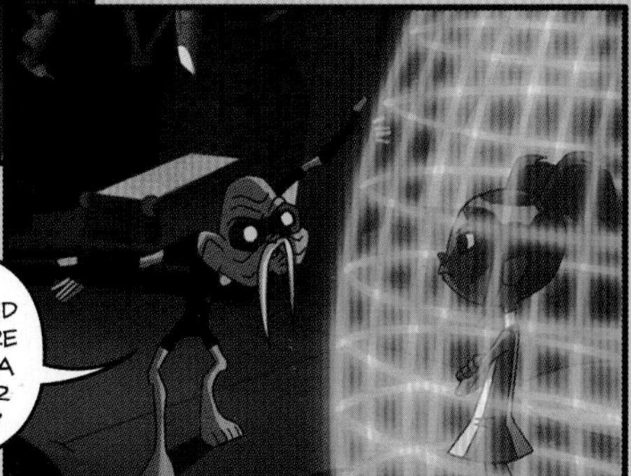
YOUR FRIENDS ARE TOAST! I SAID YOUR FRIENDS ARE TOAST! WHADAYA GOTTA SAY FOR YOURSELF NOW?

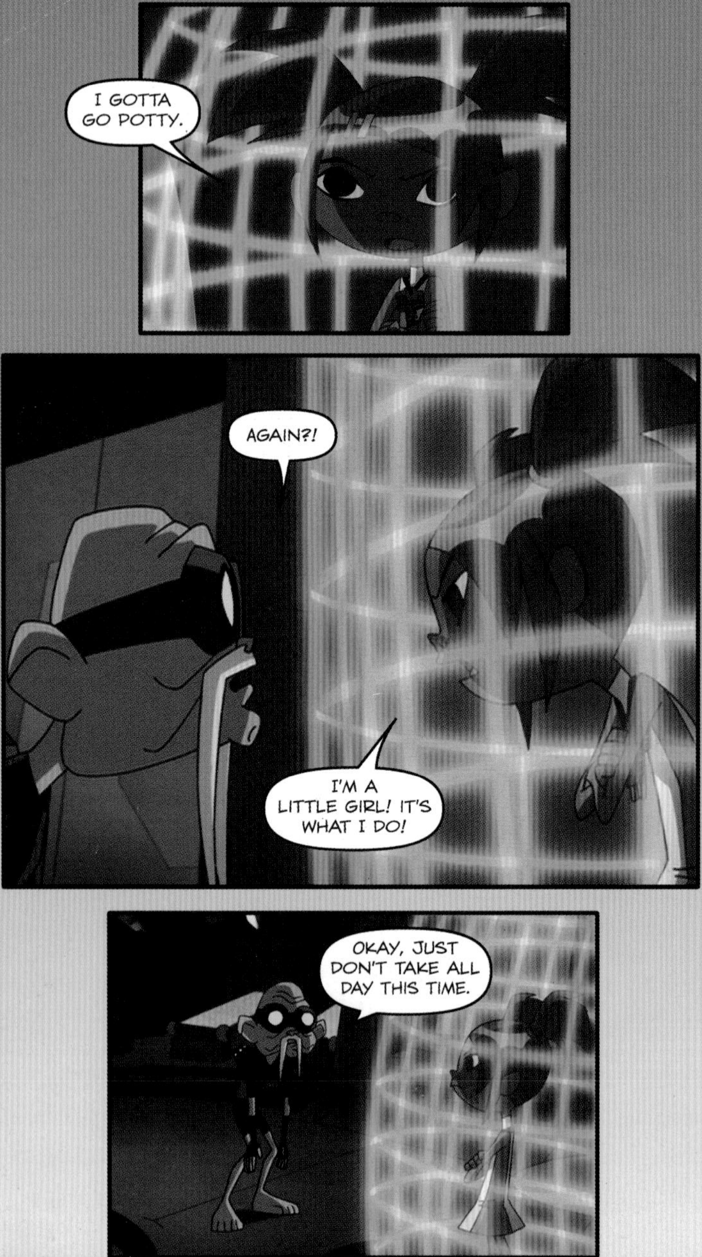
I GOTTA GO POTTY.
AGAIN?!
I'M A LITTLE GIRL! IT'S WHAT I DO!
OKAY, JUST DON'T TAKE ALL DAY THIS TIME.

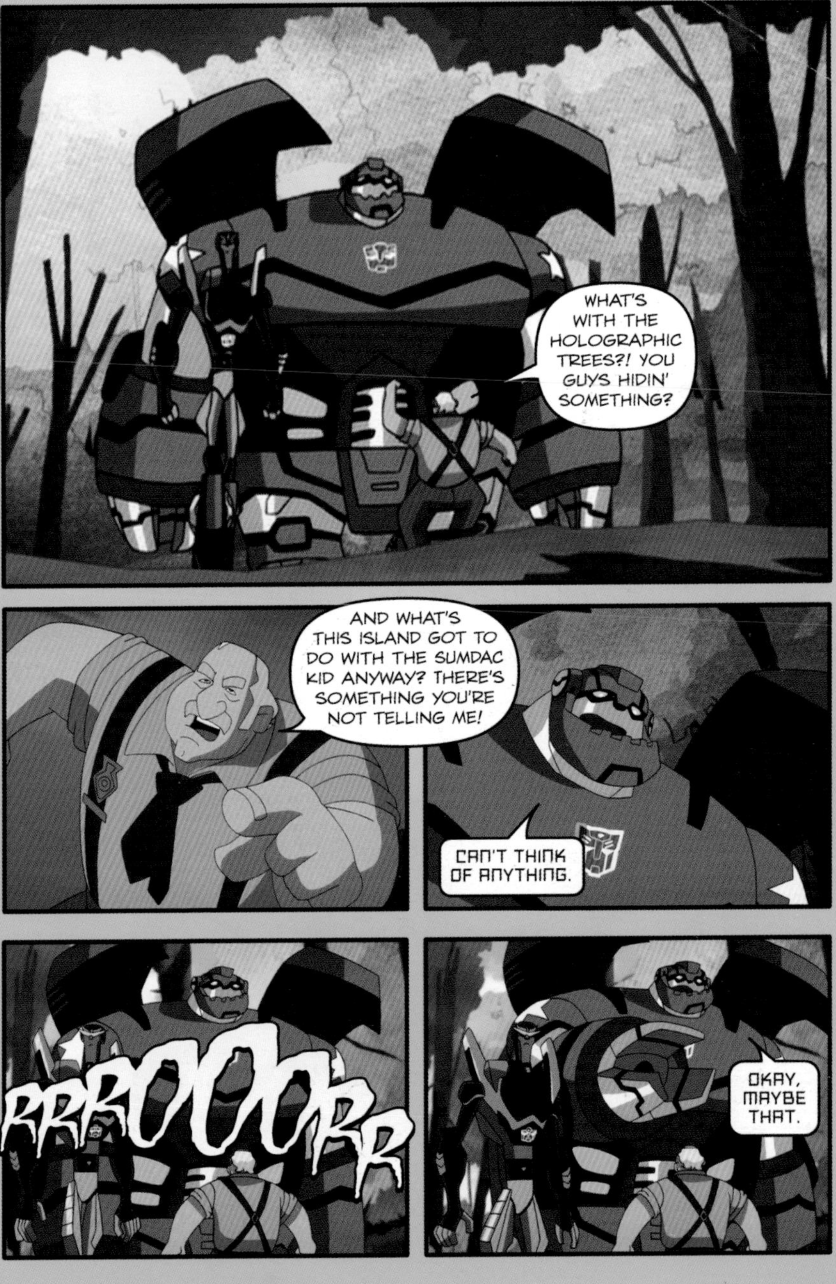
WHAT'S WITH THE HOLOGRAPHIC TREES?! YOU GUYS HIDIN' SOMETHING?
AND WHAT'S THIS ISLAND GOT TO DO WITH THE SUMDAC KID ANYWAY? THERE'S SOMETHING YOU'RE NOT TELLING ME!
CAN'T THINK OF ANYTHING.
RRROOOORR
OKAY, MAYBE THAT.

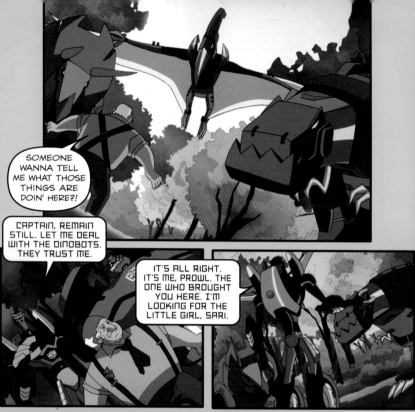

SOMEONE WANNA TELL ME WHAT THOSE THINGS ARE DOIN' HERE?!

CAPTAIN, REMAIN STILL. LET ME DEAL WITH THE DINOBOTS. THEY TRUST ME.

IT'S ALL RIGHT. IT'S ME, PROWL. THE ONE WHO BROUGHT YOU HERE. I'M LOOKING FOR THE LITTLE GIRL, SARI.

INTRUDERS! ME GRIMLOCK, DESTROY!

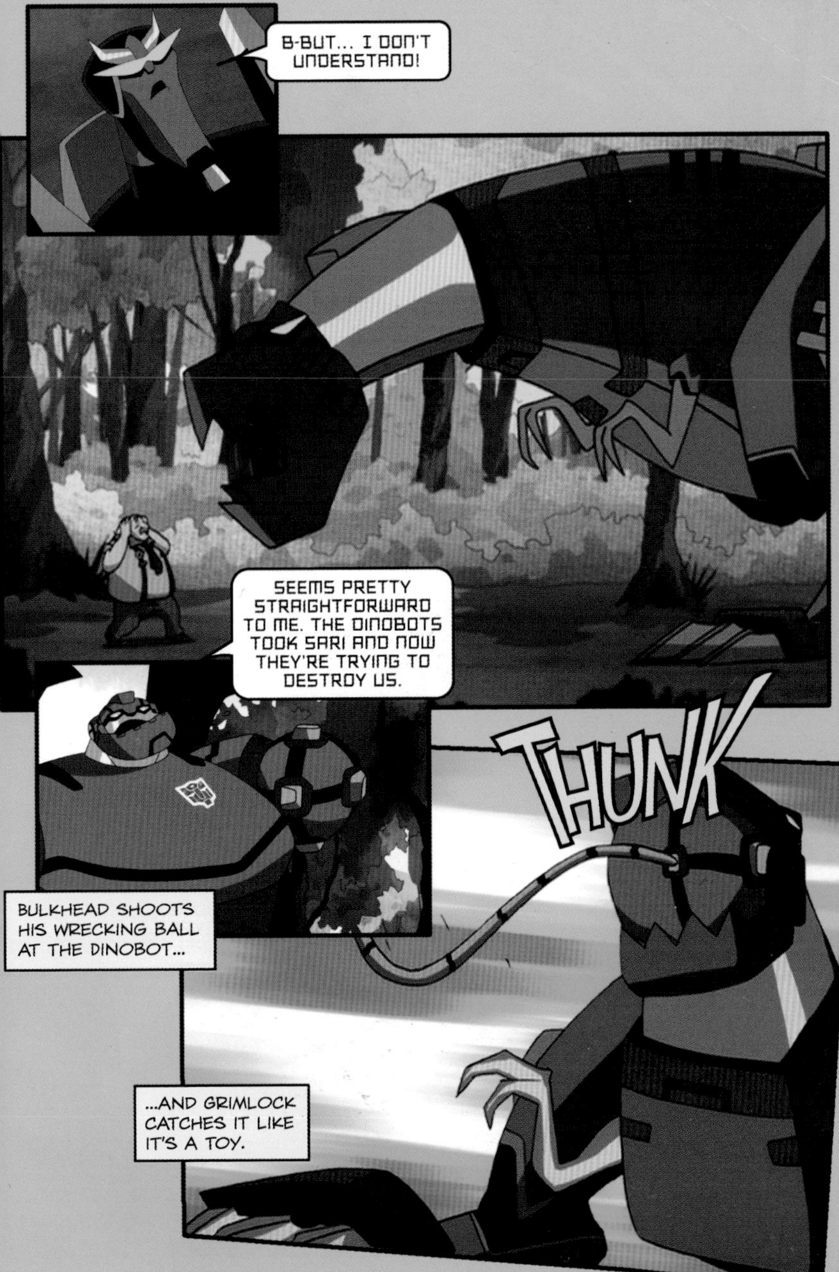
B-BUT... I DON'T UNDERSTAND!
SEEMS PRETTY STRAIGHTFORWARD TO ME. THE DINOBOTS TOOK SARI AND NOW THEY'RE TRYING TO DESTROY US.
BULKHEAD SHOOTS HIS WRECKING BALL AT THE DINOBOT...
THUNK
...AND GRIMLOCK CATCHES IT LIKE IT'S A TOY.

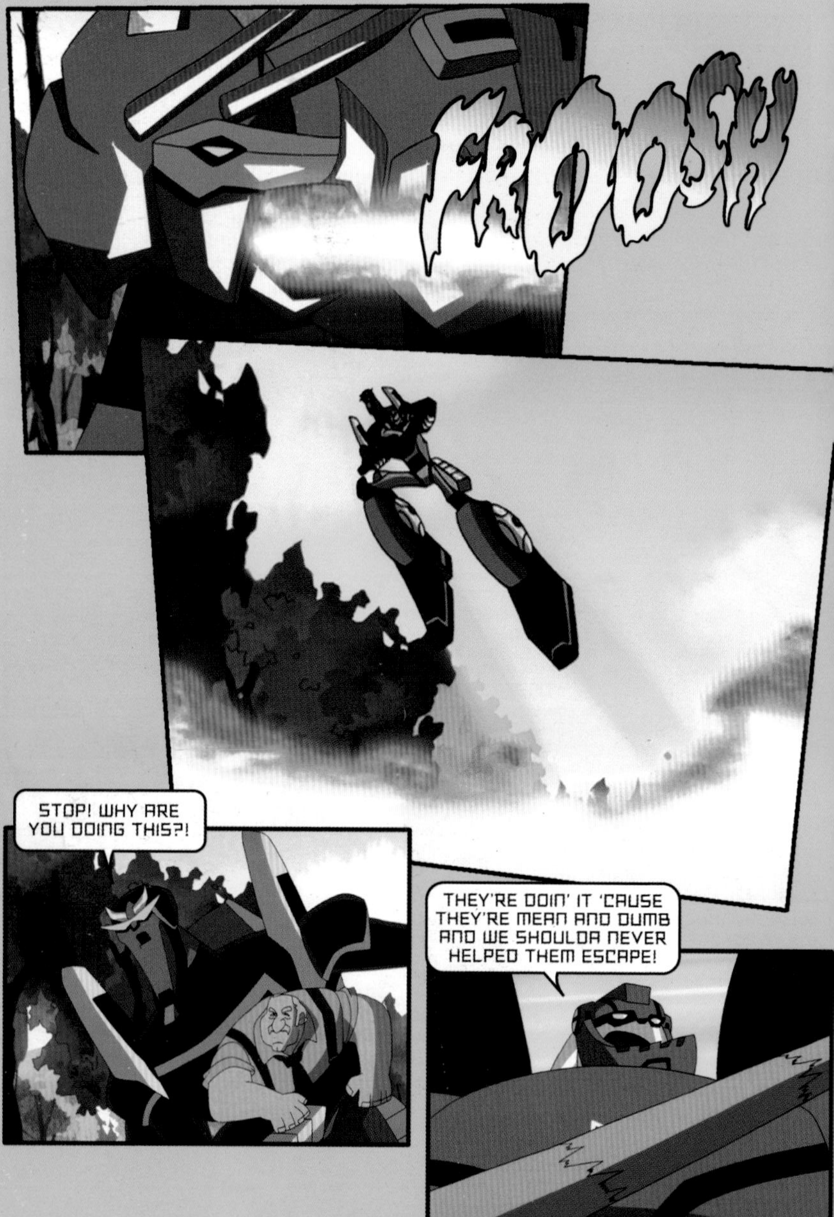
FROOSH
STOP! WHY ARE YOU DOING THIS?!
THEY'RE DOIN' IT 'CAUSE THEY'RE MEAN AND DUMB AND WE SHOULDA NEVER HELPED THEM ESCAPE!

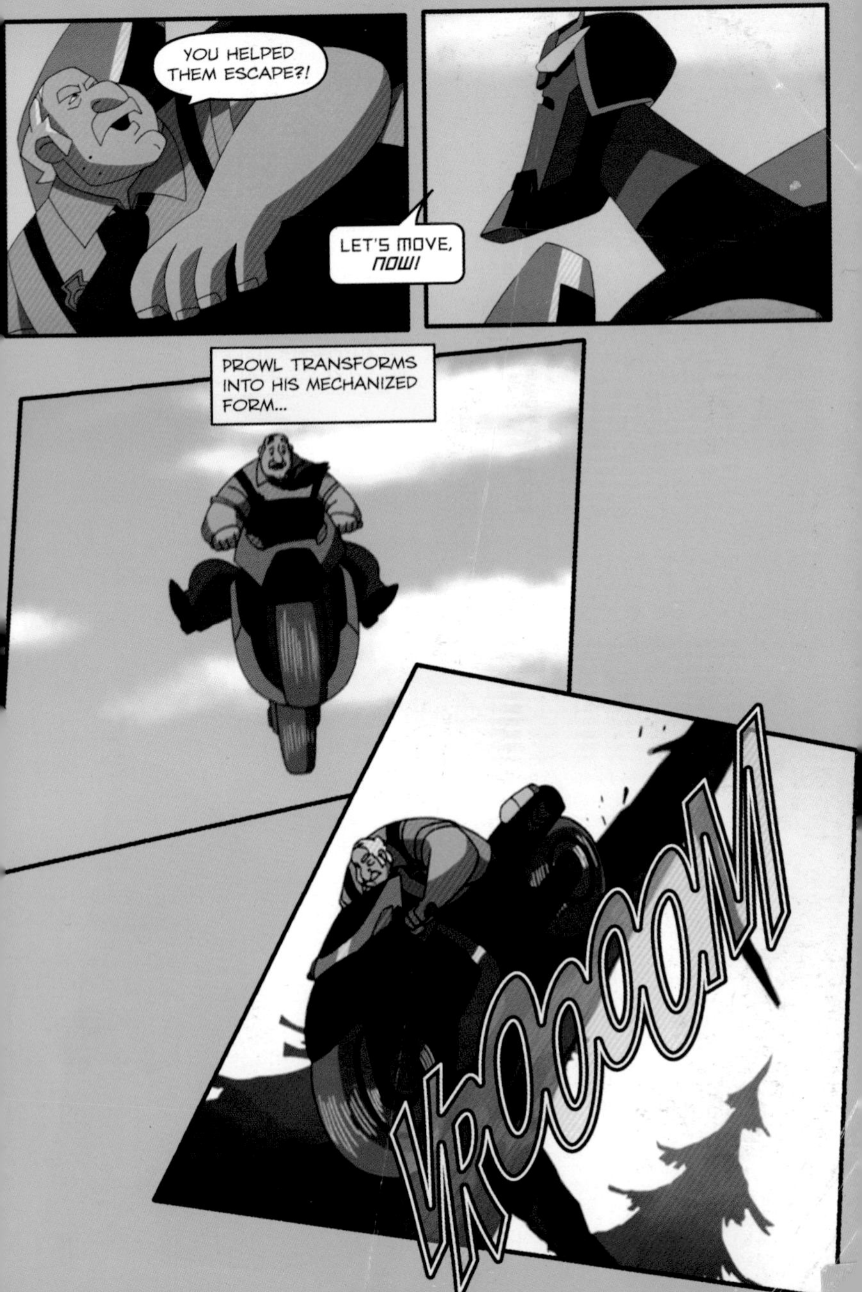
YOU HELPED THEM ESCAPE?!
LET'S MOVE, *NOW!*
PROWL TRANSFORMS INTO HIS MECHANIZED FORM...
VROOOOOM

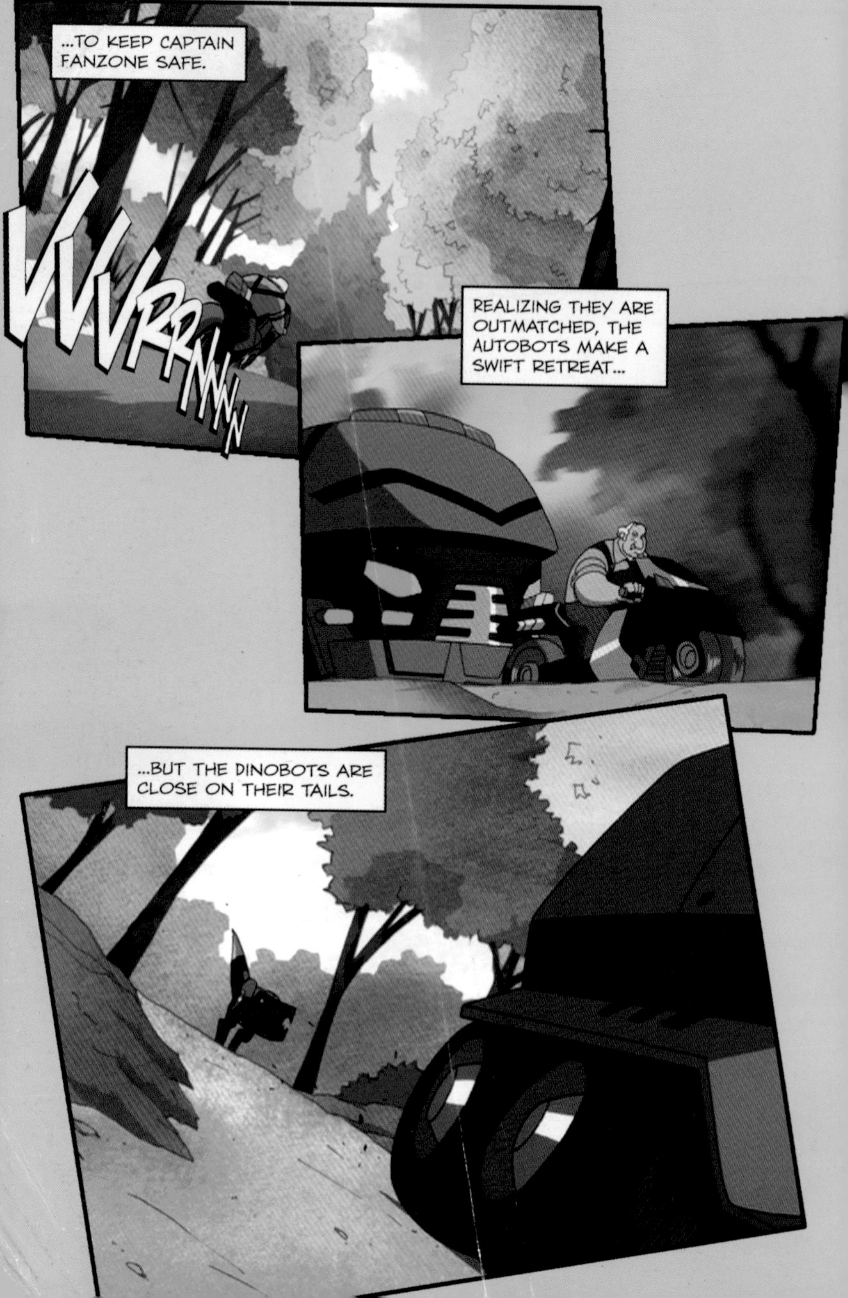
...TO KEEP CAPTAIN FANZONE SAFE.
VVVRRNNNN
REALIZING THEY ARE OUTMATCHED, THE AUTOBOTS MAKE A SWIFT RETREAT...
...BUT THE DINOBOTS ARE CLOSE ON THEIR TAILS.

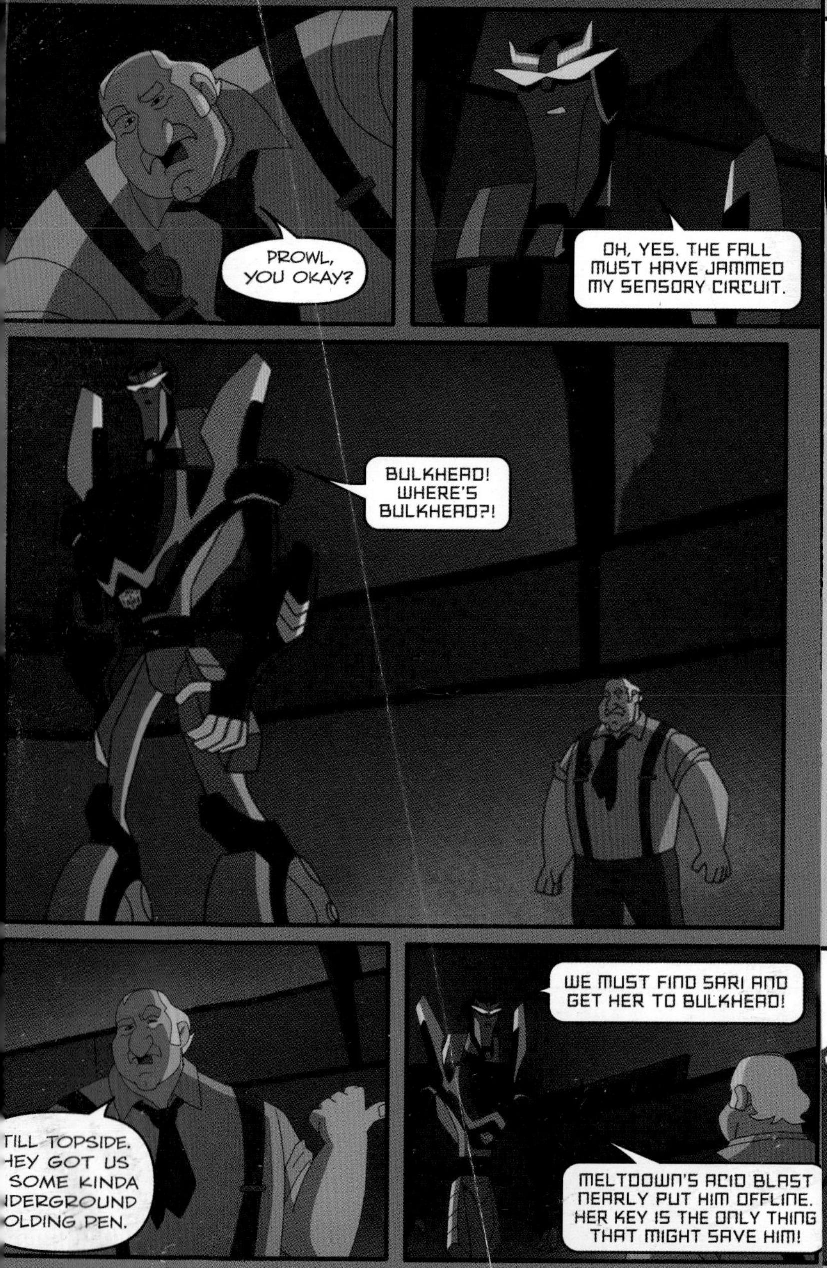
PROWL, YOU OKAY?
OH, YES. THE FALL MUST HAVE JAMMED MY SENSORY CIRCUIT.
BULKHEAD! WHERE'S BULKHEAD?!
TILL TOPSIDE. HEY GOT US SOME KINDA IDERGROUND OLDING PEN.
WE MUST FIND SARI AND GET HER TO BULKHEAD!
MELTDOWN'S ACID BLAST NEARLY PUT HIM OFFLINE. HER KEY IS THE ONLY THING THAT MIGHT SAVE HIM!

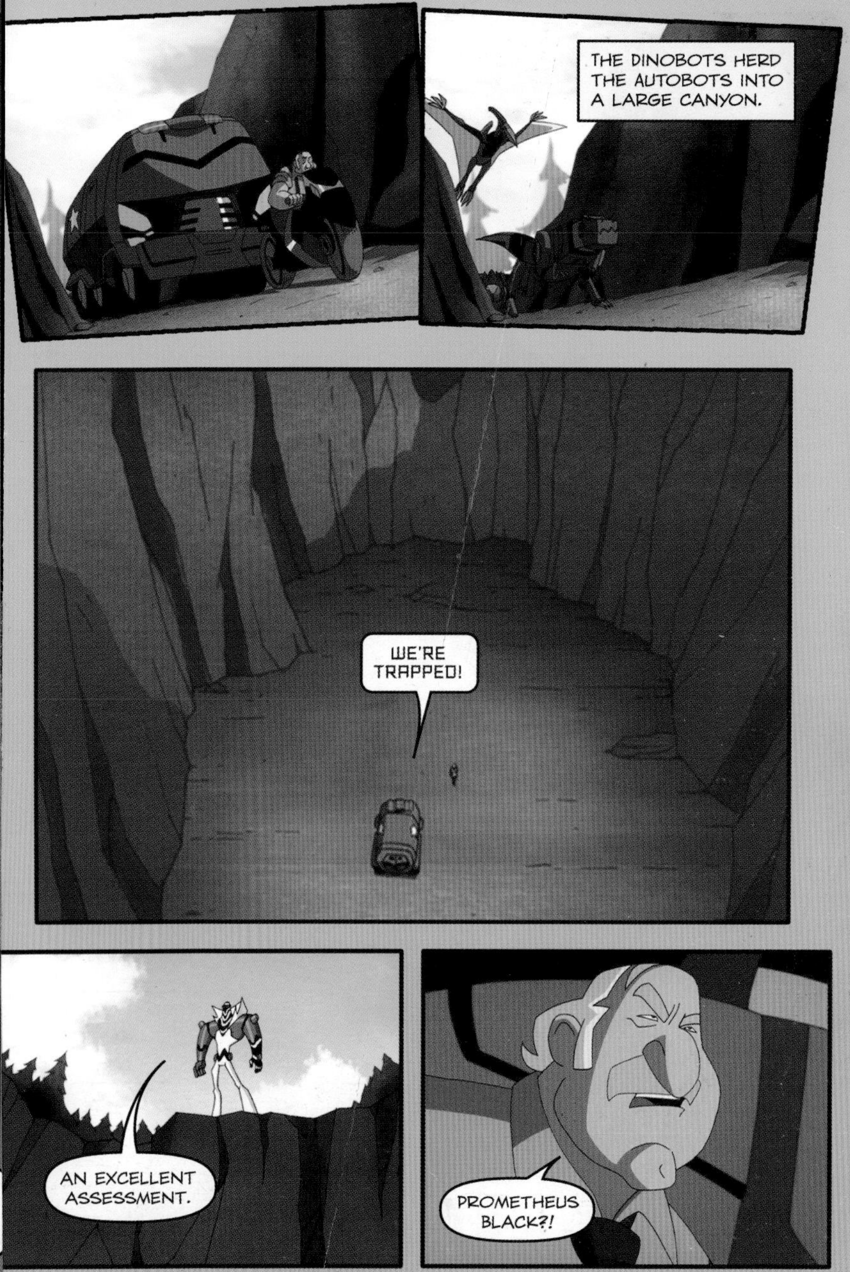
THE DINOBOTS HERD THE AUTOBOTS INTO A LARGE CANYON.
WE'RE TRAPPED!
AN EXCELLENT ASSESSMENT.
PROMETHEUS BLACK?!

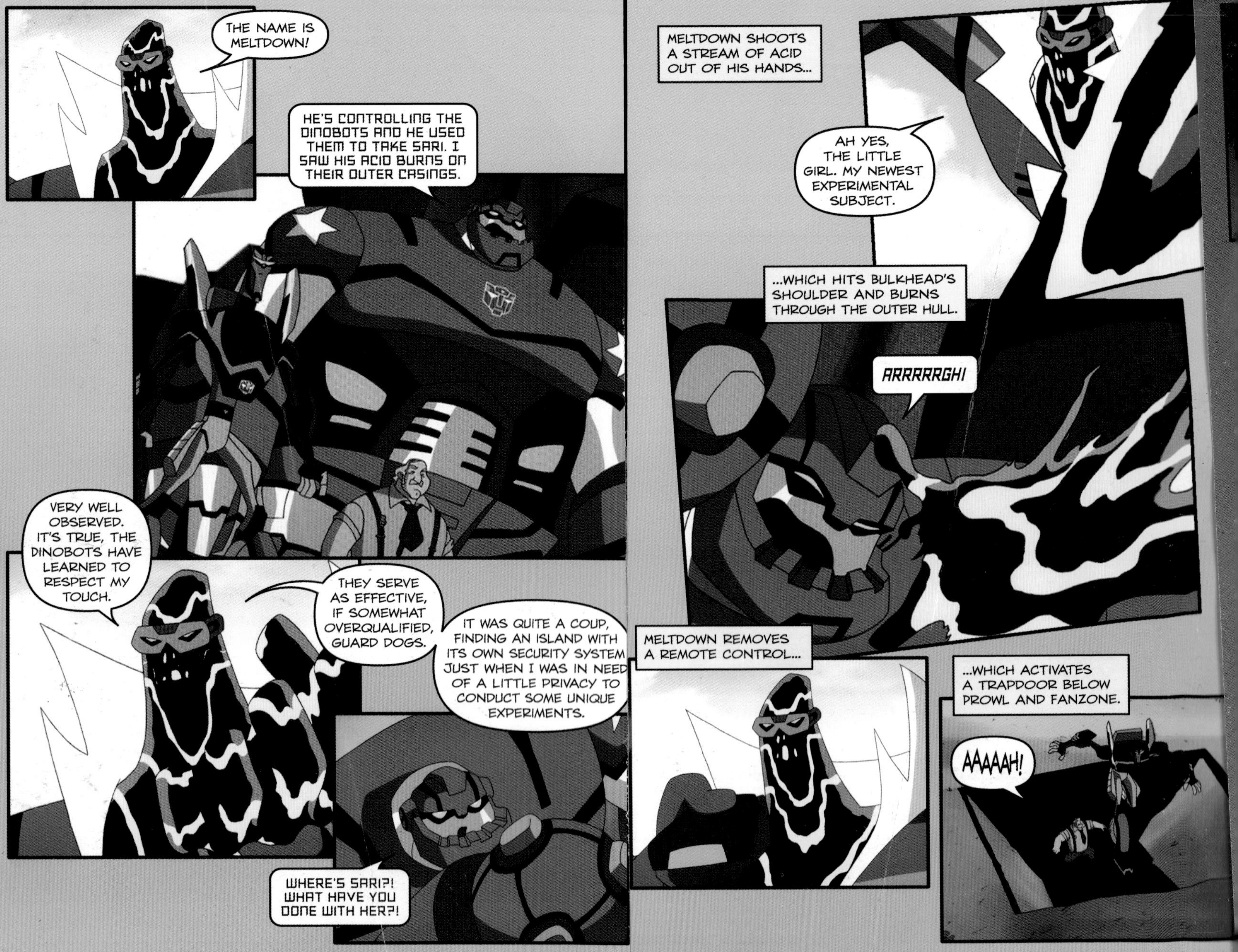
THE NAME IS MELTDOWN!
HE'S CONTROLLING THE DINOBOTS AND HE USED THEM TO TAKE SARI. I SAW HIS ACID BURNS ON THEIR OUTER CASINGS.
VERY WELL OBSERVED. IT'S TRUE, THE DINOBOTS HAVE LEARNED TO RESPECT MY TOUCH.
THEY SERVE AS EFFECTIVE, IF SOMEWHAT OVERQUALIFIED, GUARD DOGS.
IT WAS QUITE A COUP, FINDING AN ISLAND WITH ITS OWN SECURITY SYSTEM JUST WHEN I WAS IN NEED OF A LITTLE PRIVACY TO CONDUCT SOME UNIQUE EXPERIMENTS.
WHERE'S SARI?! WHAT HAVE YOU DONE WITH HER?!
MELTDOWN SHOOTS A STREAM OF ACID OUT OF HIS HANDS...
AH YES, THE LITTLE GIRL. MY NEWEST EXPERIMENTAL SUBJECT.
...WHICH HITS BULKHEAD'S SHOULDER AND BURNS THROUGH THE OUTER HULL.
ARRRRRGH!
MELTDOWN REMOVES A REMOTE CONTROL...
...WHICH ACTIVATES A TRAPDOOR BELOW PROWL AND FANZONE.
AAAAAH!

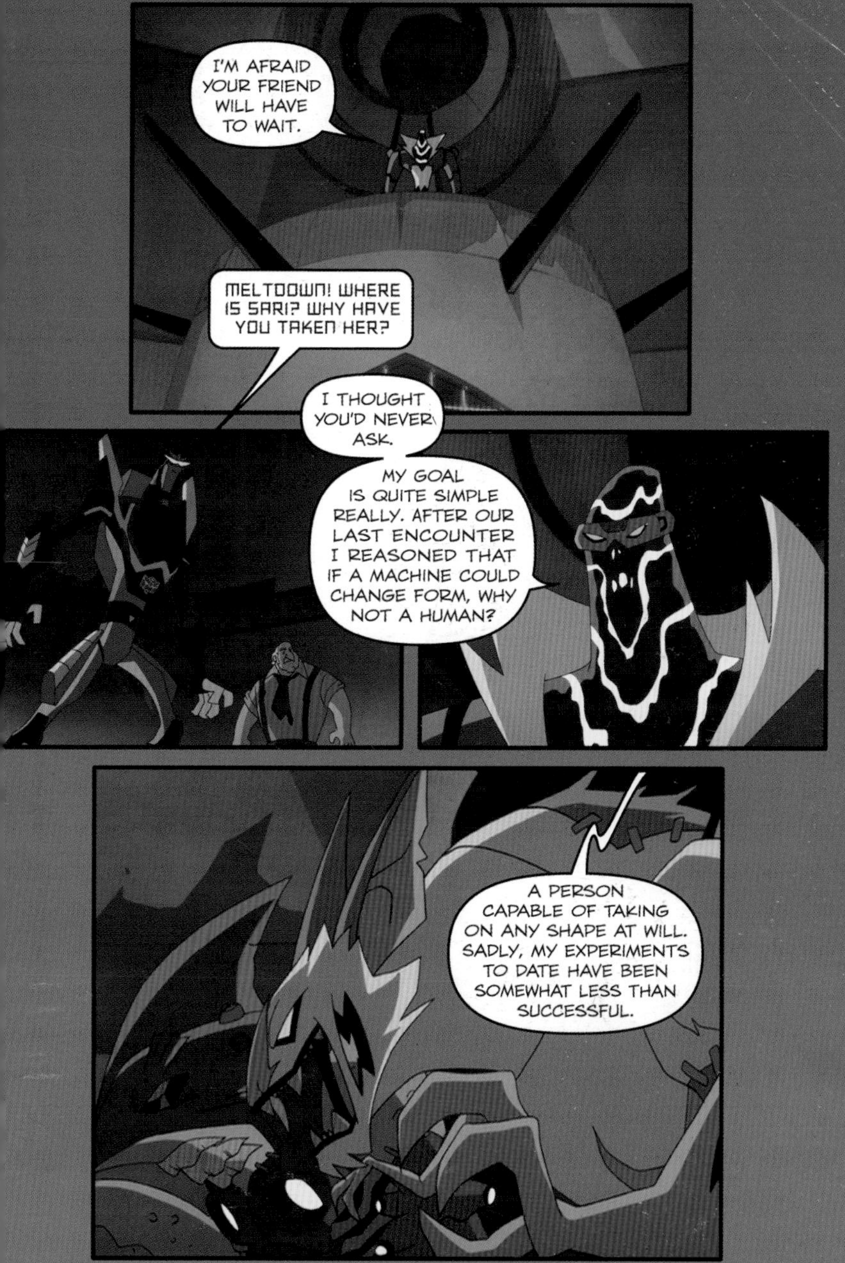
I'M AFRAID YOUR FRIEND WILL HAVE TO WAIT.
MELTDOWN! WHERE IS SARI? WHY HAVE YOU TAKEN HER?
I THOUGHT YOU'D NEVER ASK.
MY GOAL IS QUITE SIMPLE REALLY. AFTER OUR LAST ENCOUNTER I REASONED THAT IF A MACHINE COULD CHANGE FORM, WHY NOT A HUMAN?
A PERSON CAPABLE OF TAKING ON ANY SHAPE AT WILL. SADLY, MY EXPERIMENTS TO DATE HAVE BEEN SOMEWHAT LESS THAN SUCCESSFUL.

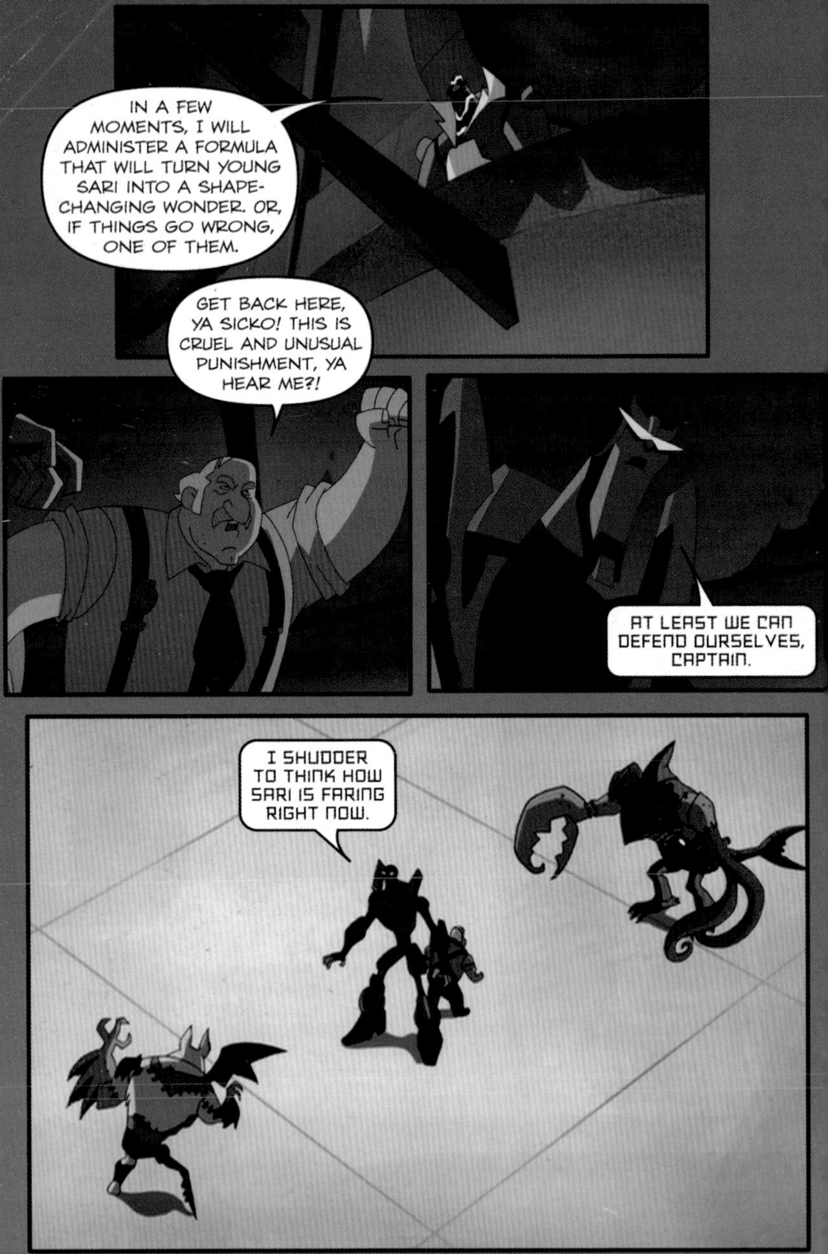
IN A FEW MOMENTS, I WILL ADMINISTER A FORMULA THAT WILL TURN YOUNG SARI INTO A SHAPE-CHANGING WONDER. OR, IF THINGS GO WRONG, ONE OF THEM.
GET BACK HERE, YA SICKO! THIS IS CRUEL AND UNUSUAL PUNISHMENT, YA HEAR ME?!
AT LEAST WE CAN DEFEND OURSELVES, CAPTAIN.
I SHUDDER TO THINK HOW SARI IS FARING RIGHT NOW.

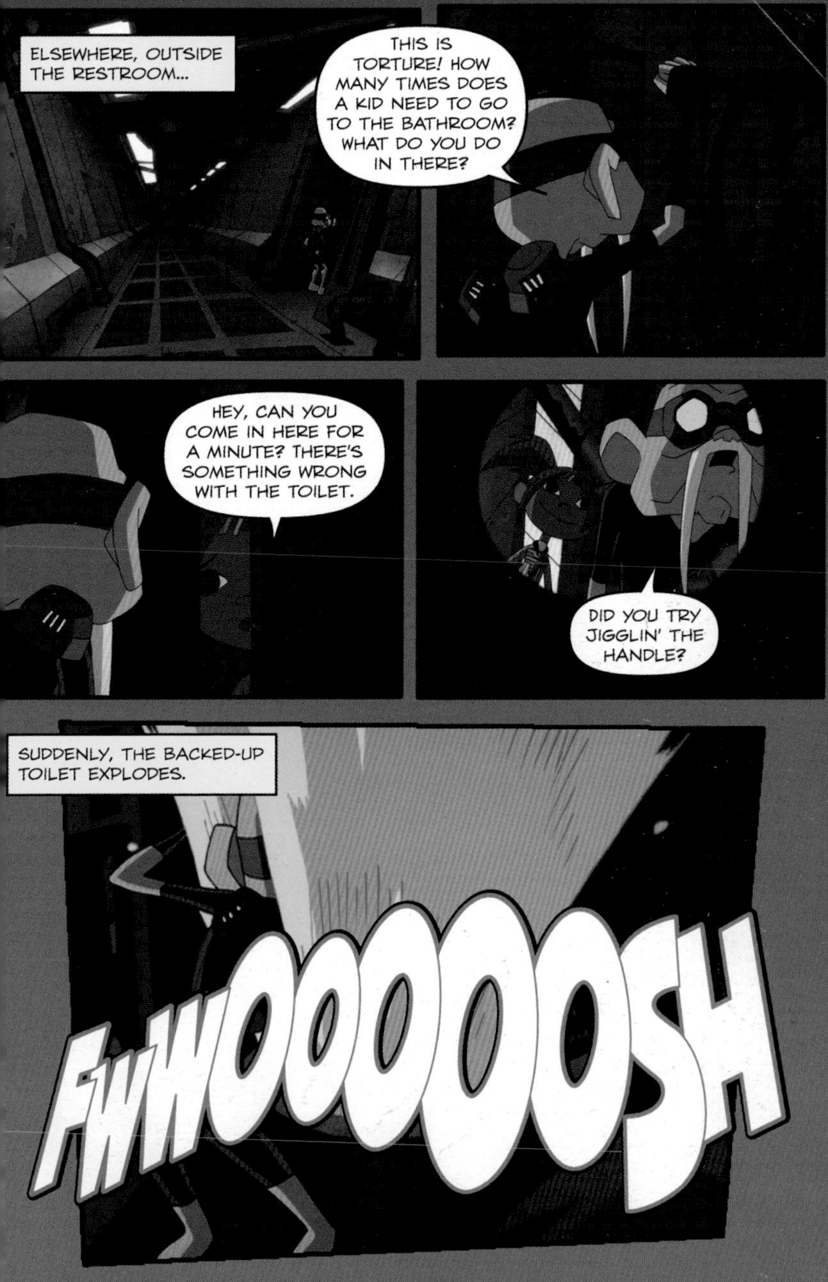
ELSEWHERE, OUTSIDE THE RESTROOM...
THIS IS TORTURE! HOW MANY TIMES DOES A KID NEED TO GO TO THE BATHROOM? WHAT DO YOU DO IN THERE?
HEY, CAN YOU COME IN HERE FOR A MINUTE? THERE'S SOMETHING WRONG WITH THE TOILET.
DID YOU TRY JIGGLIN' THE HANDLE?
SUDDENLY, THE BACKED-UP TOILET EXPLODES.
FWHOOOOOOSH

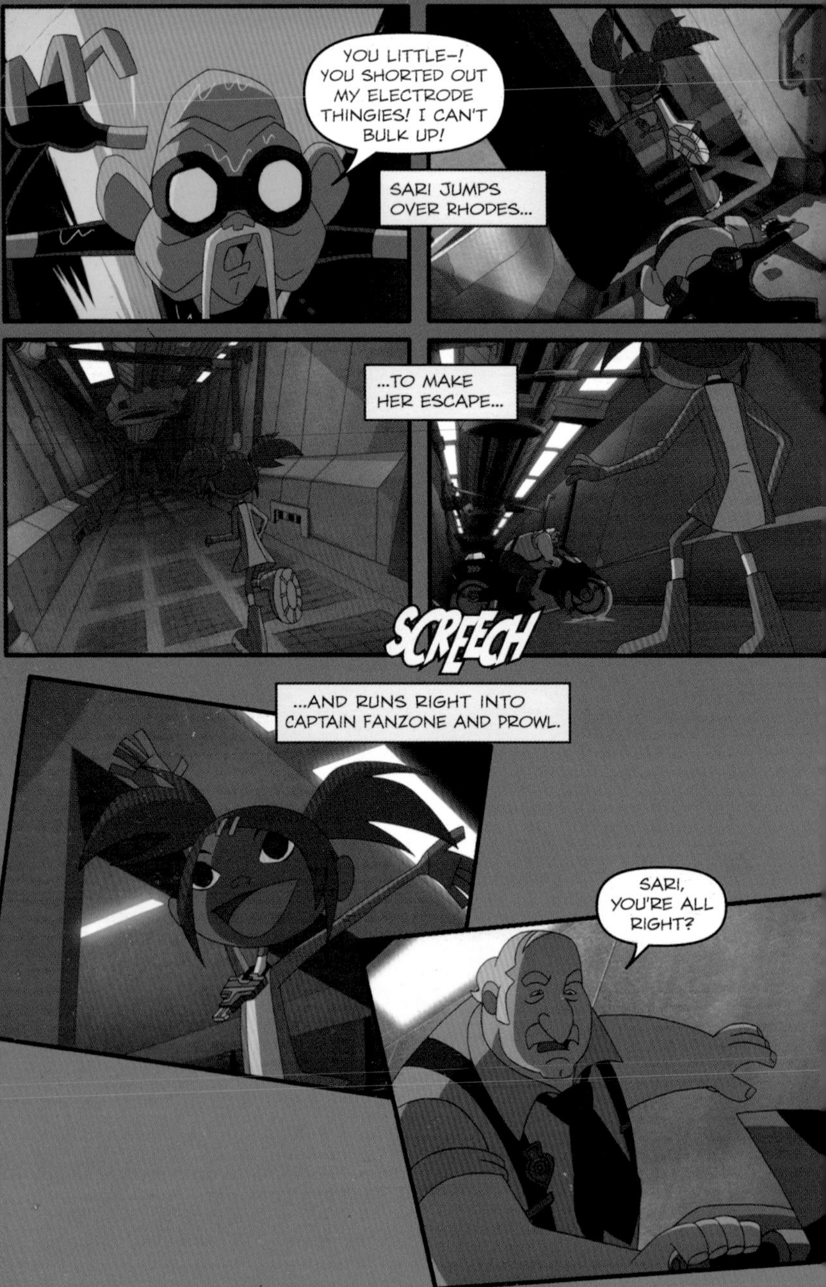
YOU LITTLE-! YOU SHORTED OUT MY ELECTRODE THINGIES! I CAN'T BULK UP!
SARI JUMPS OVER RHODES...
...TO MAKE HER ESCAPE...
SCREECH
...AND RUNS RIGHT INTO CAPTAIN FANZONE AND PROWL.
SARI, YOU'RE ALL RIGHT?

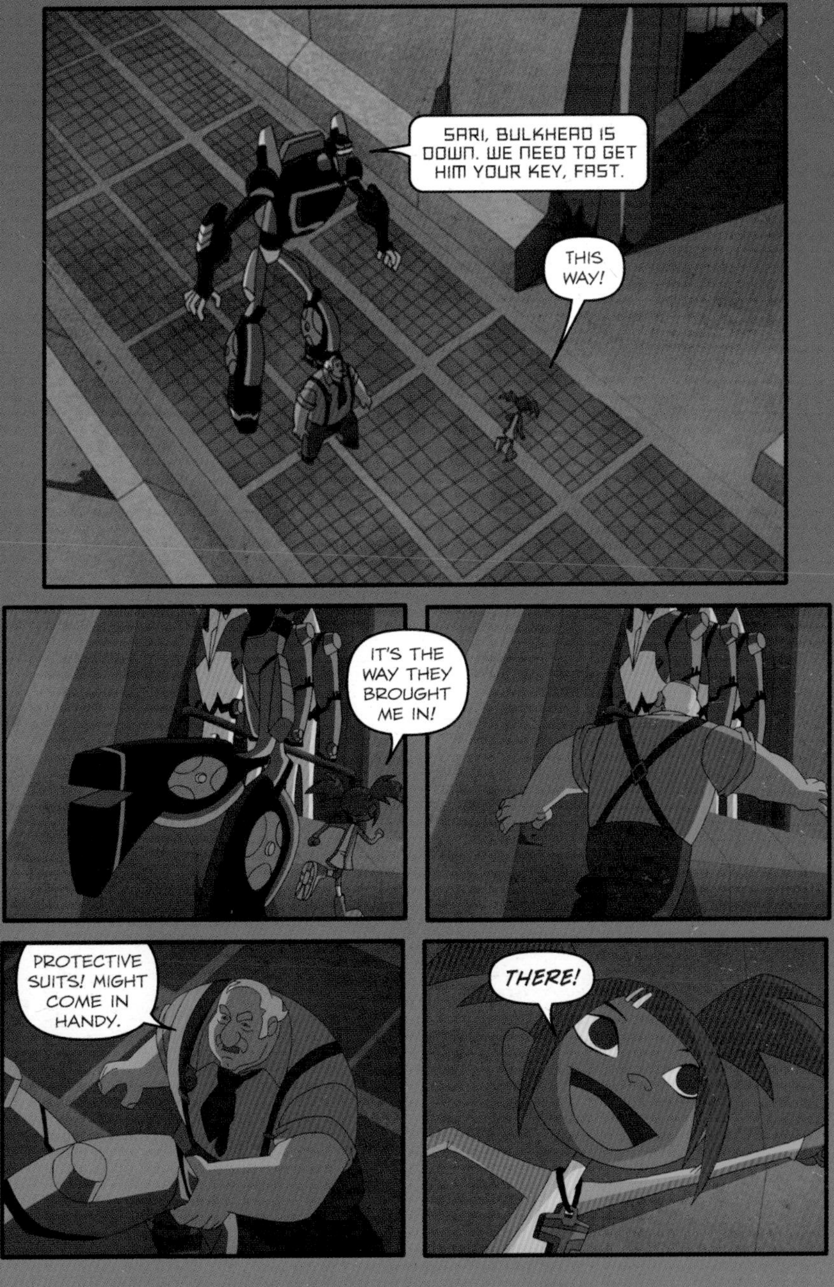
SARI, BULKHEAD IS DOWN. WE NEED TO GET HIM YOUR KEY, FAST.
THIS WAY!
IT'S THE WAY THEY BROUGHT ME IN!
PROTECTIVE SUITS! MIGHT COME IN HANDY.
THERE!

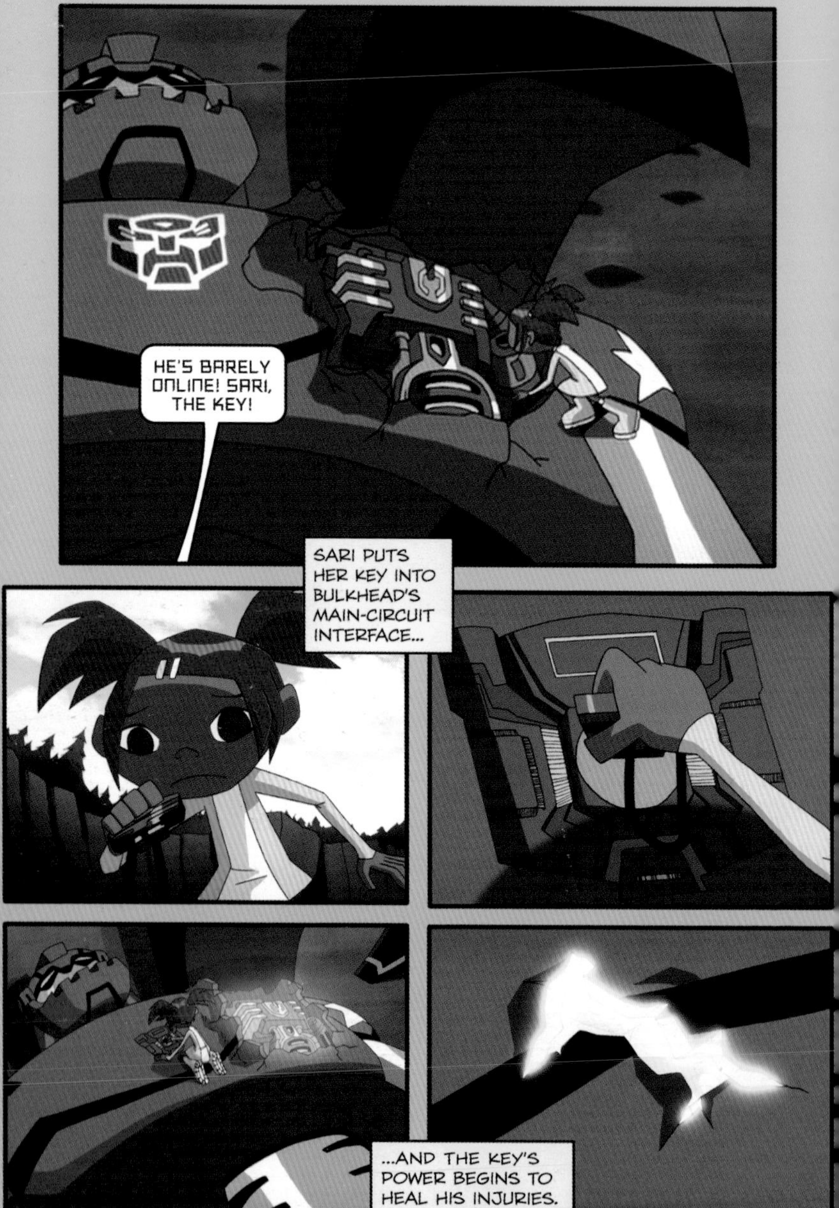
HE'S BARELY ONLINE! SARI, THE KEY!
SARI PUTS HER KEY INTO BULKHEAD'S MAIN-CIRCUIT INTERFACE...
...AND THE KEY'S POWER BEGINS TO HEAL HIS INJURIES.

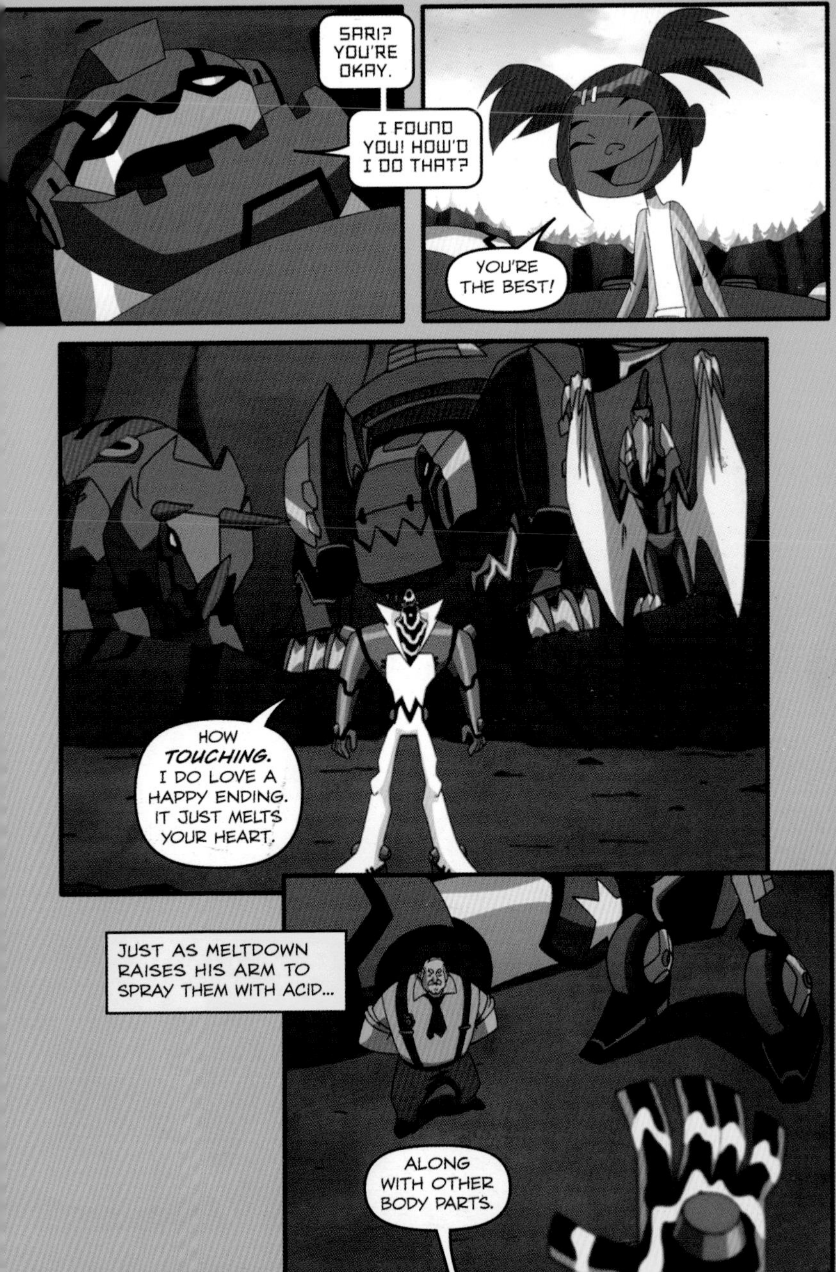
SARI? YOU'RE OKAY.
I FOUND YOU! HOW'D I DO THAT?
YOU'RE THE BEST!
HOW *TOUCHING.* I DO LOVE A HAPPY ENDING. IT JUST MELTS YOUR HEART.
JUST AS MELTDOWN RAISES HIS ARM TO SPRAY THEM WITH ACID...
ALONG WITH OTHER BODY PARTS.

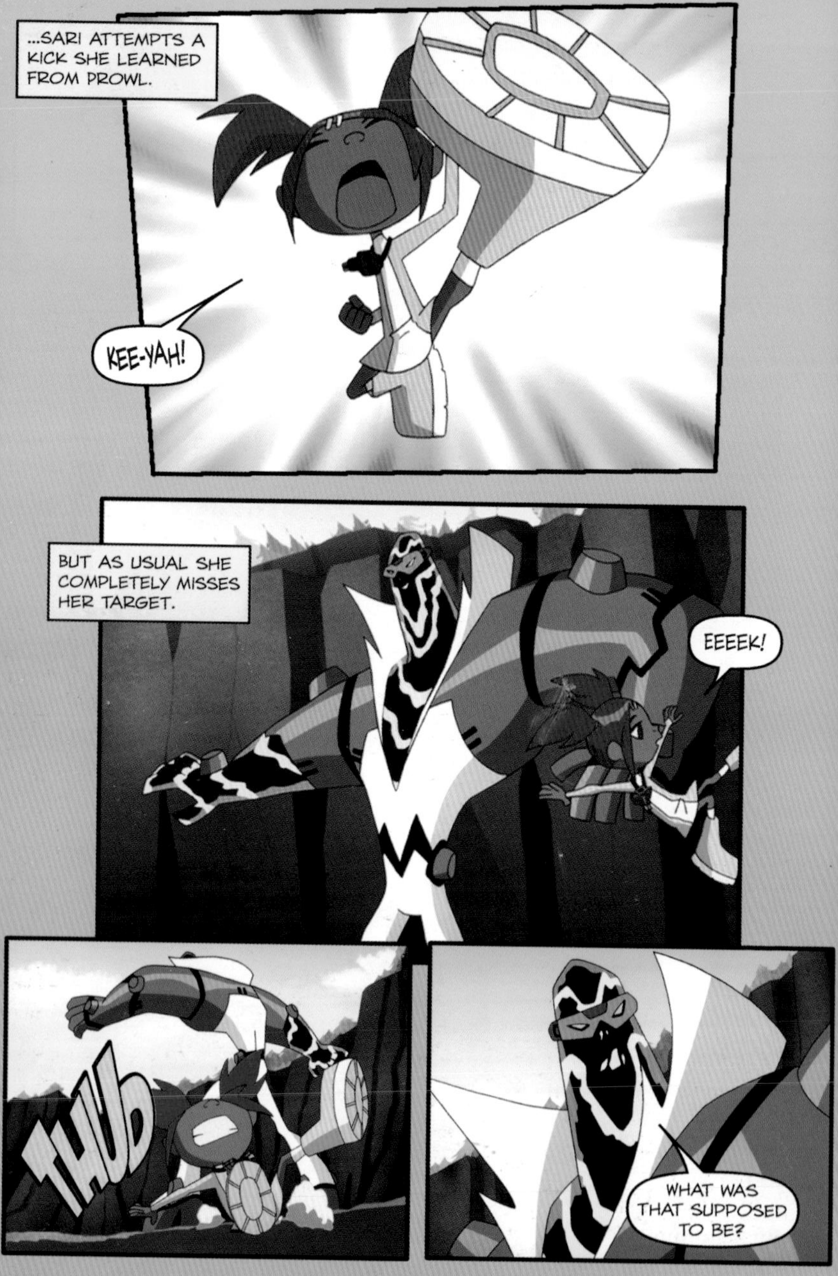
...SARI ATTEMPTS A KICK SHE LEARNED FROM PROWL.
KEE-YAH!
BUT AS USUAL SHE COMPLETELY MISSES HER TARGET.
EEEEK!
THUD
WHAT WAS THAT SUPPOSED TO BE?

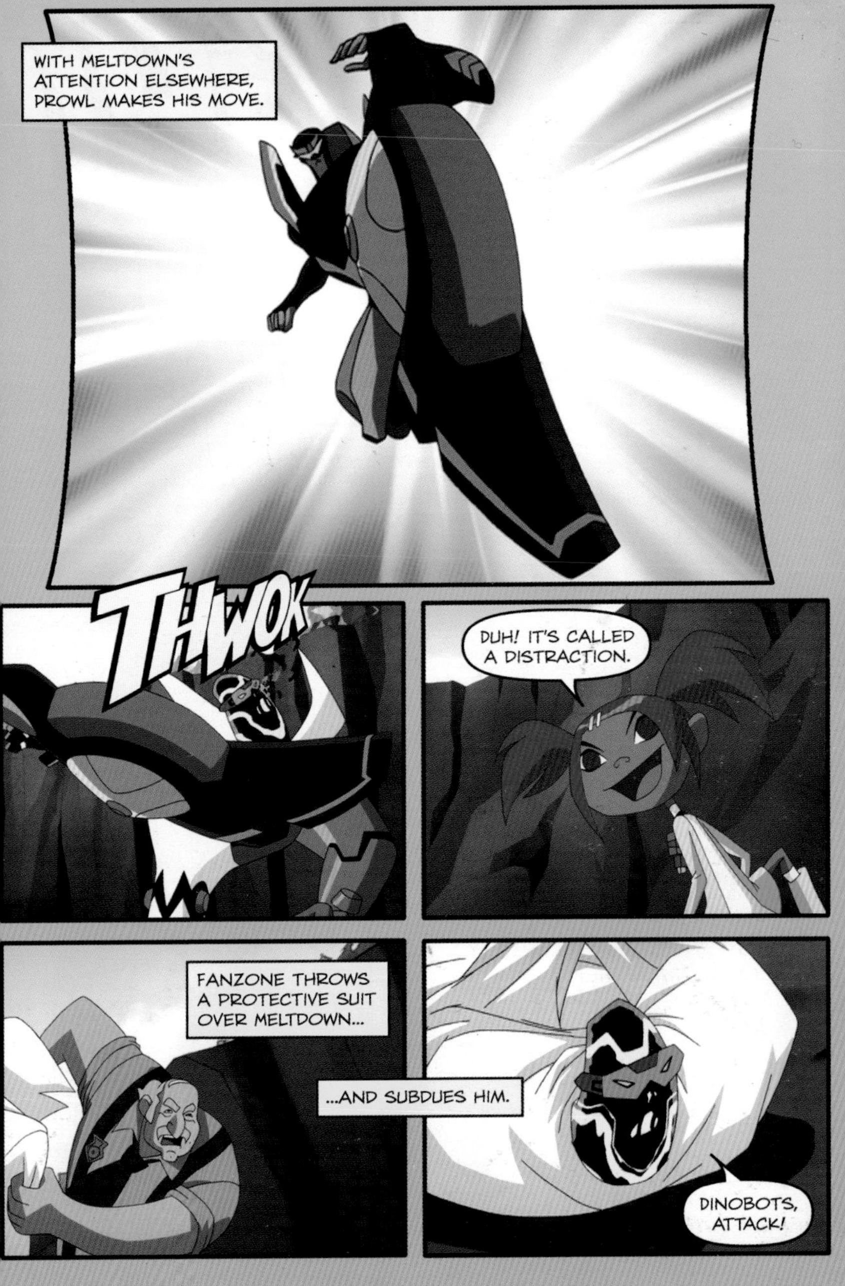
WITH MELTDOWN'S ATTENTION ELSEWHERE, PROWL MAKES HIS MOVE.
THWOK
DUH! IT'S CALLED A DISTRACTION.
FANZONE THROWS A PROTECTIVE SUIT OVER MELTDOWN...
...AND SUBDUES HIM.
DINOBOTS, ATTACK!

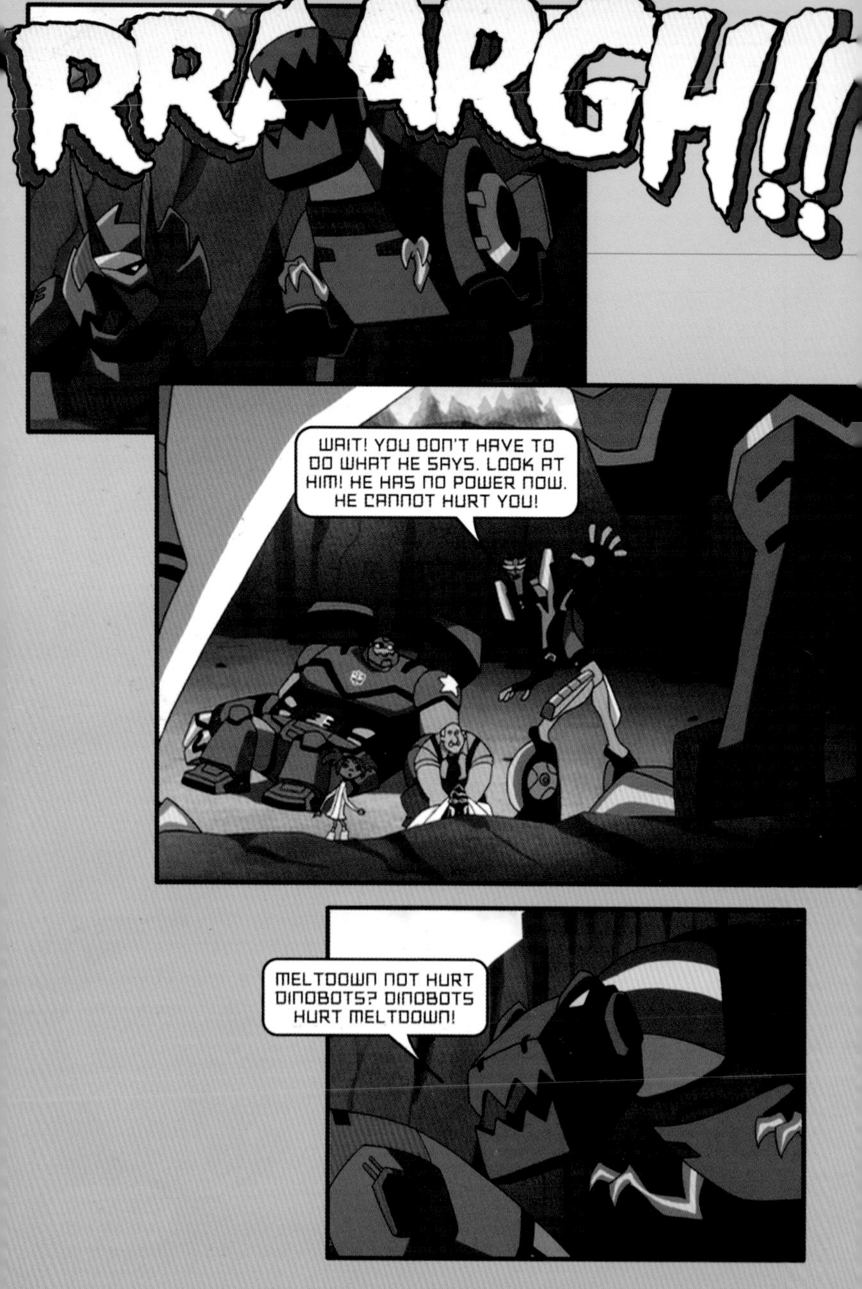
RRAARGH!!!
WAIT! YOU DON'T HAVE TO DO WHAT HE SAYS. LOOK AT HIM! HE HAS NO POWER NOW. HE CANNOT HURT YOU!
MELTDOWN NOT HURT DINOBOTS? DINOBOTS HURT MELTDOWN!

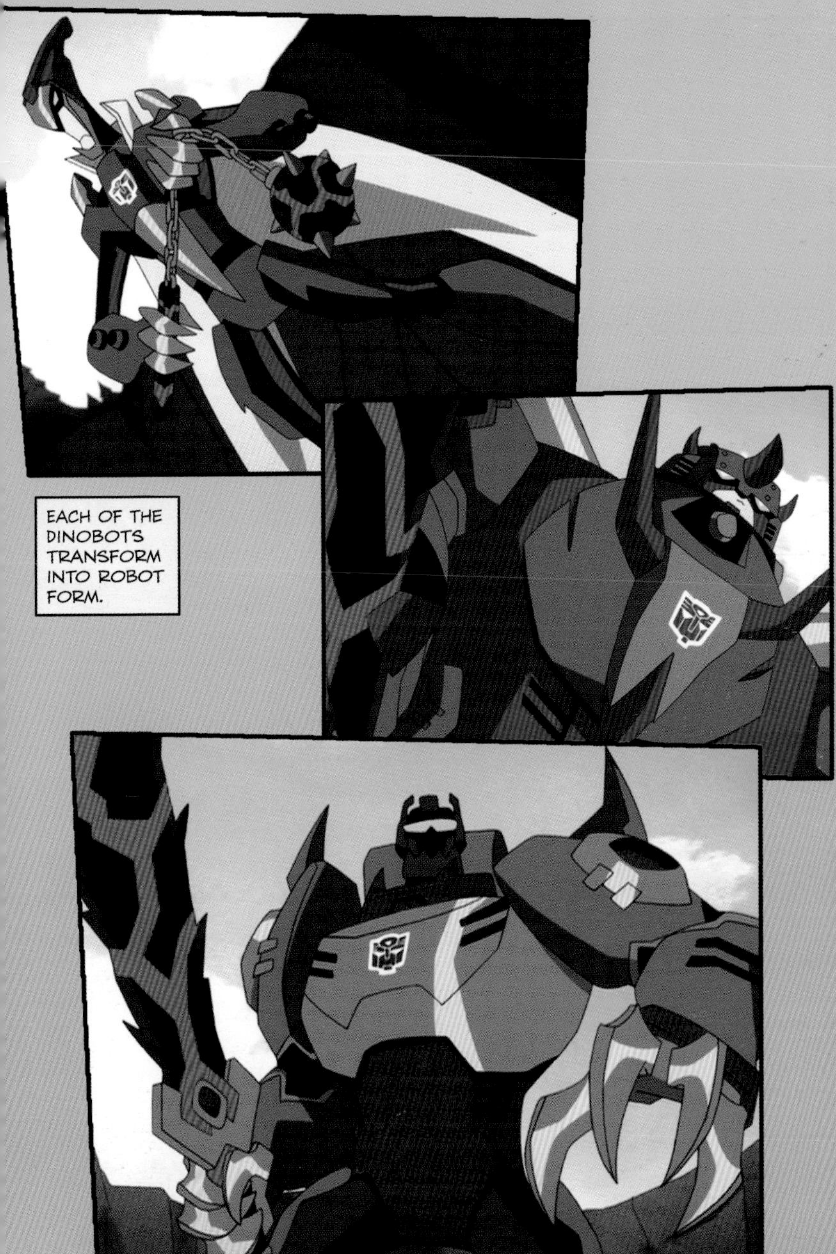
EACH OF THE DINOBOTS TRANSFORM INTO ROBOT FORM.

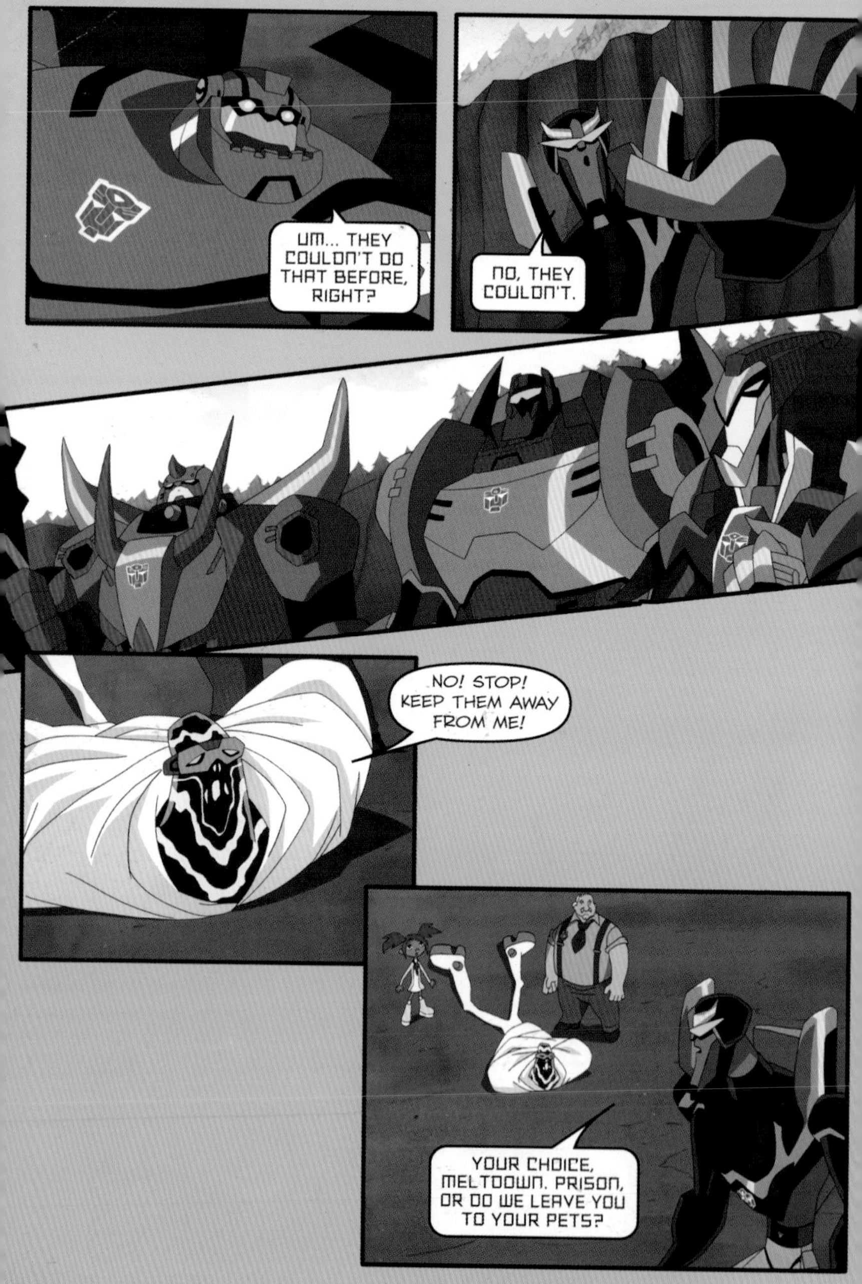
UM... THEY COULDN'T DO THAT BEFORE, RIGHT?
NO, THEY COULDN'T.
NO! STOP! KEEP THEM AWAY FROM ME!
YOUR CHOICE, MELTDOWN. PRISON, OR DO WE LEAVE YOU TO YOUR PETS?

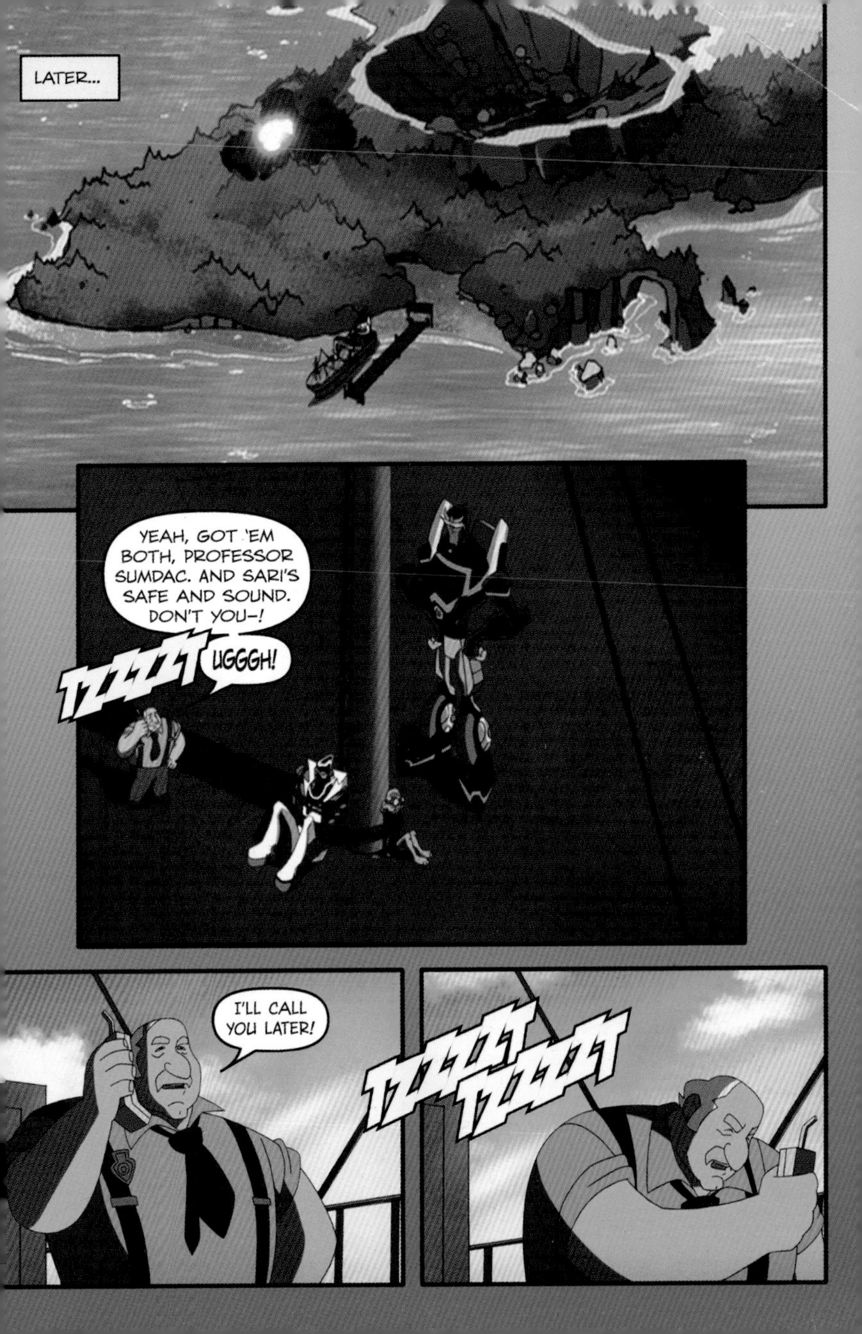
LATER...
YEAH, GOT 'EM BOTH, PROFESSOR SUMDAC. AND SARI'S SAFE AND SOUND. DON'T YOU-!
TZZZZT
UGGGH!
I'LL CALL YOU LATER!
TZZZT TZZZT

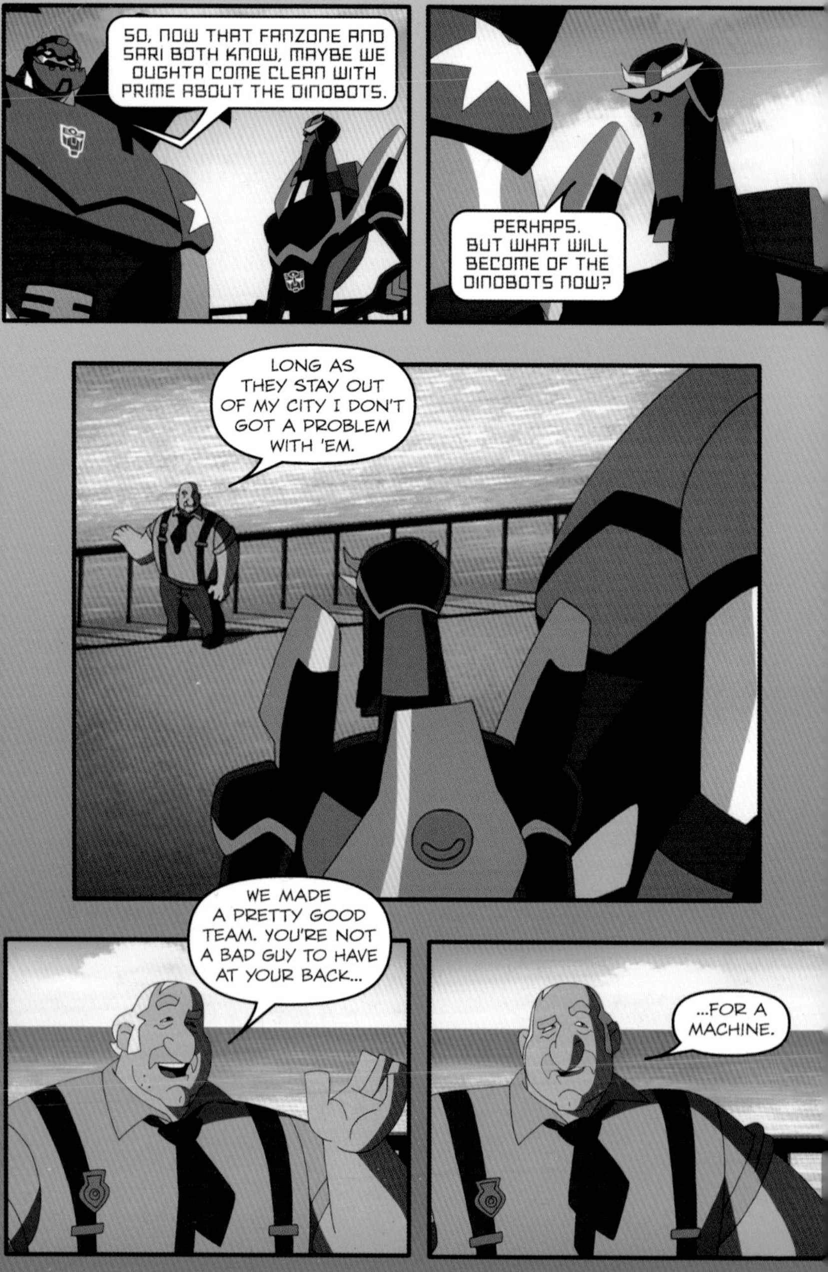
SO, NOW THAT FANZONE AND SARI BOTH KNOW, MAYBE WE OUGHTA COME CLEAN WITH PRIME ABOUT THE DINOBOTS.
PERHAPS. BUT WHAT WILL BECOME OF THE DINOBOTS NOW?
LONG AS THEY STAY OUT OF MY CITY I DON'T GOT A PROBLEM WITH 'EM.
WE MADE A PRETTY GOOD TEAM. YOU'RE NOT A BAD GUY TO HAVE AT YOUR BACK...
...FOR A MACHINE.

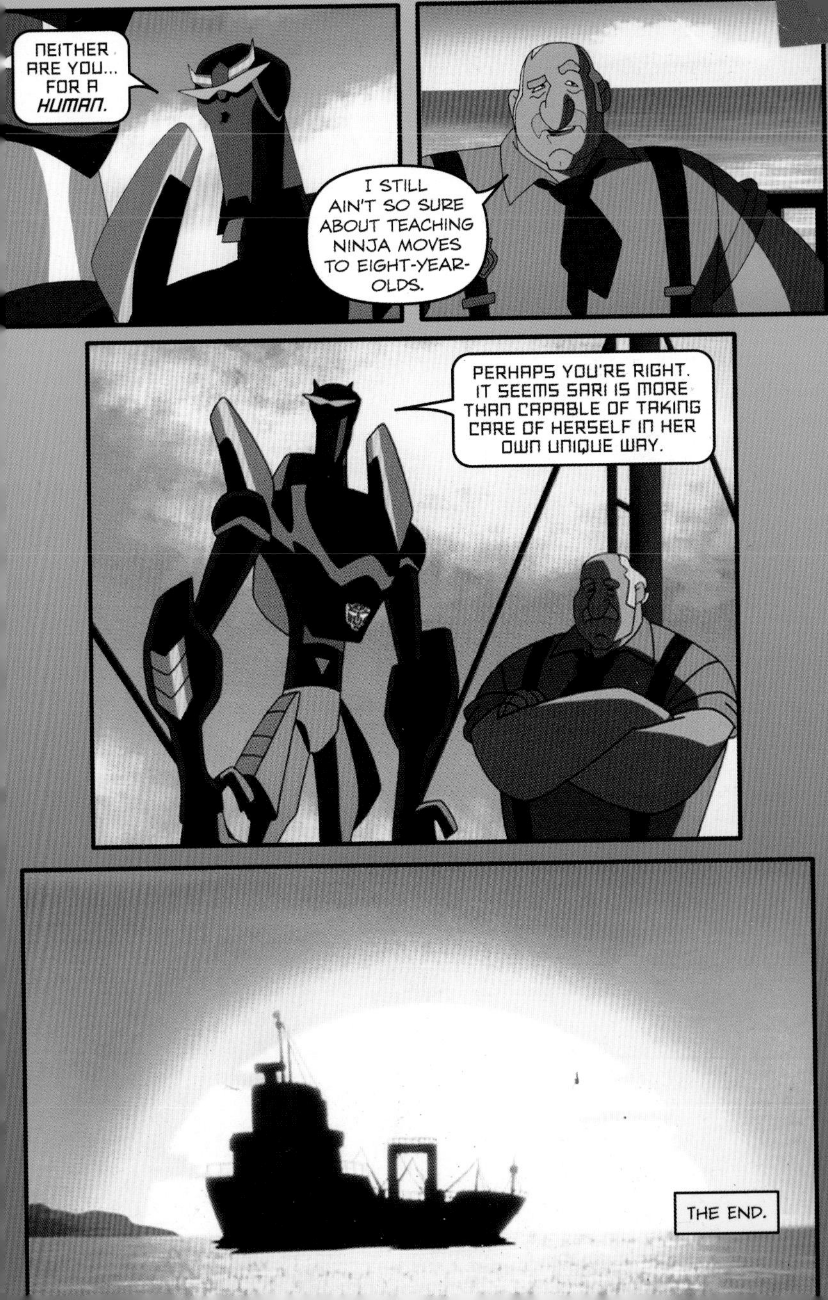
NEITHER ARE YOU... FOR A *HUMAN*.
I STILL AIN'T SO SURE ABOUT TEACHING NINJA MOVES TO EIGHT-YEAR-OLDS.
PERHAPS YOU'RE RIGHT. IT SEEMS SARI IS MORE THAN CAPABLE OF TAKING CARE OF HERSELF IN HER OWN UNIQUE WAY.
THE END.

LOST AND FOUND

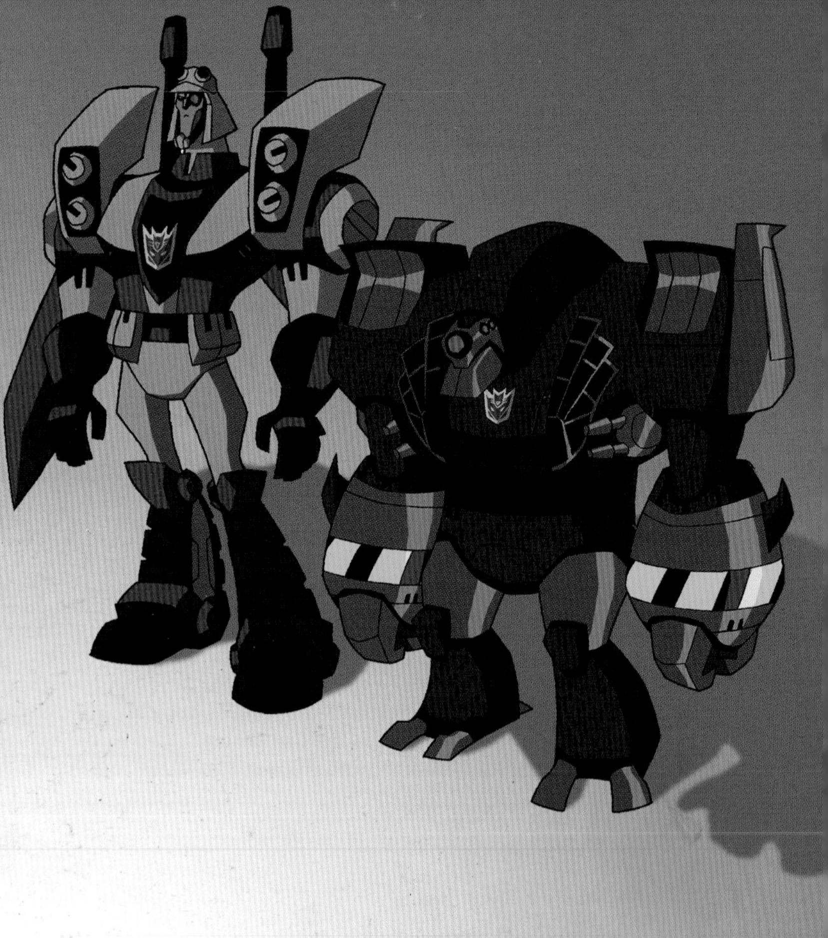

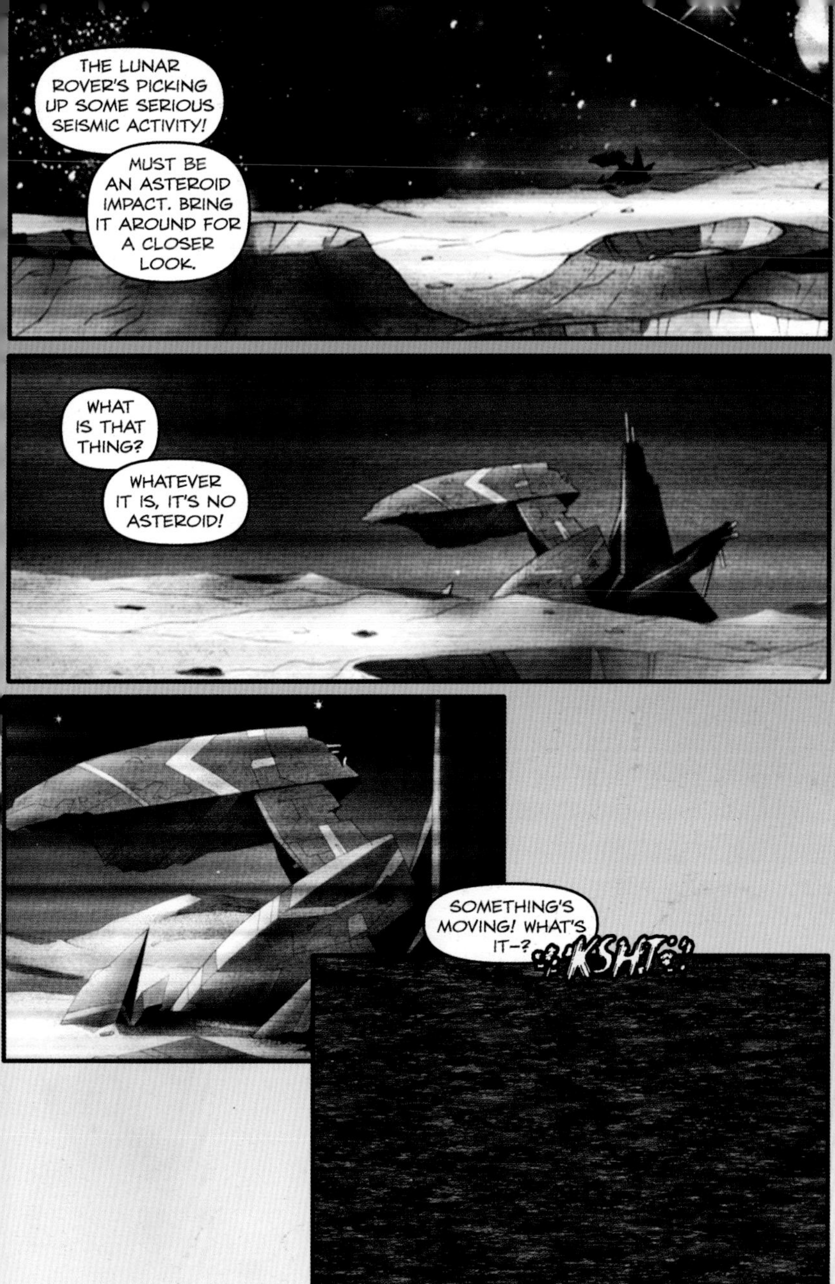
THE LUNAR ROVER'S PICKING UP SOME SERIOUS SEISMIC ACTIVITY!
MUST BE AN ASTEROID IMPACT. BRING IT AROUND FOR A CLOSER LOOK.
WHAT IS THAT THING?
WHATEVER IT IS, IT'S NO ASTEROID!
SOMETHING'S MOVING! WHAT'S IT--?
KSHT

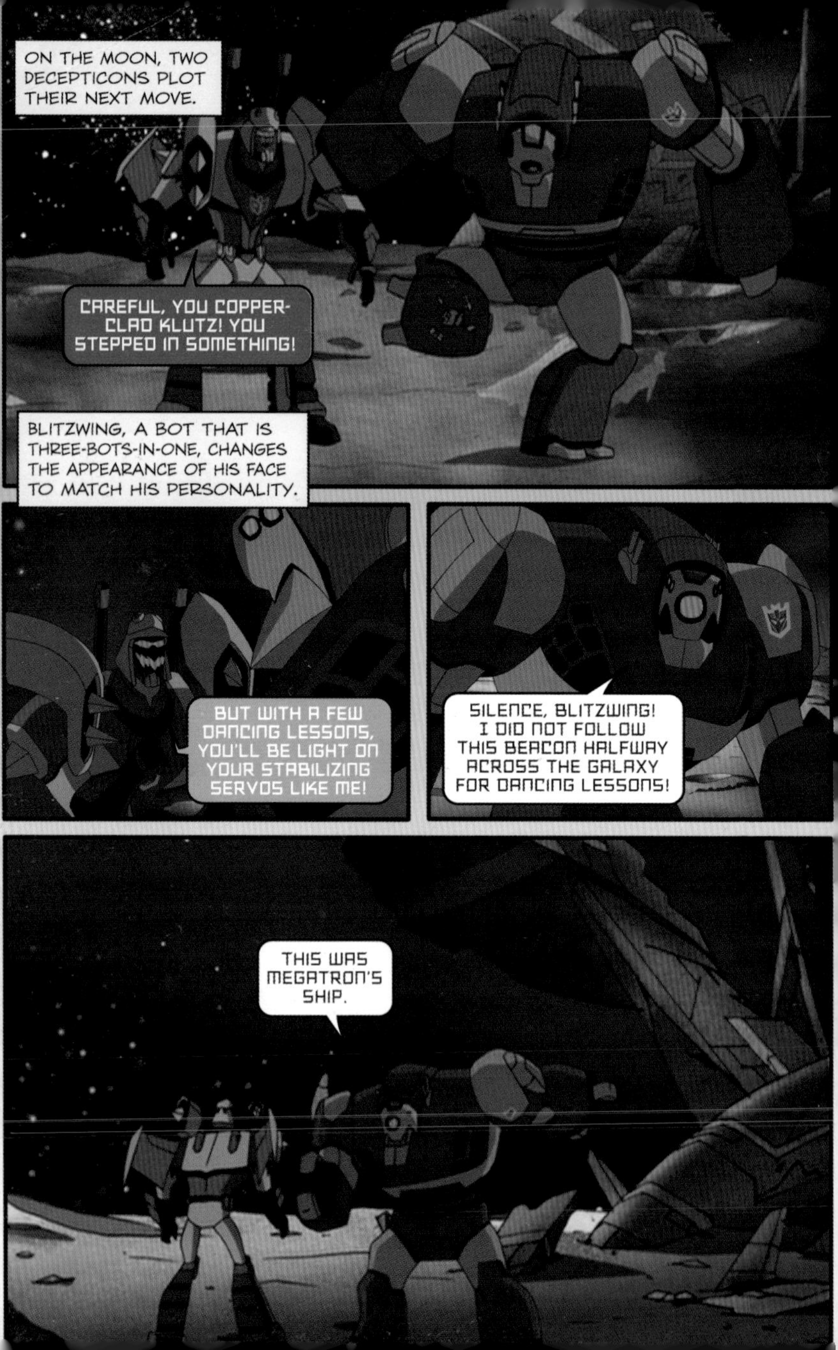
ON THE MOON, TWO DECEPTICONS PLOT THEIR NEXT MOVE.
CAREFUL, YOU COPPER-CLAD KLUTZ! YOU STEPPED IN SOMETHING!
BLITZWING, A BOT THAT IS THREE-BOTS-IN-ONE, CHANGES THE APPEARANCE OF HIS FACE TO MATCH HIS PERSONALITY.
BUT WITH A FEW DANCING LESSONS, YOU'LL BE LIGHT ON YOUR STABILIZING SERVOS LIKE ME!
SILENCE, BLITZWING! I DID NOT FOLLOW THIS BEACON HALFWAY ACROSS THE GALAXY FOR DANCING LESSONS!
THIS WAS MEGATRON'S SHIP.

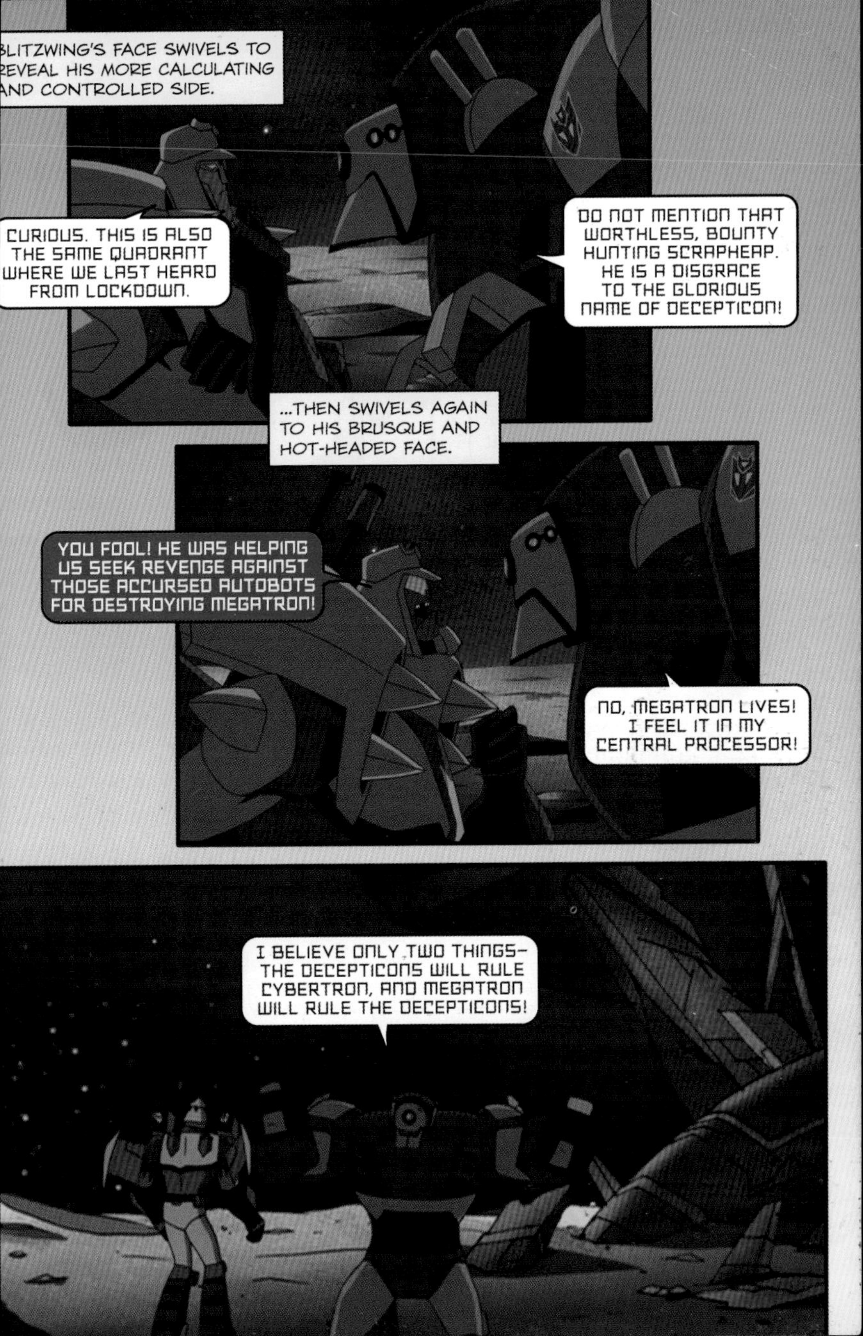
BLITZWING'S FACE SWIVELS TO REVEAL HIS MORE CALCULATING AND CONTROLLED SIDE.
CURIOUS. THIS IS ALSO THE SAME QUADRANT WHERE WE LAST HEARD FROM LOCKDOWN.
DO NOT MENTION THAT WORTHLESS, BOUNTY HUNTING SCRAPHEAP. HE IS A DISGRACE TO THE GLORIOUS NAME OF DECEPTICON!
...THEN SWIVELS AGAIN TO HIS BRUSQUE AND HOT-HEADED FACE.
YOU FOOL! HE WAS HELPING US SEEK REVENGE AGAINST THOSE ACCURSED AUTOBOTS FOR DESTROYING MEGATRON!
NO, MEGATRON LIVES! I FEEL IT IN MY CENTRAL PROCESSOR!
I BELIEVE ONLY TWO THINGS–THE DECEPTICONS WILL RULE CYBERTRON, AND MEGATRON WILL RULE THE DECEPTICONS!

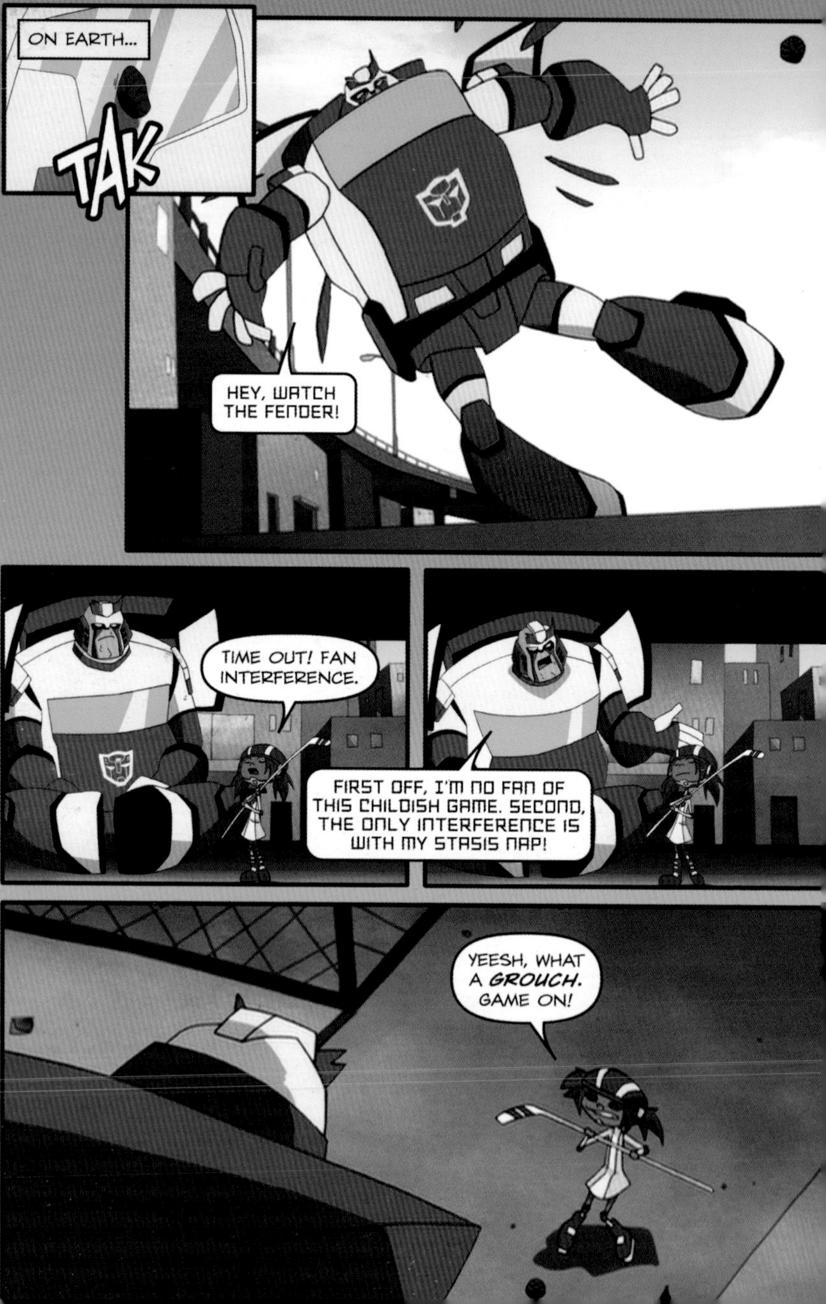
ON EARTH...
TAK
HEY, WATCH THE FENDER!
TIME OUT! FAN INTERFERENCE.
FIRST OFF, I'M NO FAN OF THIS CHILDISH GAME. SECOND, THE ONLY INTERFERENCE IS WITH MY STASIS NAP!
YEESH, WHAT A *GROUCH.* GAME ON!

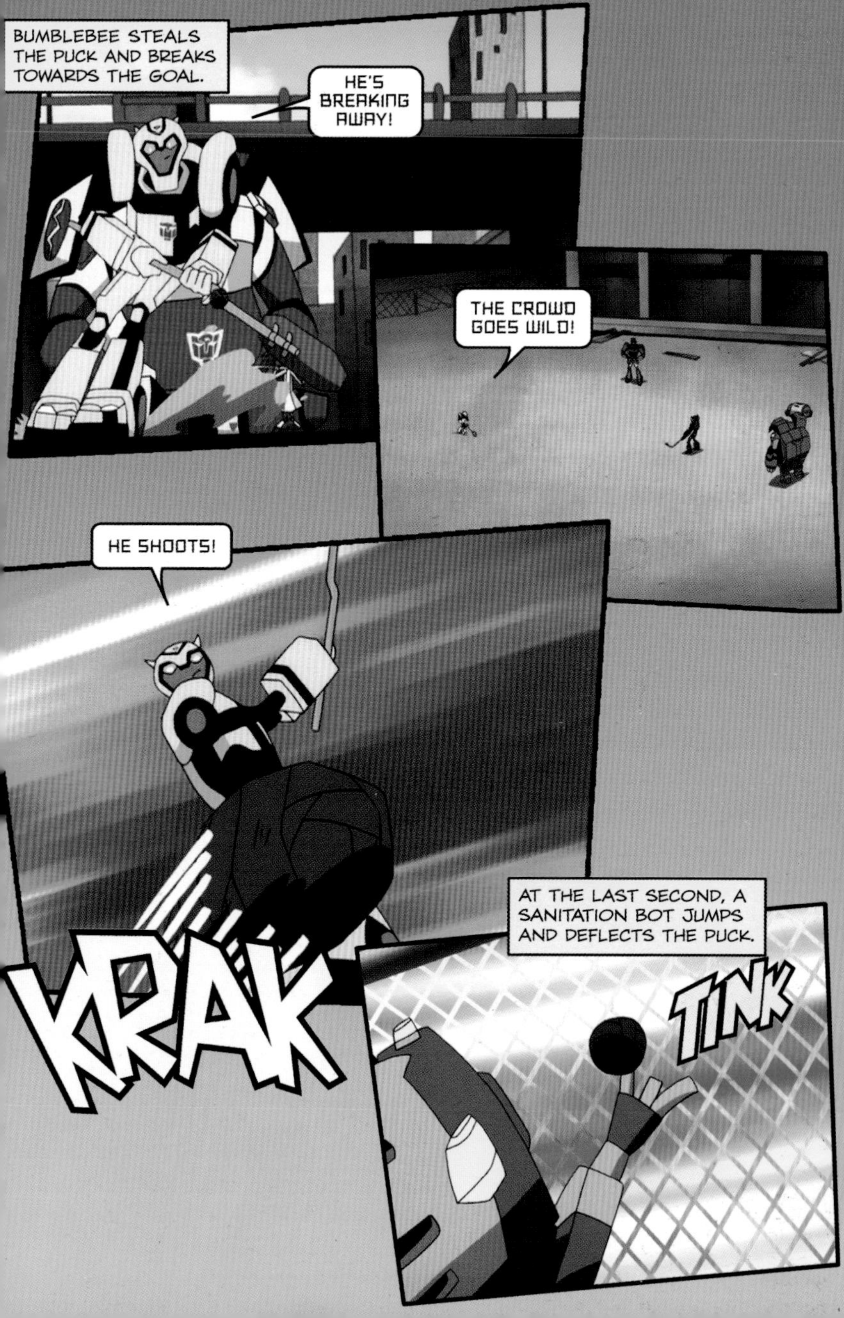
BUMBLEBEE STEALS THE PUCK AND BREAKS TOWARDS THE GOAL.
HE'S BREAKING AWAY!
THE CROWD GOES WILD!
HE SHOOTS!
KRAK
AT THE LAST SECOND, A SANITATION BOT JUMPS AND DEFLECTS THE PUCK.
TINK

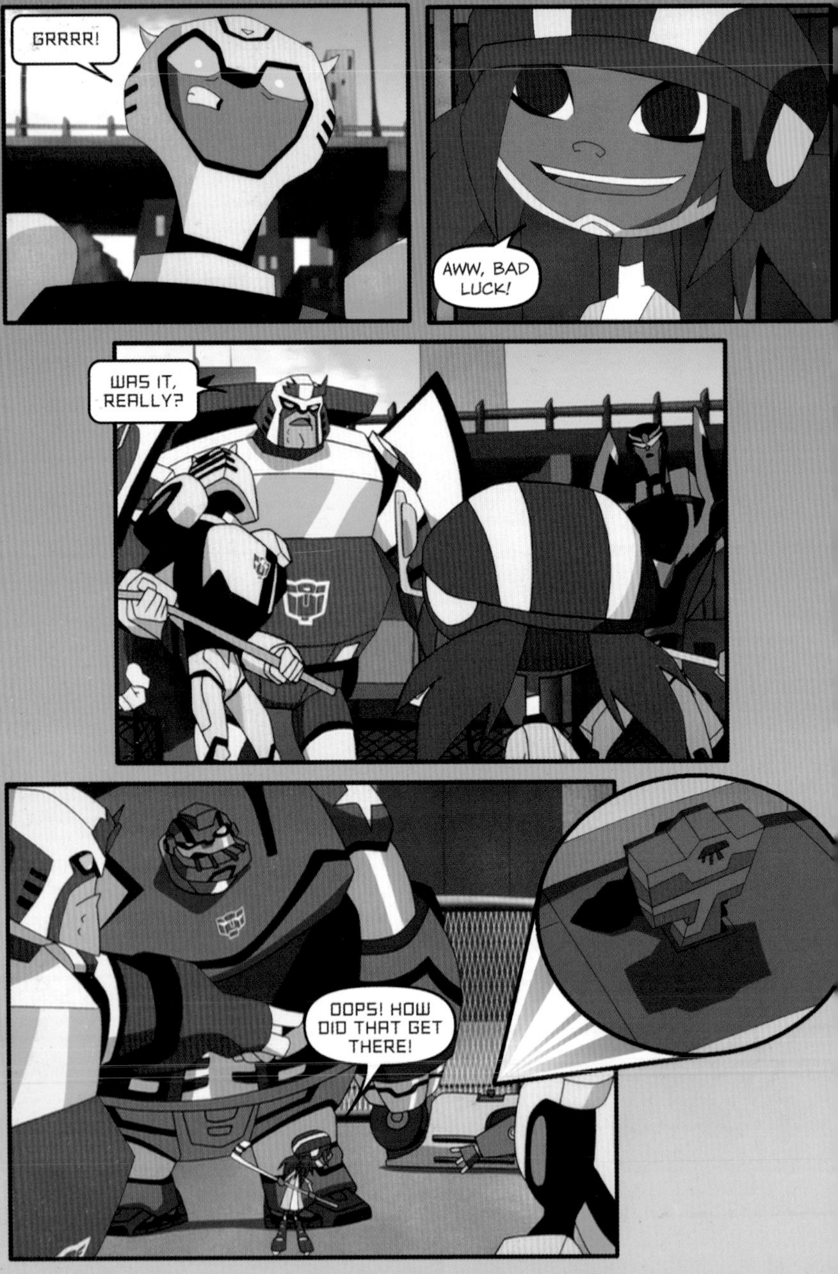
GRRRR!
AWW, BAD LUCK!
WAS IT, REALLY?
OOPS! HOW DID THAT GET THERE!

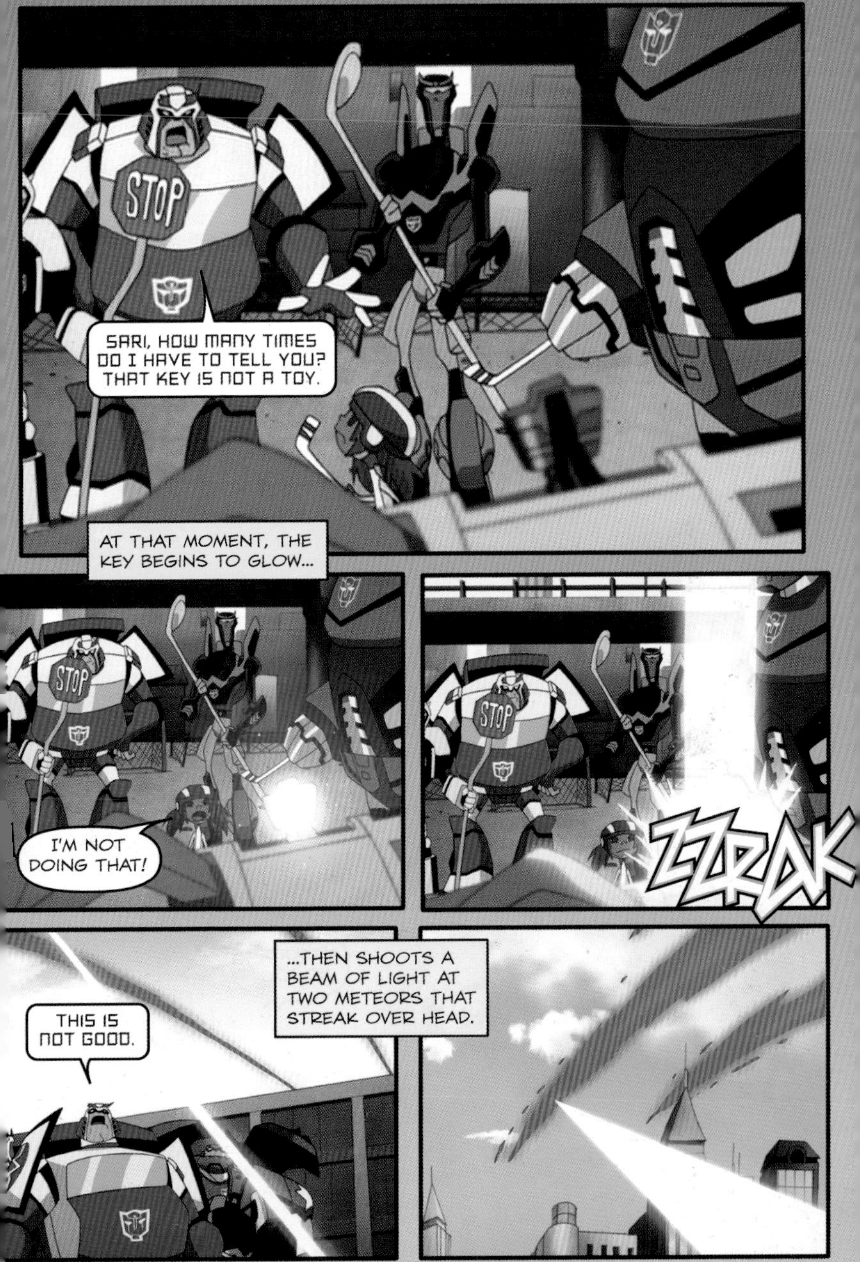
SARI, HOW MANY TIMES DO I HAVE TO TELL YOU? THAT KEY IS NOT A TOY.
AT THAT MOMENT, THE KEY BEGINS TO GLOW...
I'M NOT DOING THAT!
ZZRAK
...THEN SHOOTS A BEAM OF LIGHT AT TWO METEORS THAT STREAK OVER HEAD.
THIS IS NOT GOOD.

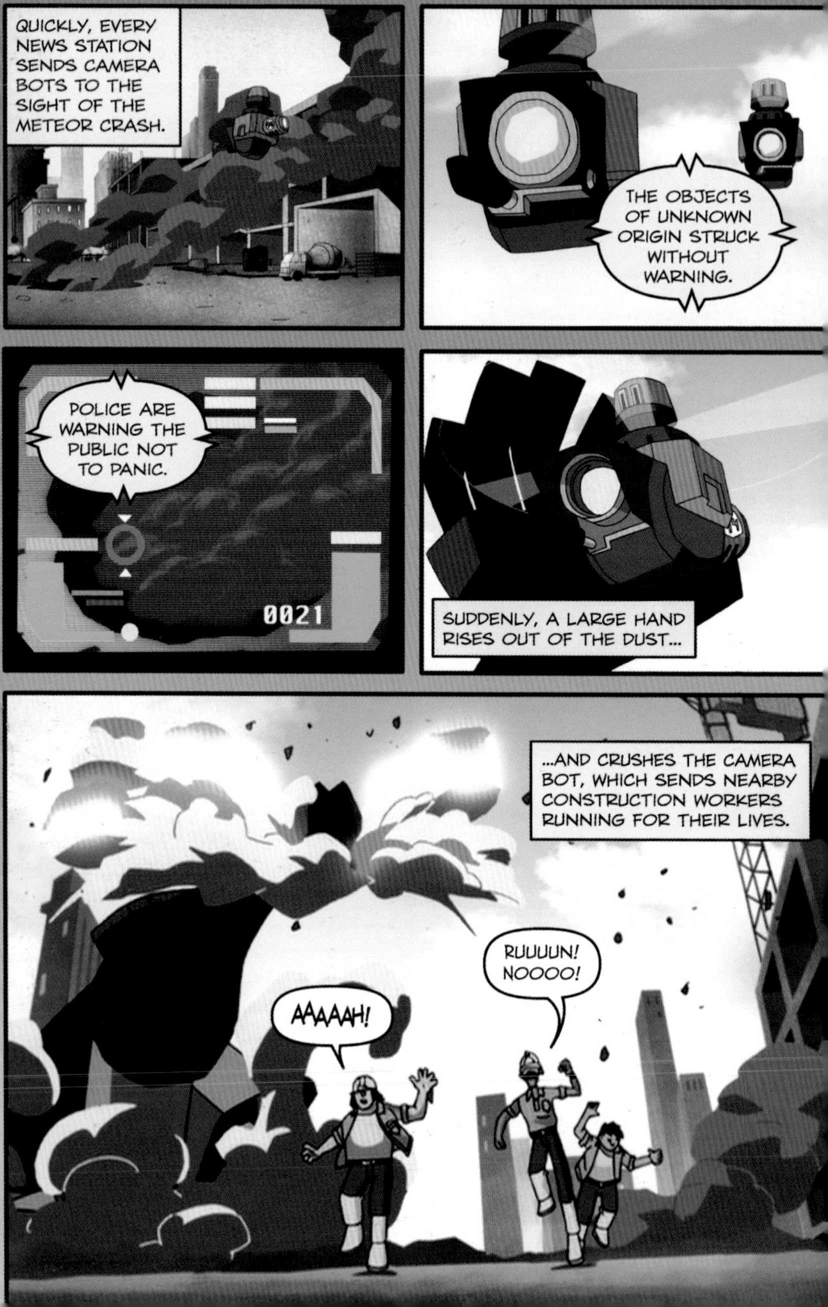
QUICKLY, EVERY NEWS STATION SENDS CAMERA BOTS TO THE SIGHT OF THE METEOR CRASH.
THE OBJECTS OF UNKNOWN ORIGIN STRUCK WITHOUT WARNING.
POLICE ARE WARNING THE PUBLIC NOT TO PANIC.
0021
SUDDENLY, A LARGE HAND RISES OUT OF THE DUST...
...AND CRUSHES THE CAMERA BOT, WHICH SENDS NEARBY CONSTRUCTION WORKERS RUNNING FOR THEIR LIVES.
AAAAAH!
RUUUUN! NOOOO!

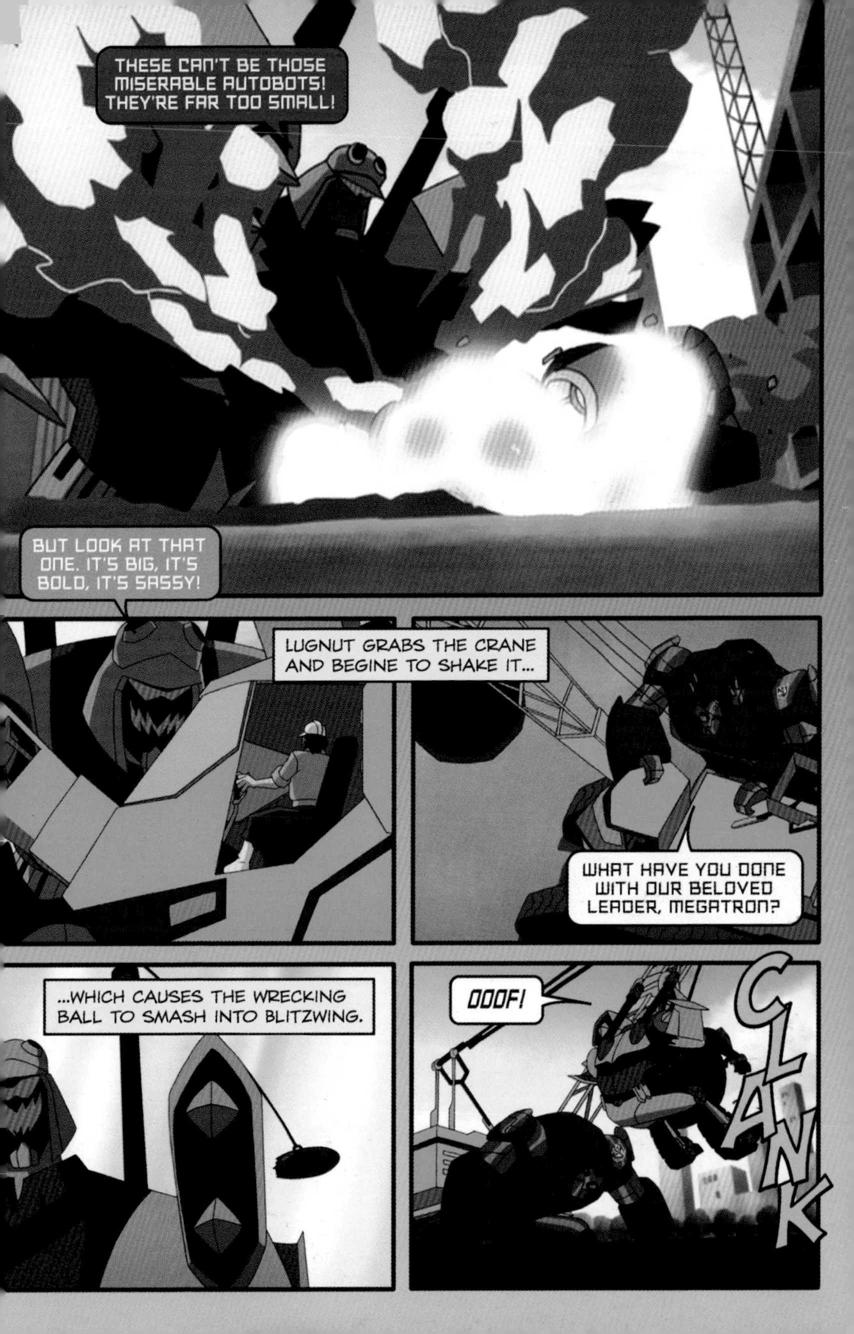
THESE CAN'T BE THOSE MISERABLE AUTOBOTS! THEY'RE FAR TOO SMALL!
BUT LOOK AT THAT ONE. IT'S BIG, IT'S BOLD, IT'S SASSY!
LUGNUT GRABS THE CRANE AND BEGINE TO SHAKE IT...
WHAT HAVE YOU DONE WITH OUR BELOVED LEADER, MEGATRON?
...WHICH CAUSES THE WRECKING BALL TO SMASH INTO BLITZWING.
OOOF!
CLANK

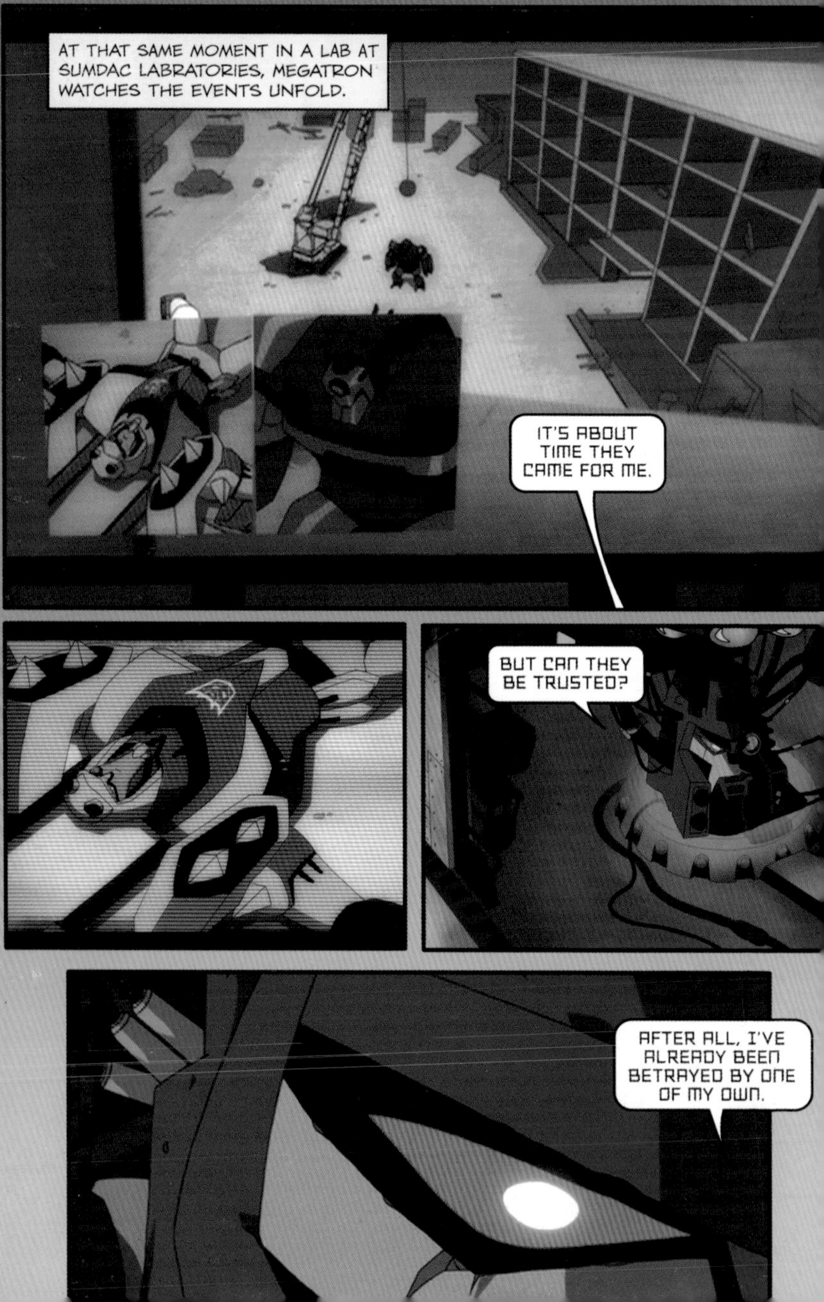
AT THAT SAME MOMENT IN A LAB AT SUMDAC LABRATORIES, MEGATRON WATCHES THE EVENTS UNFOLD.
IT'S ABOUT TIME THEY CAME FOR ME.
BUT CAN THEY BE TRUSTED?
AFTER ALL, I'VE ALREADY BEEN BETRAYED BY ONE OF MY OWN.

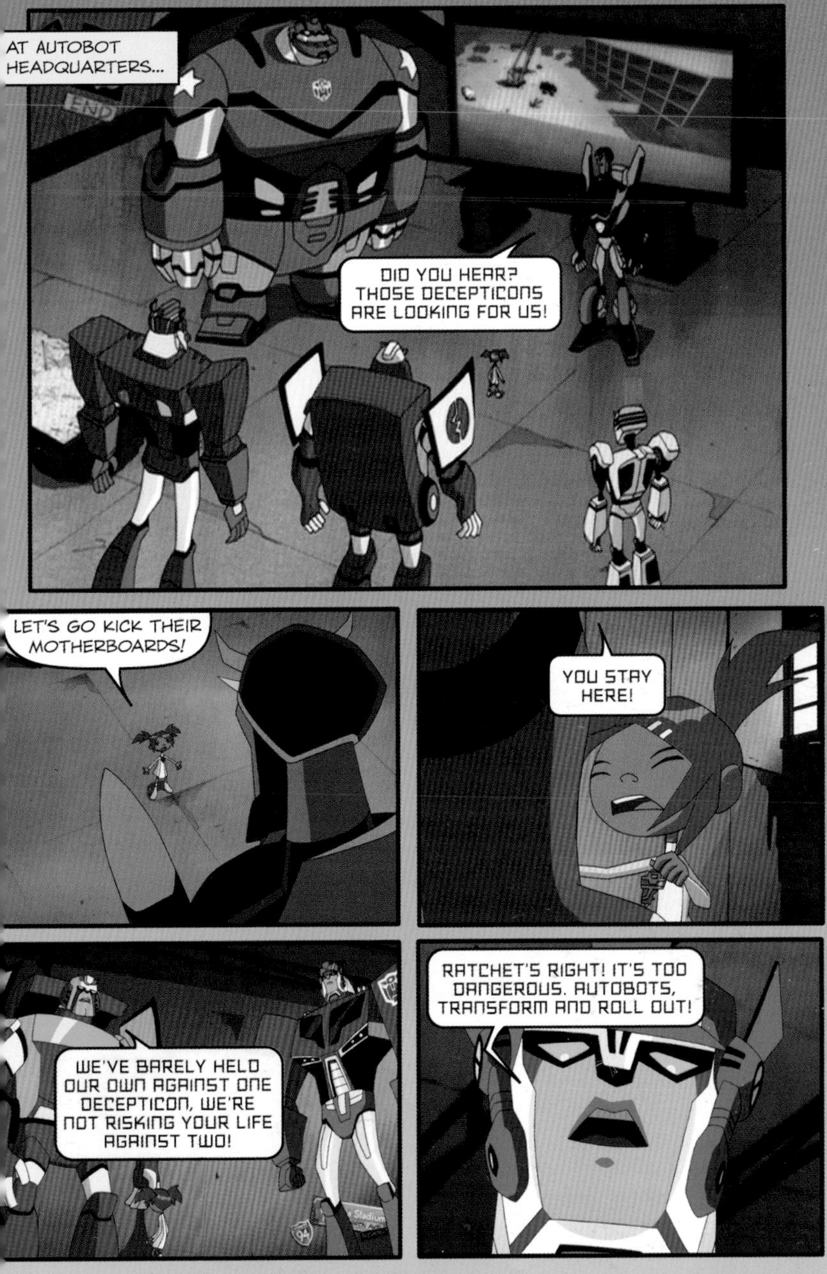
AT AUTOBOT HEADQUARTERS...
DID YOU HEAR? THOSE DECEPTICONS ARE LOOKING FOR US!
LET'S GO KICK THEIR MOTHERBOARDS!
YOU STAY HERE!
WE'VE BARELY HELD OUR OWN AGAINST ONE DECEPTICON, WE'RE NOT RISKING YOUR LIFE AGAINST TWO!
RATCHET'S RIGHT! IT'S TOO DANGEROUS. AUTOBOTS, TRANSFORM AND ROLL OUT!

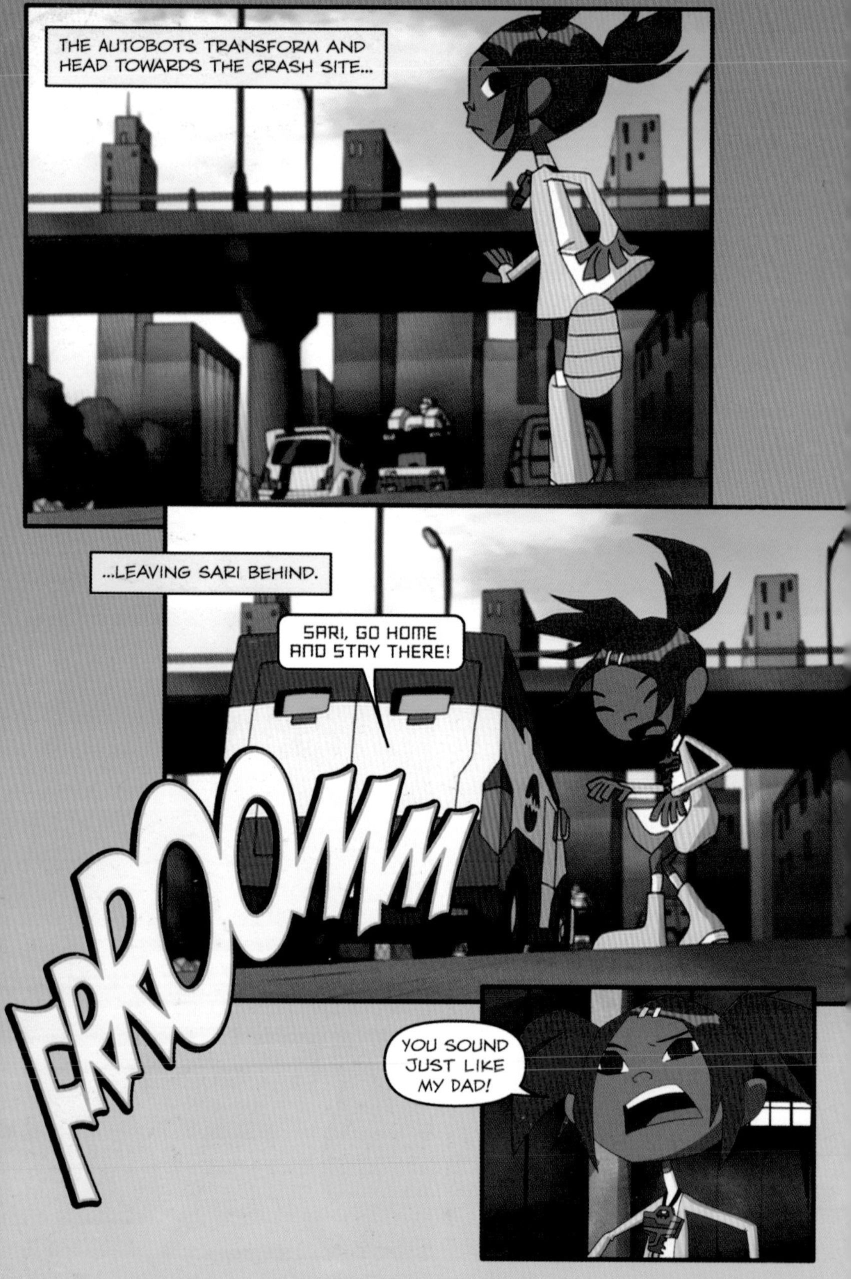
THE AUTOBOTS TRANSFORM AND HEAD TOWARDS THE CRASH SITE...
...LEAVING SARI BEHIND.
SARI, GO HOME AND STAY THERE!
FRROOMM
YOU SOUND JUST LIKE MY DAD!

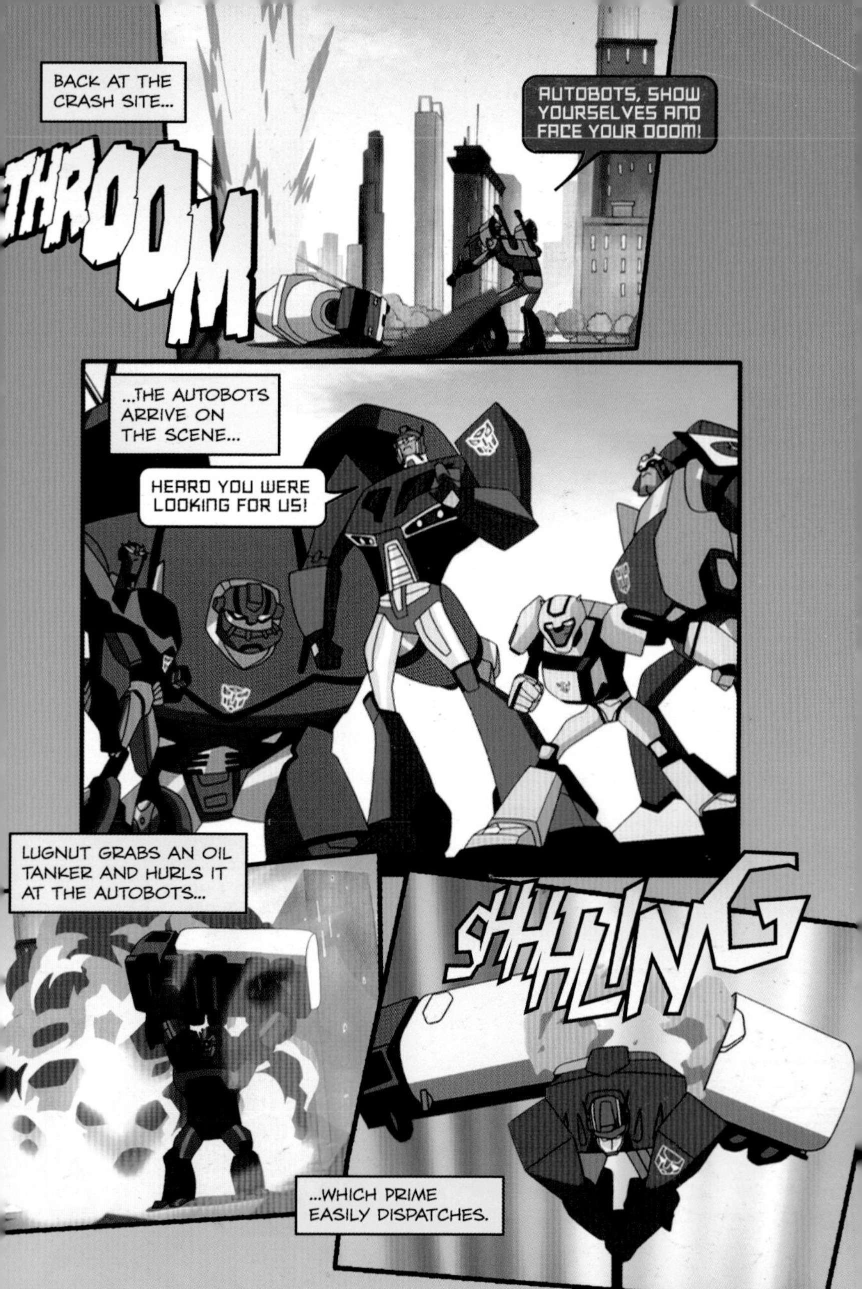
BACK AT THE CRASH SITE...
THROOM
AUTOBOTS, SHOW YOURSELVES AND FACE YOUR DOOM!
...THE AUTOBOTS ARRIVE ON THE SCENE...
HEARD YOU WERE LOOKING FOR US!
LUGNUT GRABS AN OIL TANKER AND HURLS IT AT THE AUTOBOTS...
SHHLING
...WHICH PRIME EASILY DISPATCHES.

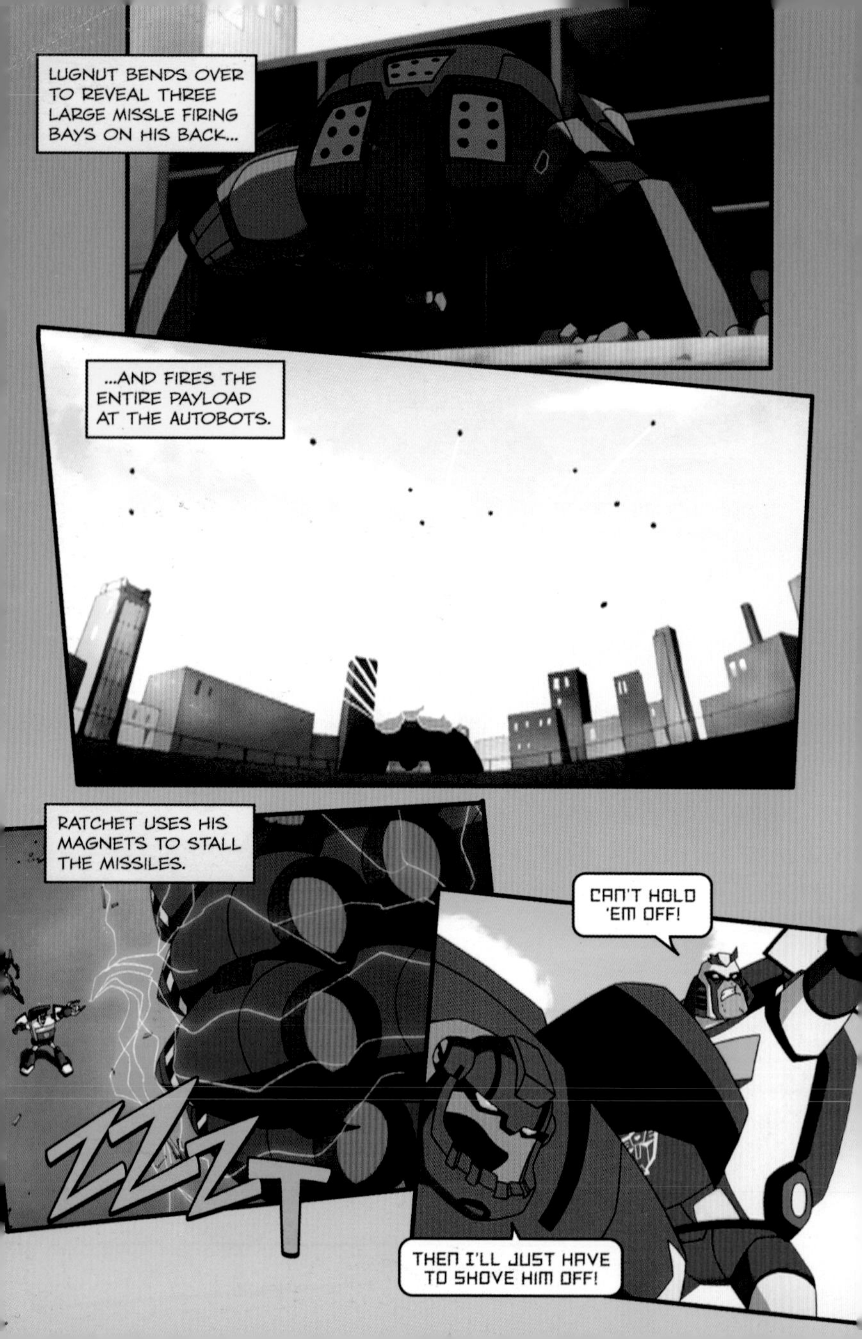
LUGNUT BENDS OVER TO REVEAL THREE LARGE MISSLE FIRING BAYS ON HIS BACK...
...AND FIRES THE ENTIRE PAYLOAD AT THE AUTOBOTS.
RATCHET USES HIS MAGNETS TO STALL THE MISSILES.
ZZZT
CAN'T HOLD 'EM OFF!
THEN I'LL JUST HAVE TO SHOVE HIM OFF!

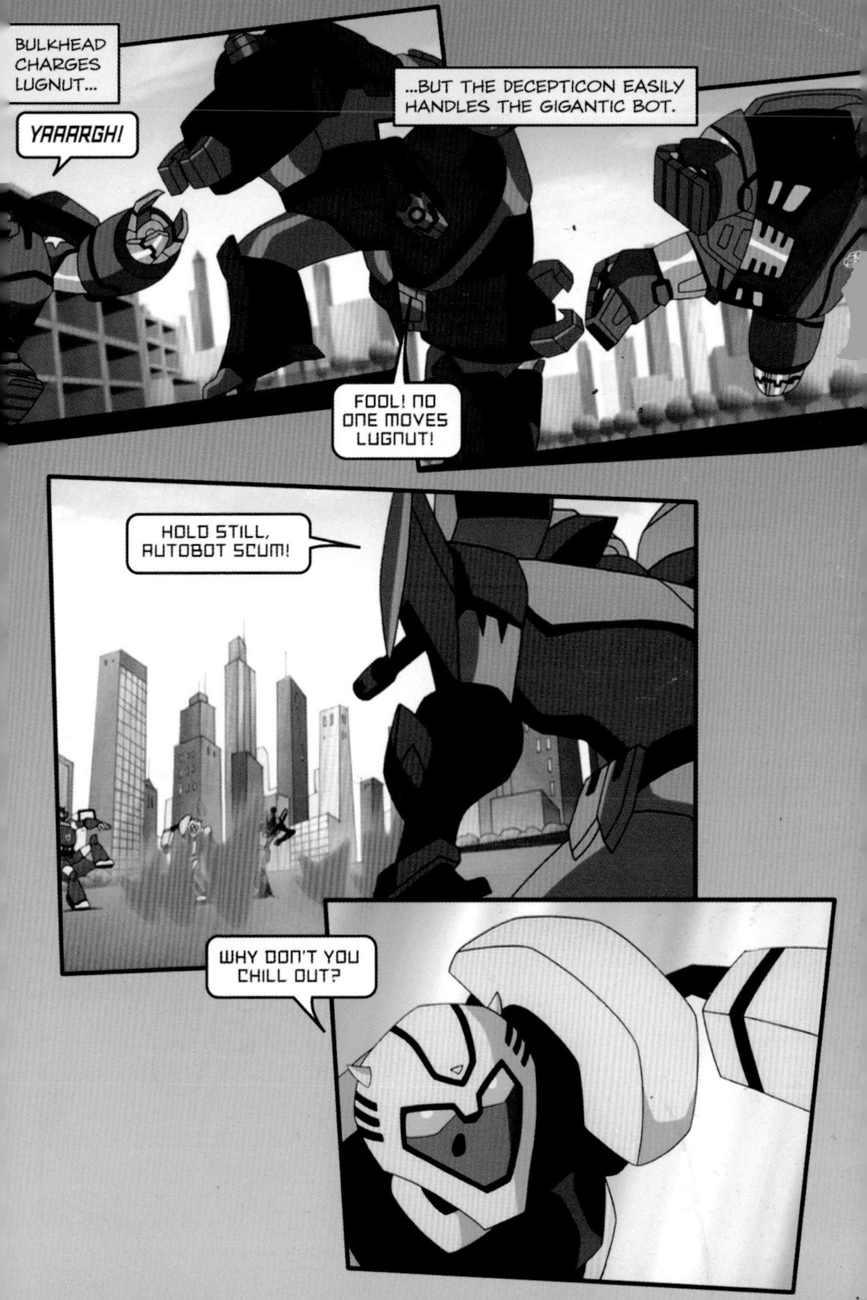
BULKHEAD CHARGES LUGNUT...
YAAARGH!
...BUT THE DECEPTICON EASILY HANDLES THE GIGANTIC BOT.
FOOL! NO ONE MOVES LUGNUT!
HOLD STILL, AUTOBOT SCUM!
WHY DON'T YOU CHILL OUT?

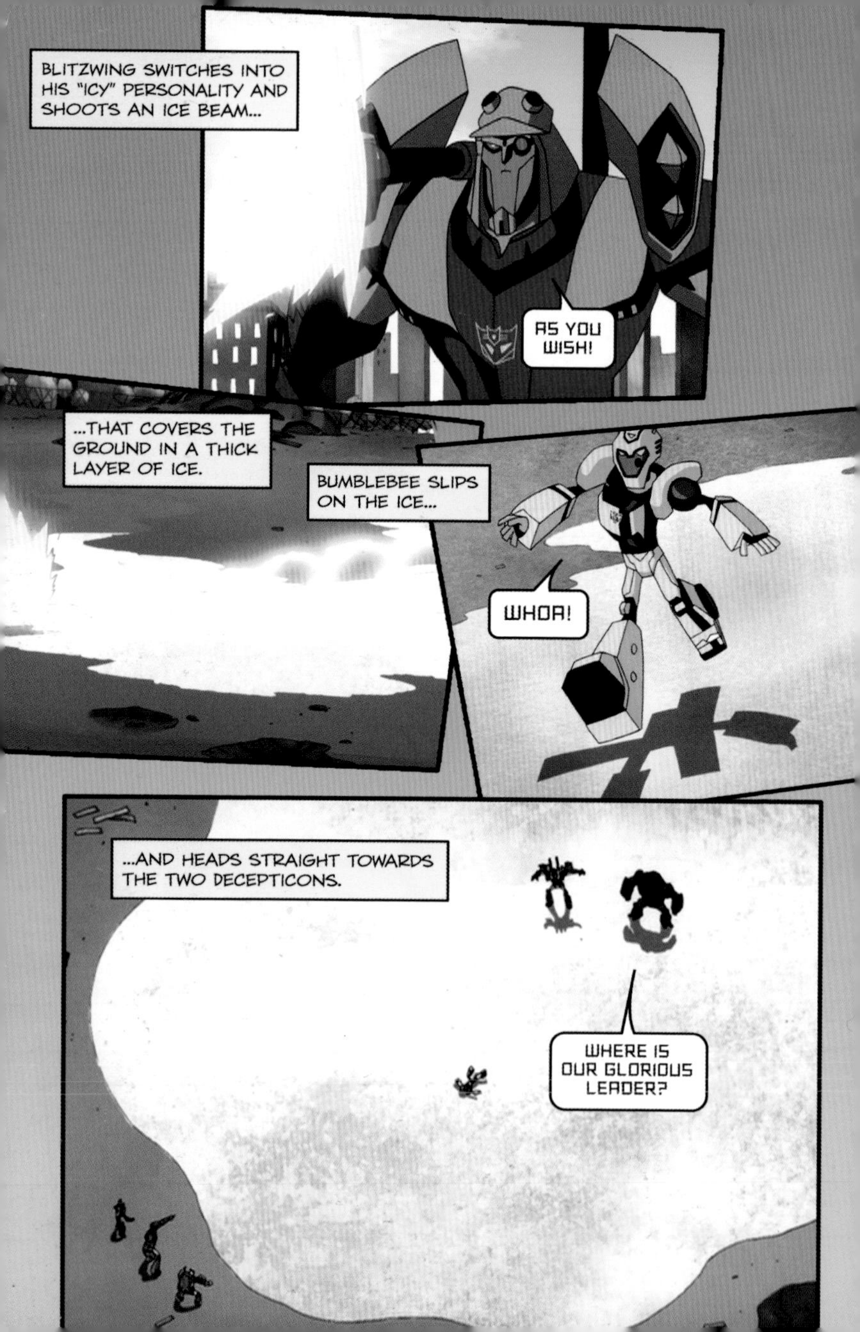
BLITZWING SWITCHES INTO HIS "ICY" PERSONALITY AND SHOOTS AN ICE BEAM...
AS YOU WISH!
...THAT COVERS THE GROUND IN A THICK LAYER OF ICE.
BUMBLEBEE SLIPS ON THE ICE...
WHOA!
...AND HEADS STRAIGHT TOWARDS THE TWO DECEPTICONS.
WHERE IS OUR GLORIOUS LEADER?

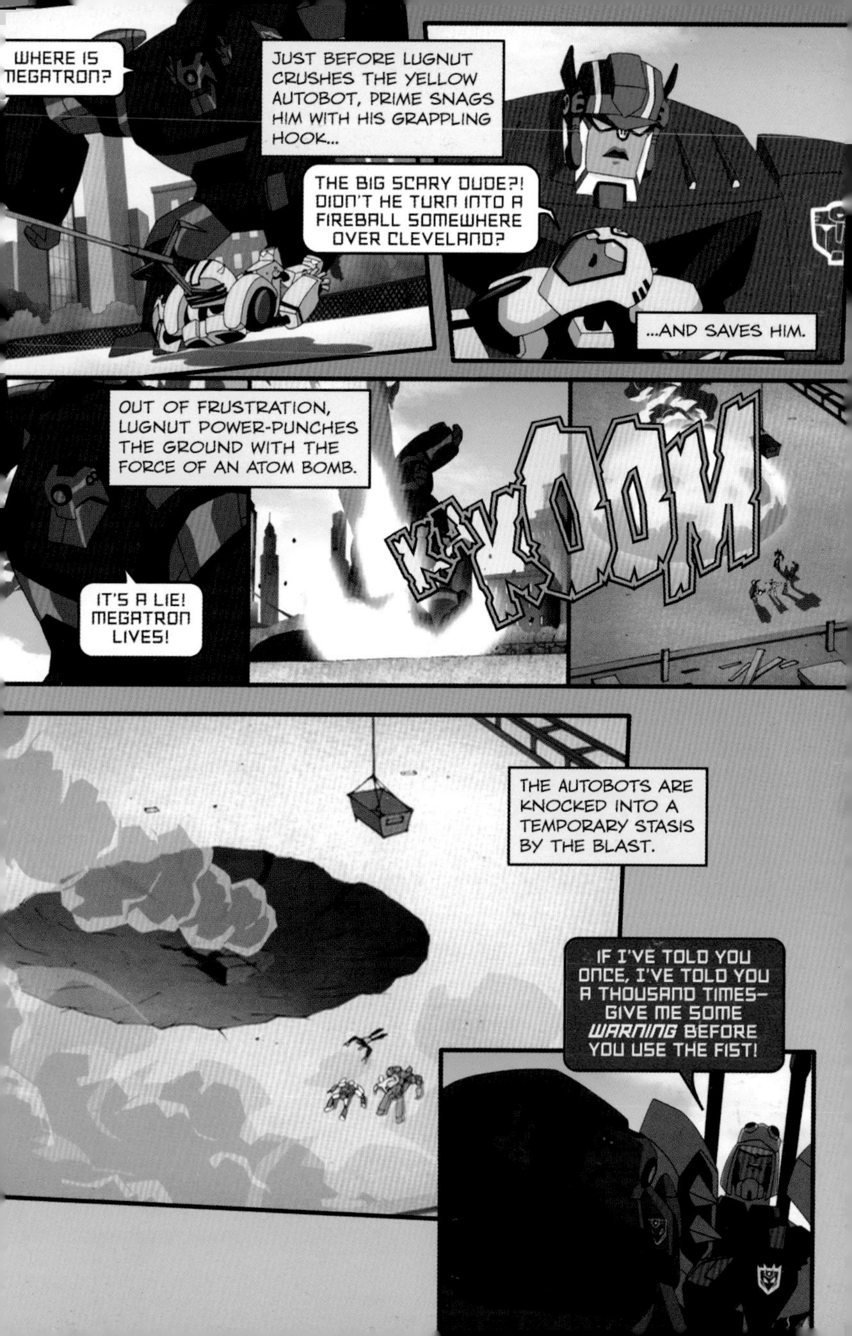
WHERE IS MEGATRON?
JUST BEFORE LUGNUT CRUSHES THE YELLOW AUTOBOT, PRIME SNAGS HIM WITH HIS GRAPPLING HOOK...
THE BIG SCARY DUDE?! DIDN'T HE TURN INTO A FIREBALL SOMEWHERE OVER CLEVELAND?
...AND SAVES HIM.
OUT OF FRUSTRATION, LUGNUT POWER-PUNCHES THE GROUND WITH THE FORCE OF AN ATOM BOMB.
IT'S A LIE! MEGATRON LIVES!
KA-BOOM
THE AUTOBOTS ARE KNOCKED INTO A TEMPORARY STASIS BY THE BLAST.
IF I'VE TOLD YOU ONCE, I'VE TOLD YOU A THOUSAND TIMES– GIVE ME SOME *WARNING* BEFORE YOU USE THE FIST!

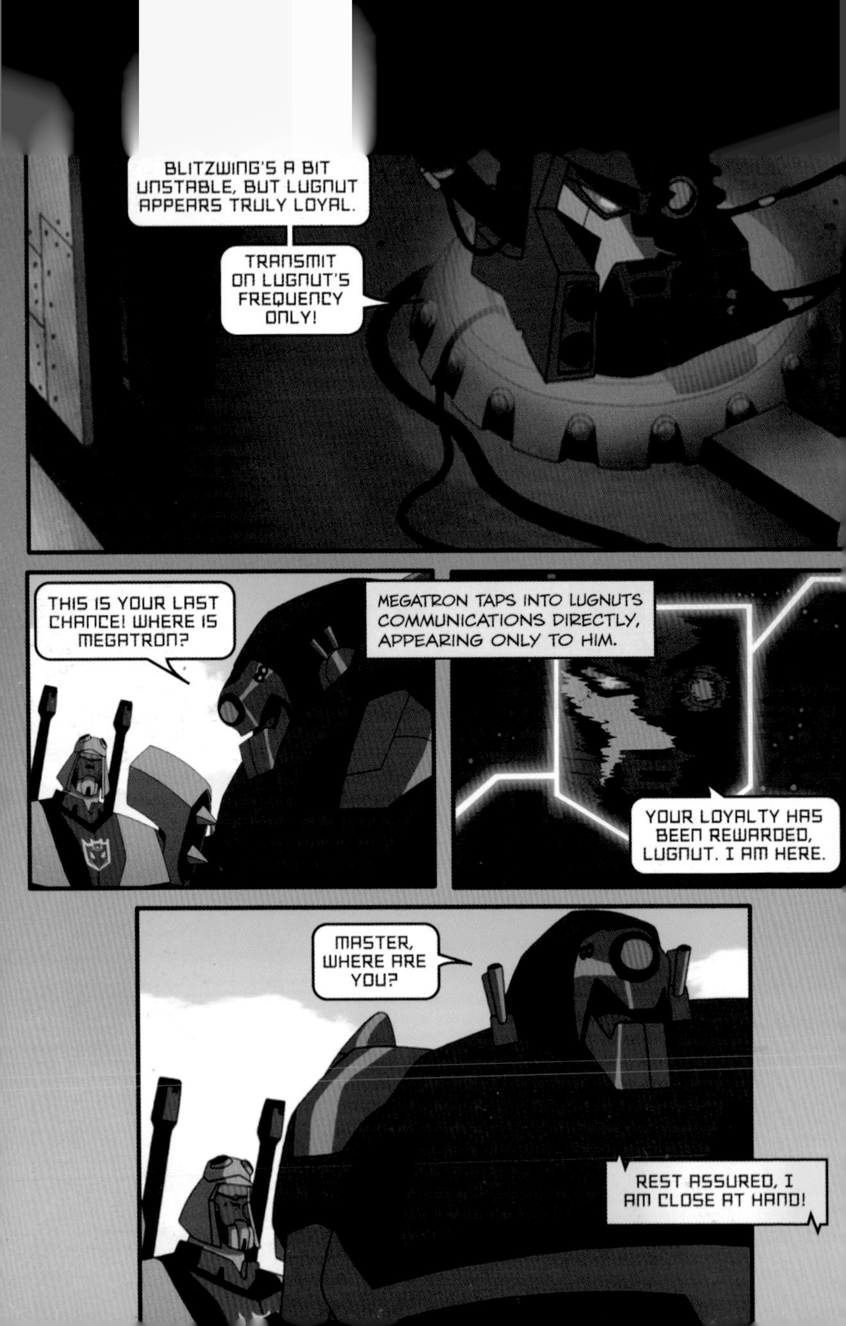
BLITZWING'S A BIT UNSTABLE, BUT LUGNUT APPEARS TRULY LOYAL.
TRANSMIT ON LUGNUT'S FREQUENCY ONLY!
THIS IS YOUR LAST CHANCE! WHERE IS MEGATRON?
MEGATRON TAPS INTO LUGNUTS COMMUNICATIONS DIRECTLY, APPEARING ONLY TO HIM.
YOUR LOYALTY HAS BEEN REWARDED, LUGNUT. I AM HERE.
MASTER, WHERE ARE YOU?
REST ASSURED, I AM CLOSE AT HAND!

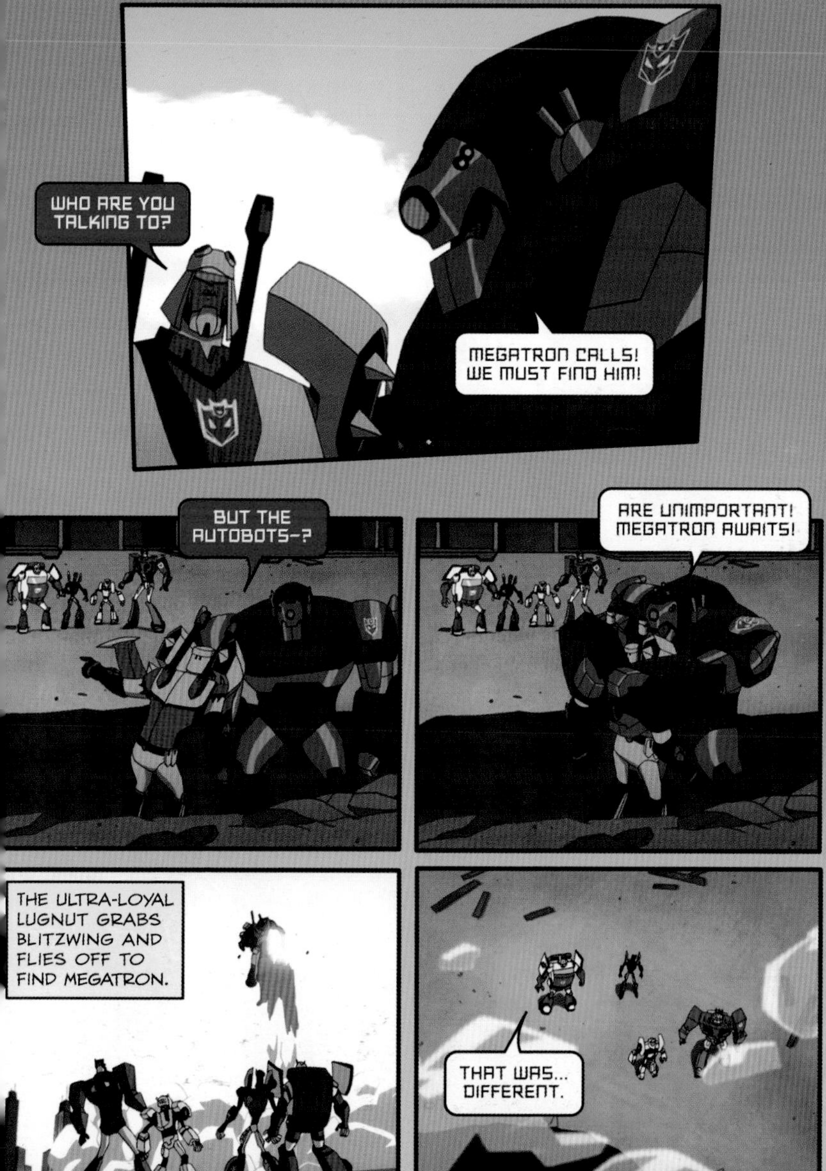
WHO ARE YOU TALKING TO?
MEGATRON CALLS! WE MUST FIND HIM!
BUT THE AUTOBOTS--?
ARE UNIMPORTANT! MEGATRON AWAITS!
THE ULTRA-LOYAL LUGNUT GRABS BLITZWING AND FLIES OFF TO FIND MEGATRON.
THAT WAS... DIFFERENT.

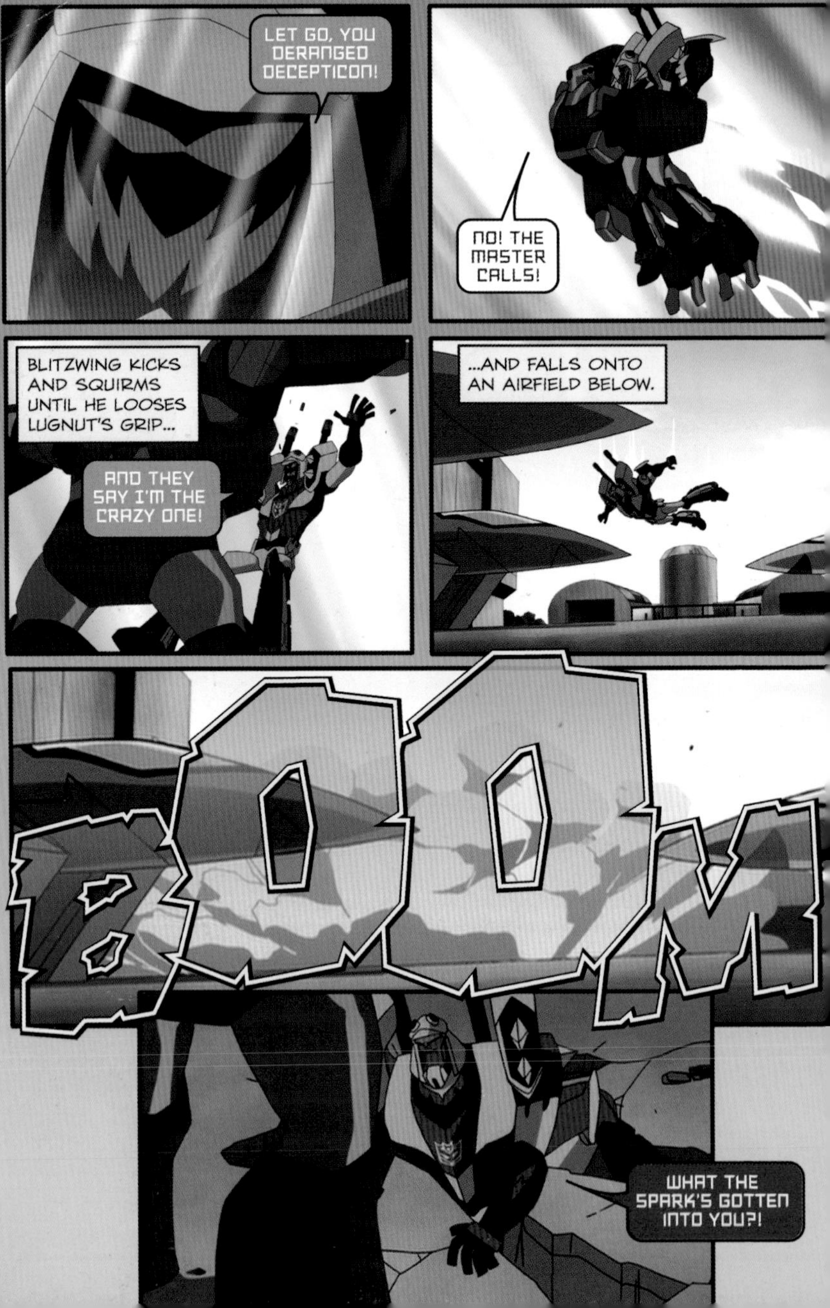
LET GO, YOU DERANGED DECEPTICON!
NO! THE MASTER CALLS!
BLITZWING KICKS AND SQUIRMS UNTIL HE LOOSES LUGNUT'S GRIP...
AND THEY SAY I'M THE CRAZY ONE!
...AND FALLS ONTO AN AIRFIELD BELOW.
BOOM
WHAT THE SPARK'S GOTTEN INTO YOU?!

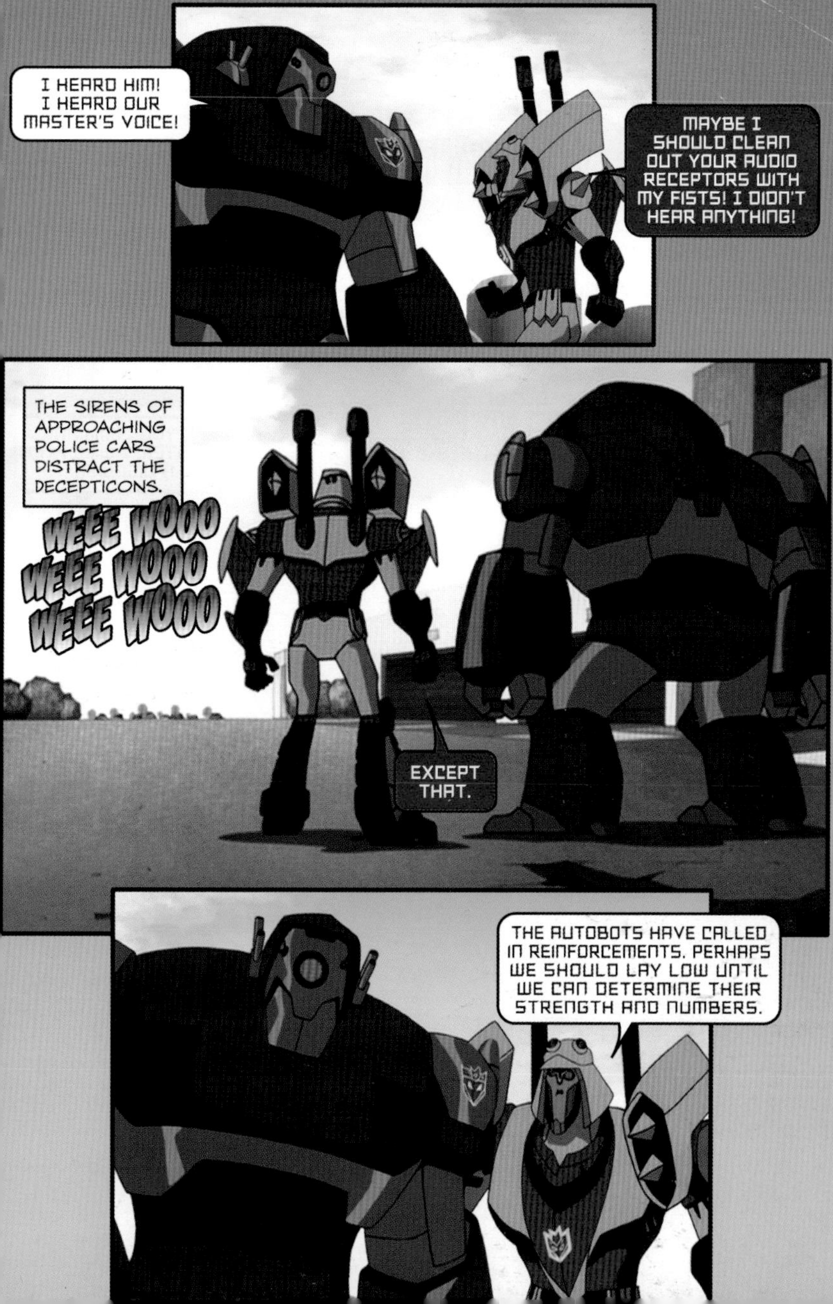
I HEARD HIM! I HEARD OUR MASTER'S VOICE!
MAYBE I SHOULD CLEAN OUT YOUR AUDIO RECEPTORS WITH MY FISTS! I DIDN'T HEAR ANYTHING!
THE SIRENS OF APPROACHING POLICE CARS DISTRACT THE DECEPTICONS.
WEEE WOOO WEEE WOOO WEEE WOOO
EXCEPT THAT.
THE AUTOBOTS HAVE CALLED IN REINFORCEMENTS. PERHAPS WE SHOULD LAY LOW UNTIL WE CAN DETERMINE THEIR STRENGTH AND NUMBERS.

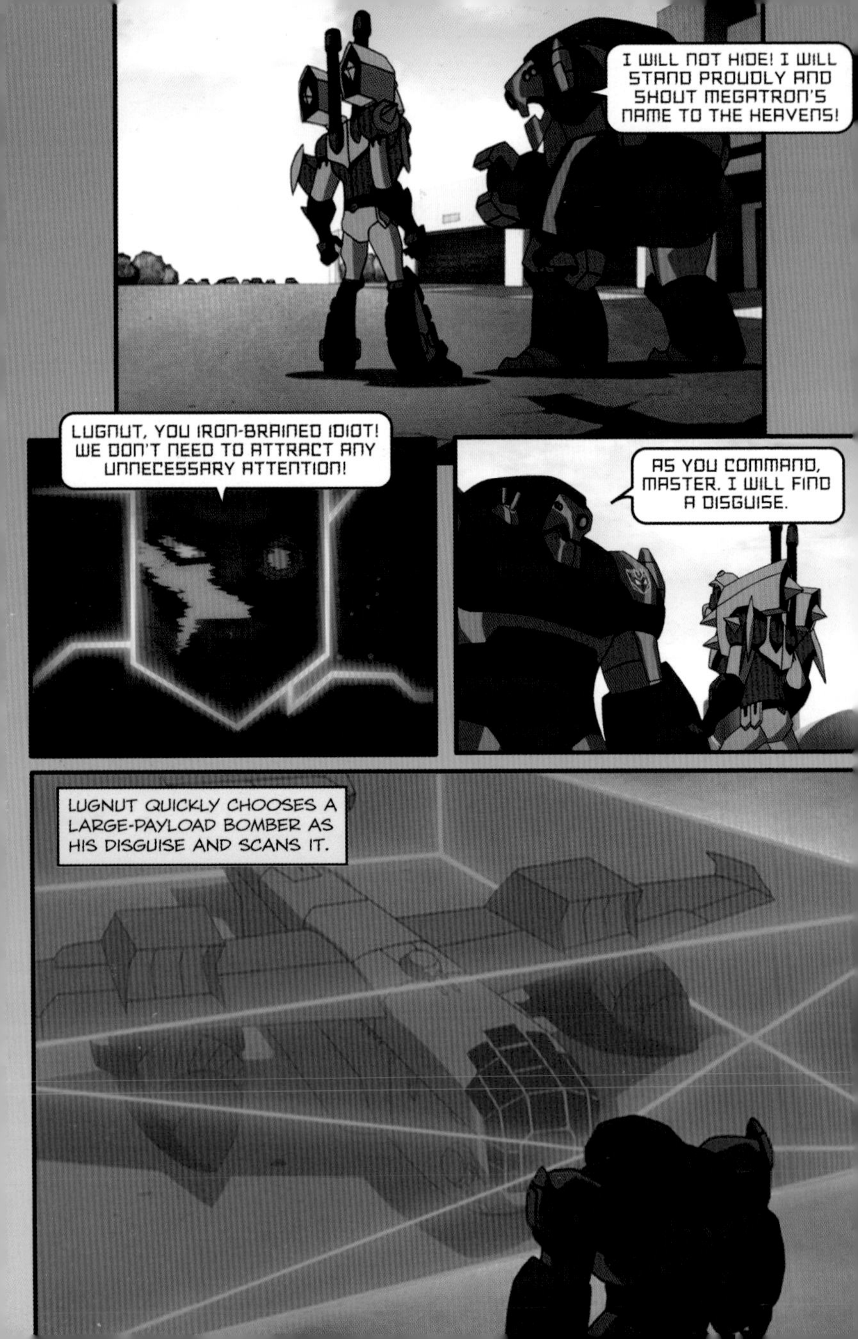
I WILL NOT HIDE! I WILL STAND PROUDLY AND SHOUT MEGATRON'S NAME TO THE HEAVENS!
LUGNUT, YOU IRON-BRAINED IDIOT! WE DON'T NEED TO ATTRACT ANY UNNECESSARY ATTENTION!
AS YOU COMMAND, MASTER. I WILL FIND A DISGUISE.
LUGNUT QUICKLY CHOOSES A LARGE-PAYLOAD BOMBER AS HIS DISGUISE AND SCANS IT.

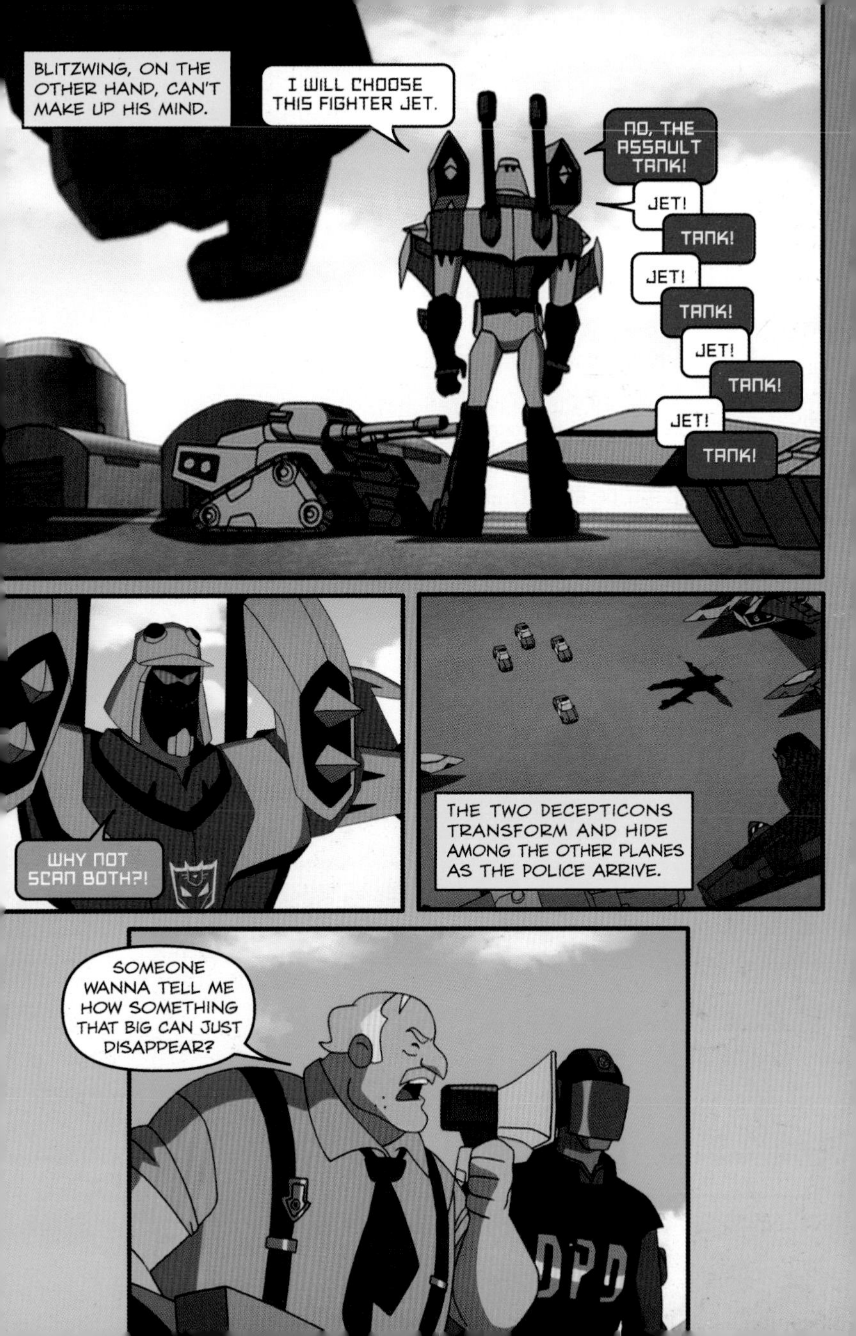
BLITZWING, ON THE OTHER HAND, CAN'T MAKE UP HIS MIND.
I WILL CHOOSE THIS FIGHTER JET.
NO, THE ASSAULT TANK!
JET!
TANK!
JET!
TANK!
JET!
TANK!
JET!
TANK!
WHY NOT SCAN BOTH?!
THE TWO DECEPTICONS TRANSFORM AND HIDE AMONG THE OTHER PLANES AS THE POLICE ARRIVE.
SOMEONE WANNA TELL ME HOW SOMETHING THAT BIG CAN JUST DISAPPEAR?
DPD

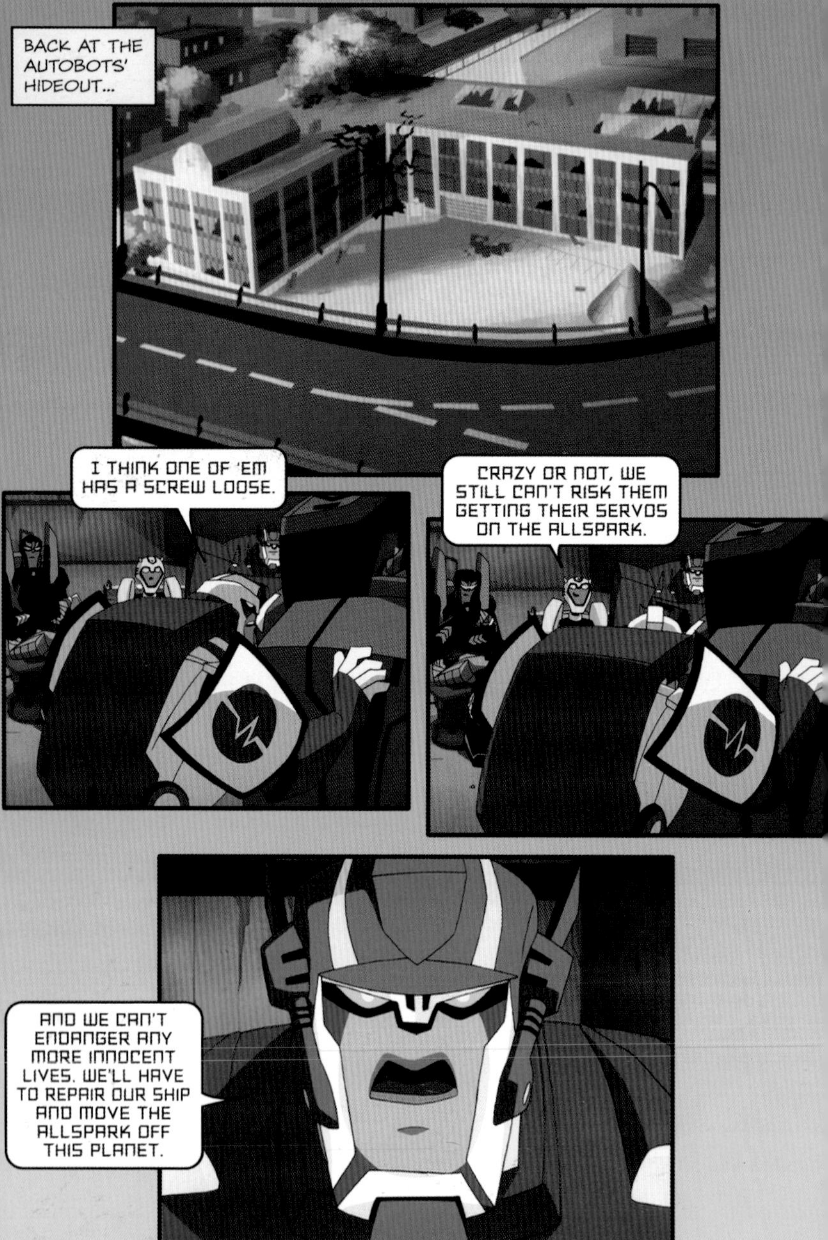
BACK AT THE AUTOBOTS' HIDEOUT...
I THINK ONE OF 'EM HAS A SCREW LOOSE.
CRAZY OR NOT, WE STILL CAN'T RISK THEM GETTING THEIR SERVOS ON THE ALLSPARK.
AND WE CAN'T ENDANGER ANY MORE INNOCENT LIVES. WE'LL HAVE TO REPAIR OUR SHIP AND MOVE THE ALLSPARK OFF THIS PLANET.

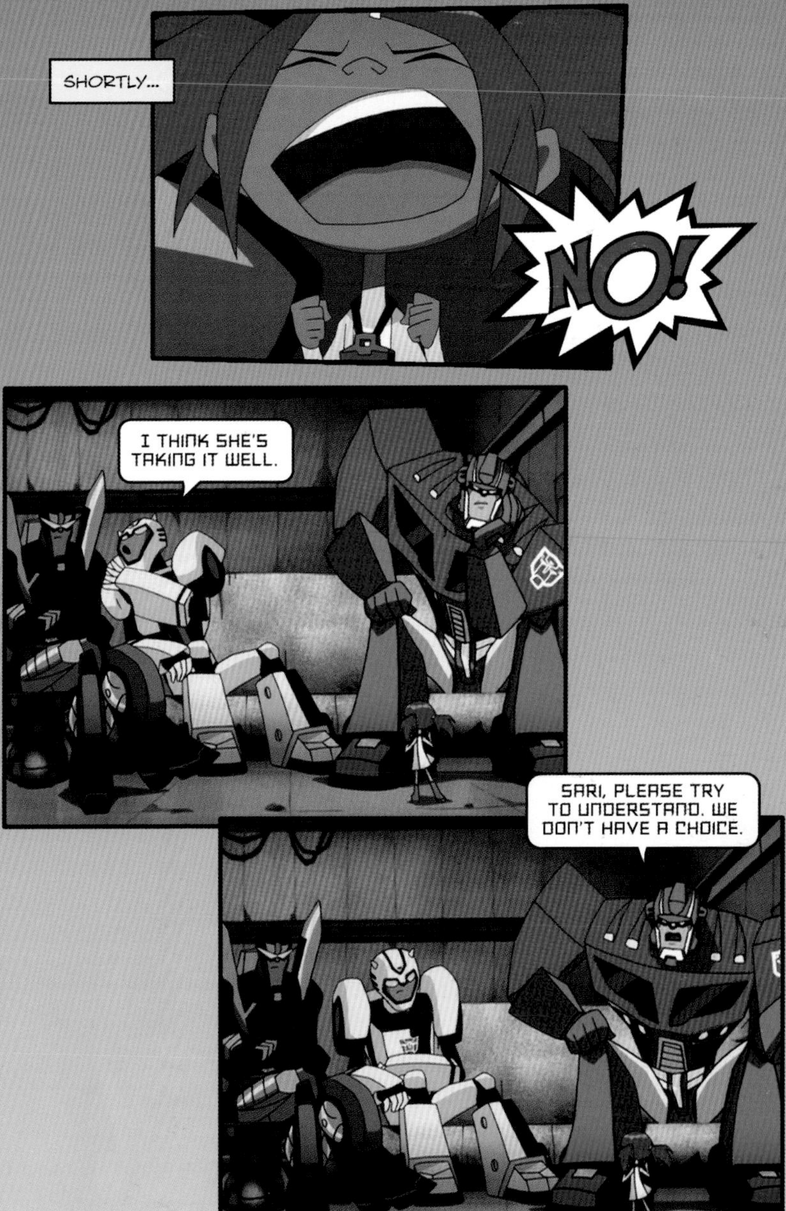
SHORTLY...
NO!
I THINK SHE'S TAKING IT WELL.
SARI, PLEASE TRY TO UNDERSTAND. WE DON'T HAVE A CHOICE.

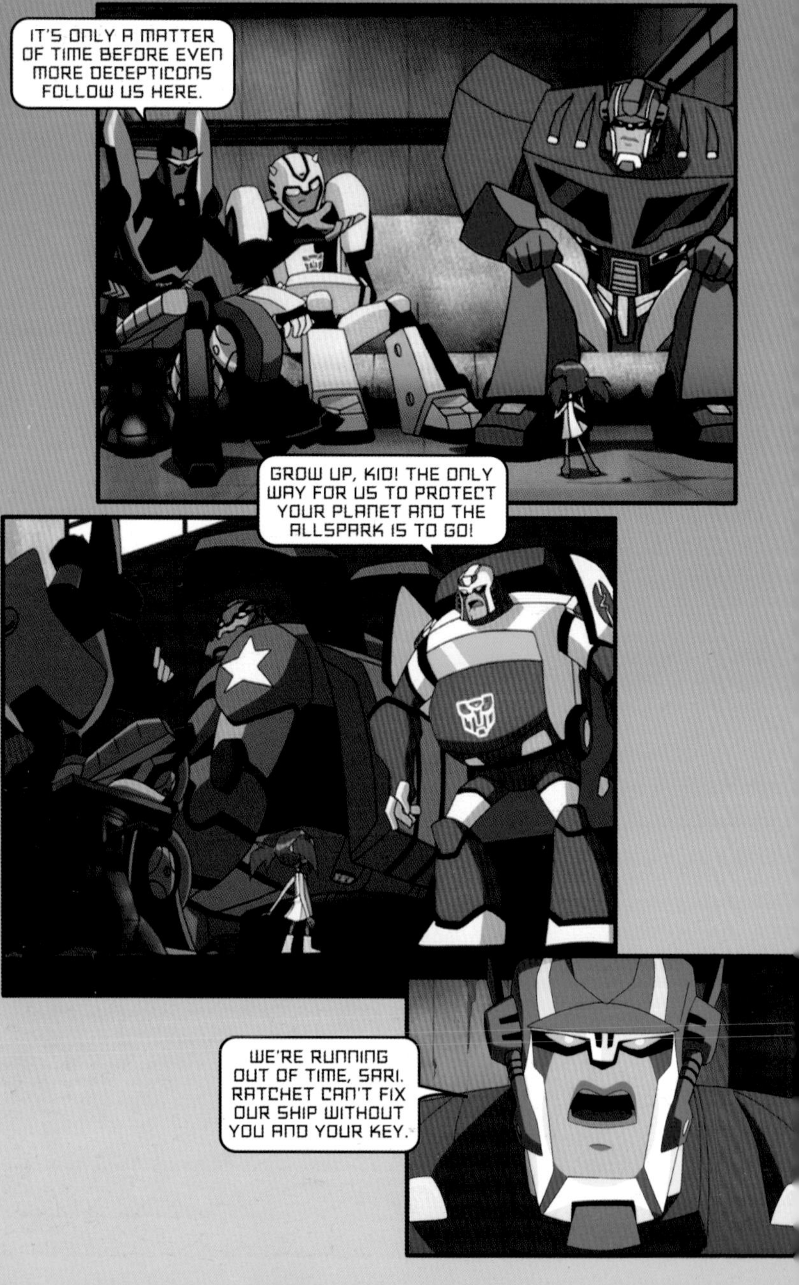
IT'S ONLY A MATTER OF TIME BEFORE EVEN MORE DECEPTICONS FOLLOW US HERE.
GROW UP, KID! THE ONLY WAY FOR US TO PROTECT YOUR PLANET AND THE ALLSPARK IS TO GO!
WE'RE RUNNING OUT OF TIME, SARI. RATCHET CAN'T FIX OUR SHIP WITHOUT YOU AND YOUR KEY.

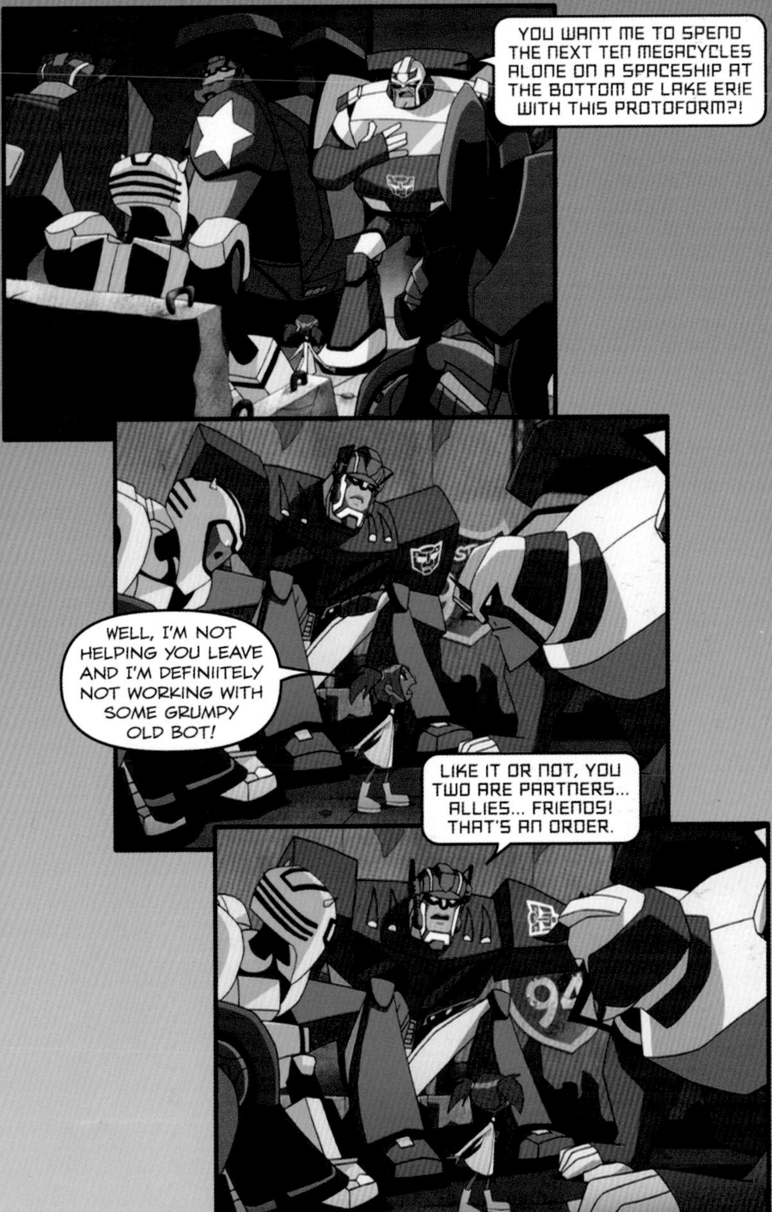
YOU WANT ME TO SPEND THE NEXT TEN MEGACYCLES ALONE ON A SPACESHIP AT THE BOTTOM OF LAKE ERIE WITH THIS PROTOFORM?!
WELL, I'M NOT HELPING YOU LEAVE AND I'M DEFINIITELY NOT WORKING WITH SOME GRUMPY OLD BOT!
LIKE IT OR NOT, YOU TWO ARE PARTNERS... ALLIES... FRIENDS! THAT'S AN ORDER.

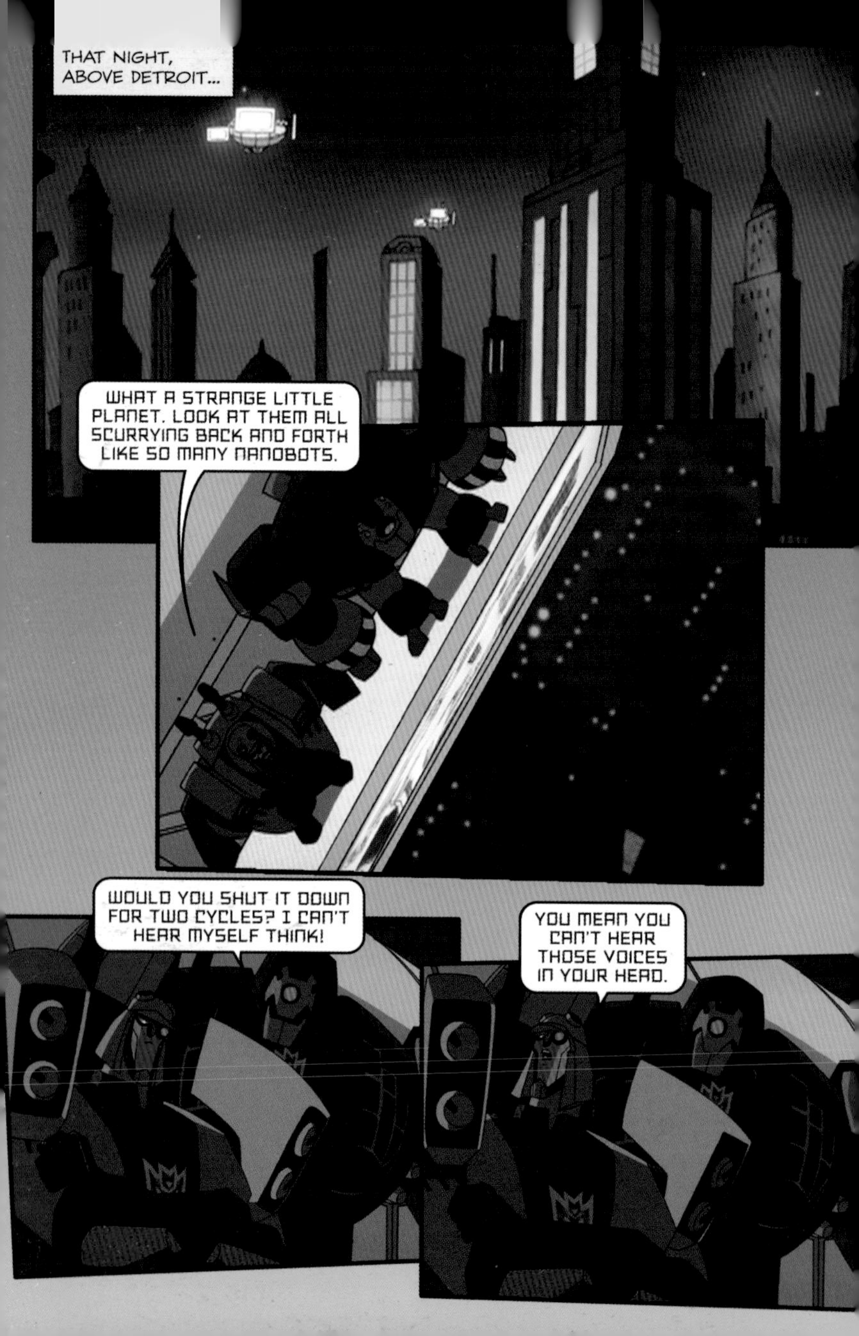
THAT NIGHT, ABOVE DETROIT...
WHAT A STRANGE LITTLE PLANET. LOOK AT THEM ALL SCURRYING BACK AND FORTH LIKE SO MANY NANOBOTS.
WOULD YOU SHUT IT DOWN FOR TWO CYCLES? I CAN'T HEAR MYSELF THINK!
YOU MEAN YOU CAN'T HEAR THOSE VOICES IN YOUR HEAD.

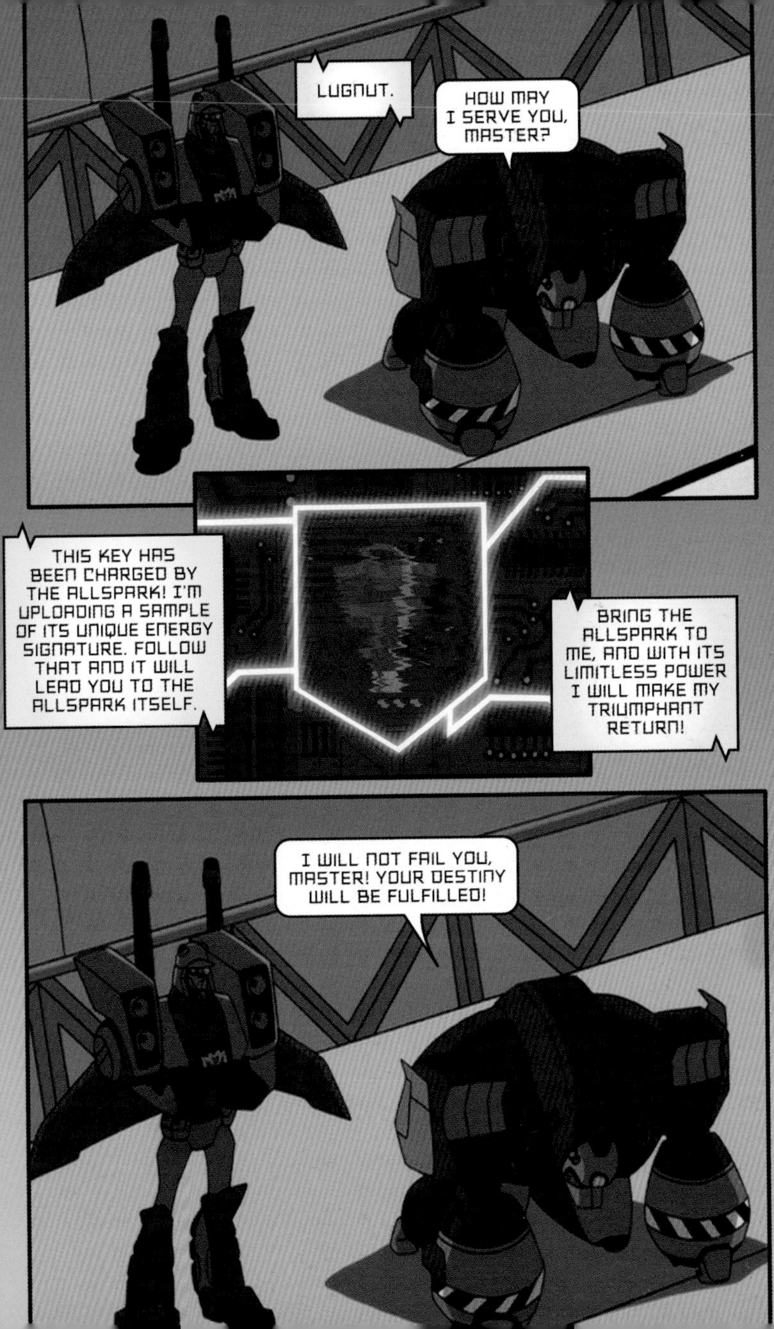
LUGNUT.
HOW MAY I SERVE YOU, MASTER?
THIS KEY HAS BEEN CHARGED BY THE ALLSPARK! I'M UPLOADING A SAMPLE OF ITS UNIQUE ENERGY SIGNATURE. FOLLOW THAT AND IT WILL LEAD YOU TO THE ALLSPARK ITSELF.
BRING THE ALLSPARK TO ME, AND WITH ITS LIMITLESS POWER I WILL MAKE MY TRIUMPHANT RETURN!
I WILL NOT FAIL YOU, MASTER! YOUR DESTINY WILL BE FULFILLED!

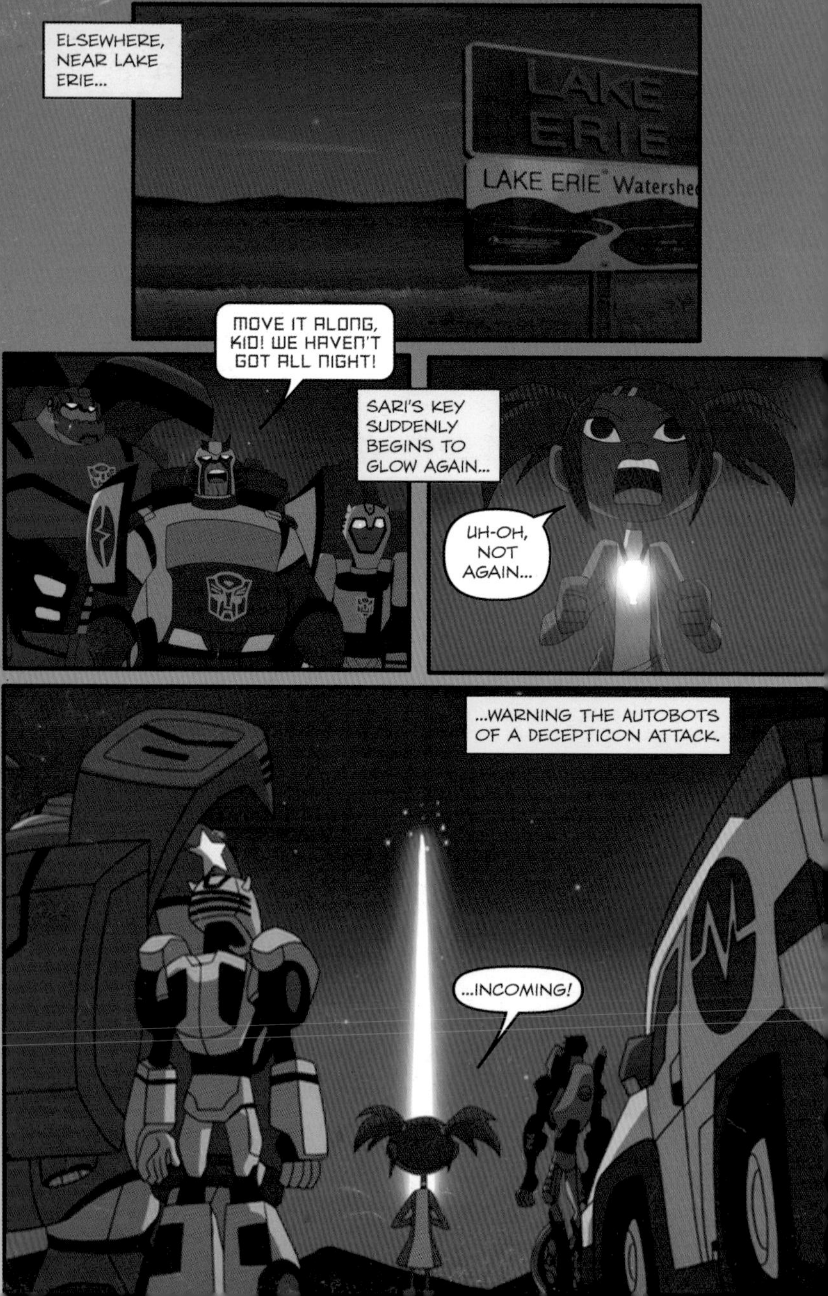
ELSEWHERE, NEAR LAKE ERIE...
LAKE ERIE
LAKE ERIE Watershe
MOVE IT ALONG, KID! WE HAVEN'T GOT ALL NIGHT!
SARI'S KEY SUDDENLY BEGINS TO GLOW AGAIN...
UH-OH, NOT AGAIN...
...WARNING THE AUTOBOTS OF A DECEPTICON ATTACK.
...INCOMING!

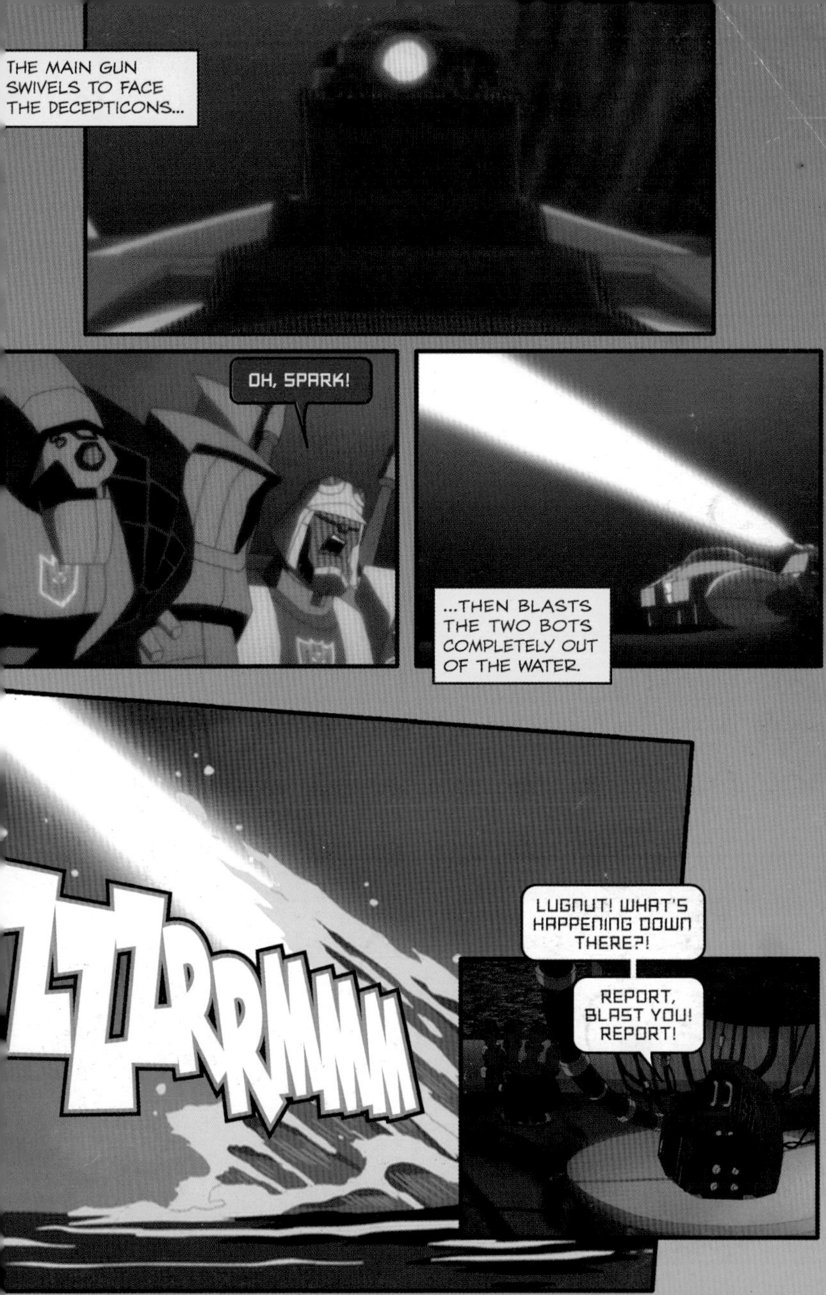
THE MAIN GUN SWIVELS TO FACE THE DECEPTICONS...
OH, SPARK!
...THEN BLASTS THE TWO BOTS COMPLETELY OUT OF THE WATER.
ZZRRMMMM
LUGNUT! WHAT'S HAPPENING DOWN THERE?!
REPORT, BLAST YOU! REPORT!

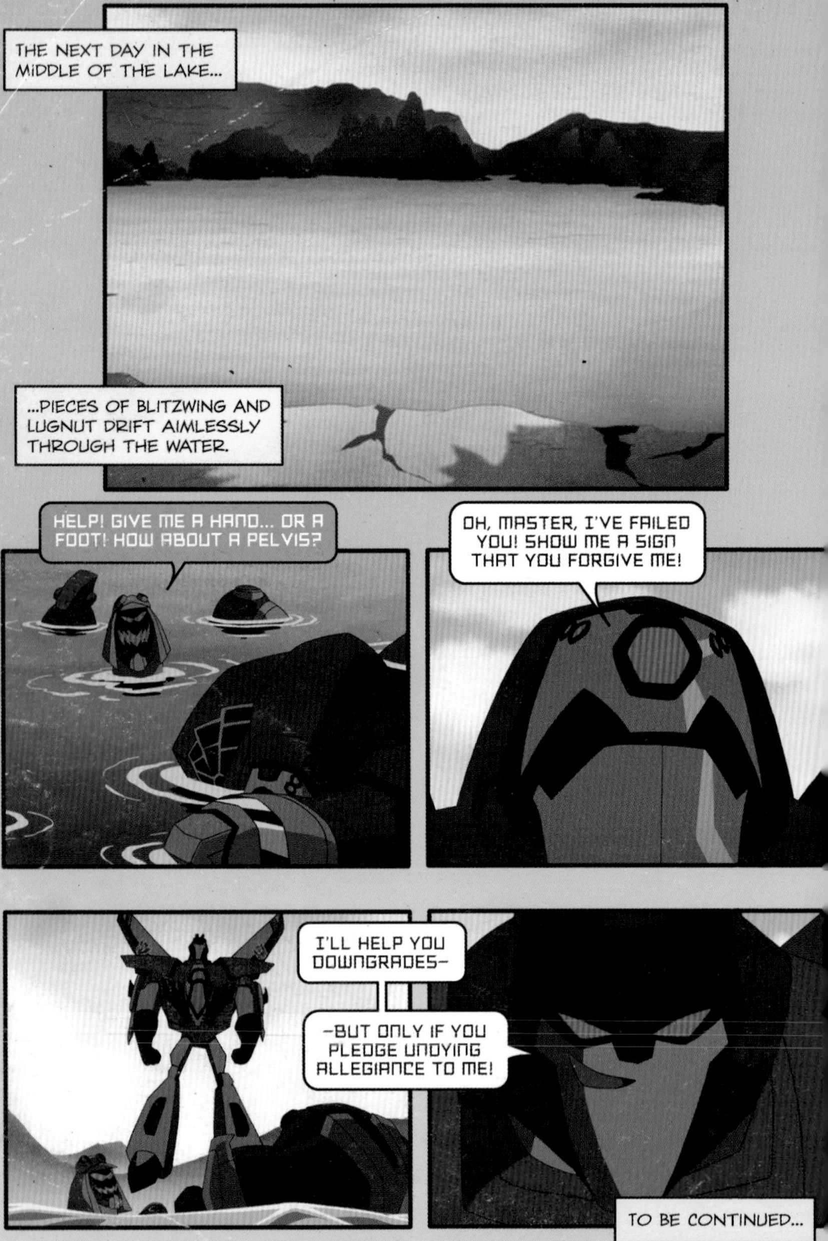
THE NEXT DAY IN THE MIDDLE OF THE LAKE...
...PIECES OF BLITZWING AND LUGNUT DRIFT AIMLESSLY THROUGH THE WATER.
HELP! GIVE ME A HAND... OR A FOOT! HOW ABOUT A PELVIS?
OH, MASTER, I'VE FAILED YOU! SHOW ME A SIGN THAT YOU FORGIVE ME!
I'LL HELP YOU DOWNGRADES—
—BUT ONLY IF YOU PLEDGE UNDYING ALLEGIANCE TO ME!
TO BE CONTINUED...